HARRIE

BLUE MURDER

HARRIET Rutland was the pen-name of Olive Shimwell. She was born Olive Seers in 1901, the daughter of a prosperous Birmingham builder and decorator.

Little is known of the author's early life but in 1926 she married microbiologist John Shimwell, with whom she moved to a small village near Cork in Ireland. This setting, transplanted to Devon, inspired her first mystery novel *Knock, Murderer, Knock!* which was published in 1938. The second of Harriet Rutland's mysteries, *Bleeding Hooks*, came out in 1940, and the third and last, *Blue Murder*, was published in November 1942. All three novels are remarkable for their black comedy, innovative plots, and pin-sharp portraits of human behaviour, especially concerning relationships between men and women.

Olive and John were divorced in the early forties, and Olive apparently did not publish anything further. She died in Newton Abbot in 1962.

HARRIET RUTLAND

BLUE MURDER

With an introduction by
Curtis Evans

DEAN STREET PRESS

Published by Dean Street Press 2015

Copyright © 1942 Harriet Rutland

Introduction © 2015 Curtis Evans

Published by licence, issued under the UK Orphan Works Licensing
Scheme.

First published in 1942 by Skeffington & Son

Cover by DSP

ISBN 978 1 910570 86 9

www.deanstreetpress.co.uk

"Story! Lord bless you, I have none to tell, Sir!"

CANNING—*The Needy Knifegrinder.*

INTRODUCTION

BLUE Murder, the third and final detective novel by Harriet Rutland (the pen name of Olive Shimwell), was published in November 1942, almost three years after the appearance of the author's second mystery, *Bleeding Hooks*, which itself had contrastingly followed hard upon the heels of her debut, *Knock, Murderer, Knock!* The first two detective novels had been well received on both sides of the Atlantic--in the seminal genre history *Murder for Pleasure: The Life and Times of the Detective Story* (1941), American critic Howard Haycraft included Harriet Rutland on his list of English character-driven mystery "new-comers of especial promise"--and doubtlessly the author's publishers in the United Kingdom and the United States eagerly anticipated the timely receipt of a third Rutland tale. This makes the long delay in Olive Shimwell's delivery of *Blue Murder* surprising—but only at first blush.

Certainly at this time there was much in Olive Shimwell's life that might have driven the rising detective fiction writer to distraction. Most obviously there were the dire events of the Second World War, but also her raising of an infant son and apparent marital difficulties that soon would lead Olive to a divorce from her husband, microbiologist John Lester Shimwell. In 1939 the Shimwells had moved from Ireland, where they had resided for most of the decade, to London, where in October Olive gave birth to the couple's son. In September 1940 the Nazis commenced their punishing and prolonged aerial bombing campaign against the United Kingdom, launching over seventy raids on London alone over the next eight months. Olive and her son may have evacuated England's capital, with all the ensuing dislocation that would have entailed. Yet amidst all these challenges the author managed to complete a final mystery under the Harriet Rutland name that is fully up to the high standard set by the first two detective novels, albeit rather darker all round, reflecting the trying times in which the book was conceived and written.

Set in the cleverly-named Nether Naughton, in "North-shire" (Yorkshire?), *Blue Murder* dispenses, when murder strikes, with the investigative services of Mr. Winkley, the sleuth of Harriet Rutland's first two detective novels, in favor of Northshire's Superintendent Cheam and Scotland Yard's Chief Inspector Alan Driver, the latter assisted by the inconvenient-ly-named Sergeant Lovely. The central observing character in the novel is Arnold Smith, a fifty-year old novelist who has fled wartime London for the more pacific charms of Nether Naugh-ton. Smith, an author of "novels of weak adventure, sugared with ladylike romance," has decided, at his agent's behest, to try his hand at another, now more popular, form of escapist fiction: the detective novel. In Nether Naughton he unexpect-edly finds copy for his book in his strife-ridden lodgings: the home of the Hardstaffes, husband, wife and daughter.

Mr. Hardstaffe, the Headmaster of the village school, is a choleric, lustful sadist, his wife a tiresomely neurasthenic hypochondriac, and Leda, their thirty-two year old daughter, a horsey and hopelessly hearty countrywoman familiar from classic English mystery fiction, clad in tweeds "of a colour which must surely have been the least attractive of any woven by the islanders of Harris." Soon Arnold Smith finds himself enmeshed in a real-life death drama as murder overtakes this most unpleasant household. Suspects abound, for the Hard-staffes are indeed a singularly aggravating family.

Like the first two detective novels, *Blue Murder* is rich in Olive Shimwell's characteristically sardonic humour, although in this final mystery the mirth is even sharper-edged than in the previous two books. Leda Hardstaffe keeps a kennel of rambunctious Sealyhams and insists on letting the brutes over-run the house, though they are not quite so well housetrained as one might desire. Most strikingly jaundiced is the novel's view

of marriage, especially that of the senior Hardstaffes. Mr. Hardstaffe only wed Mrs. Hardstaffe for her money, we learn, and,
though in his sixties, he is currently pursuing Charity Fuller, a
teacher in his school young enough to be his granddaughter and
easily the most alluring woman in Nether Naughton. ("Charity
always begins at home," is how one village wit summarizes the
young woman's romantic escapades.) The negative portrayal
of marriage and restrictive divorce laws in *Blue Murder* may
have reflected unpleasant circumstances in the author's own
life, for not long after the novel was published Olive and John
Shimwell divorced. John remarried in 1947 and with his new
wife had a daughter in 1948, the year Olive herself remarried.
In his professional life, at least, John could be disagreeable,
according to a 1992 article in the Journal of the Institute of
Brewing, often finding himself at "the centre of acrimonious
scientific exchanges," for "he did not suffer fools gladly."

However much the author's intimate personal circumstances may have influenced *Blue Murder*, unquestionably
the novel includes an abundance of fascinating wartime social
detail, especially concerning the household challenges posed
by domestic rationing and servant scarcity, the changing roles
of women in English life and the entry into the country of
desperate war refugees from continental Europe. Reflecting on British women's disinclination to don formal evening
attire for the duration of the conflict with Germany, Shimwell
with a feminist flourish declares: "This was war-time, and you
could not deal effectively with incendiary bombs, or stand by
with a First Aid Party, in a gown which swirled around your
ankles. There was, in fact, little scope at all for femininity
in Total War, which for the time being, and possibly for all
time, had destroyed the slogan that Woman's Place is in the
Home." Conversely the traditionalist matron Mrs. Hardstaffe
laments how the war has given female servants new options
in life and made them, in her judgment, uppish in their atti-

tudes toward their domestic superiors. Briggs, the lone maid to whom the Hardstaffes had recently been reduced--their other young woman, Mary, having left them to work in a munitions factory--has only lately been supplemented by a scatty young German Jewish refugee named Frieda Braun. "Girls are quite above themselves nowadays, with all these uniforms and high wages," complains Mrs. Hardstaffe. "I shudder to think what they'll be like after this war. Our other maid [besides Frieda] was christened Victoria Alexandra [after the British queen and a later queen consort]. Did you ever hear of such names for a village girl? Of course, we call her Briggs."

Even more problematic for the Hardstaffes than Victoria Alexandra Briggs, who by the end of the novel also has joined Mary in factory work, is Frieda Braun. Some modern readers may be shocked by the casual anti-Semitism that the Hardstaffes express in *Blue Murder*, yet as I see it Olive Shimwell was too forthright an author to shy at portraying the extreme unlikableness of these characters. A victim of the Hardstaffe's casual anti-semitism, in later chapters the novel shines a sympathetic light on Frieda, emphasizing the manifold terrors to which Jews were subjected in Germany and the daily indignities and slights that are inflicted upon her in England. Concerning her experiences in Germany, Frieda herself informs Superintendent Cheam:

You do not understand? No. Because you are not a German Jew. You say 'Itler is a bad man, must be kill. But if you are not Jew, you do not know how bad. You understand bombs and Luftwaffe, but you do not understand Gestapo and torture if you are not Jew like me. I am told to get up from my bed one night. I must go to the frontier. If I do not go, I am sent to Poland in cattletruck or to concentration camp.

Unsophisticated yet essentially kinder than her employers, the Hardstaffe cook allows to Superintendent Cheam that Frieda is a "bit queer" in the head, "but so'd we be if we'd been though half what she has. I never did hold with Jews, me being a good Church of England Christian, but I don't hold with torturing an animal, let alone a decent-living human-being, and the bits of tales that girl manages to tell you would fair make your hair curl." In a pointed commentary on the anodyne nature of escapist classic English detective fiction Shimwell has Arnold Smith, while ruminating on his detective novel, for which he is drawing on the Hardstaffe household, conclude that he must omit Frieda, because "such a passionate creature could have no place in the world of unreality which housed the scintillating figure of Noel Delare," his posh gentleman amateur sleuth.

Writing at a time when lights were going out all over the world and frightened people cowered in the dark, the author of *Blue Murder* dared in her detective novel to open the door to darker human passions taking part in her little parlor game of murder. Accordingly the novel makes a bracing read even for jaded modern mystery readers. Certainly contemporary reviewers noted, and frequently commended, this aspect of the book. "'Blue Murder' has a novel plot and some characters who are more interesting than attractive," observed the *New York Times Book Review*, while *Kirkus*, noting that all of the disagreeable Hardstaffes made "good prospects for murder," pronounced that the novel offered mystery fans "a neat, nasty case." *Blue Murder* indeed does this, and it also serves as a memorably acerbic coda for Harriet Rutland, one of Golden Age English mystery fiction's most original and interesting writers.

Curtis Evans

CHAPTER 1

MR. HARDSTAFFE had reached the critical time of life when elderly gentlemen gaze at the legs of schoolgirls in railway carriages.

Mr. Hardstaffe was definitely elderly, and he looked very much like a clergyman when he read the lessons at Sunday morning services in an Oxford drawl, pitched in a slightly falsetto voice guaranteed to hit the back of the church.

But his eyes were not engaged, at the moment, in the above-mentioned occupation.

He was seated in a leather-covered armchair in front of a meagre fire in his study in the village school of Nether Naughton, to which he had succeeded as Headmaster some thirty years ago. And although the youngest and prettiest of his staff, Miss Charity Fuller, was sitting near him, wearing a knee-length skirt which showed the slim beauty of her near-silk-clad legs, his protuberant blue eyes were gazing unmistakably at her elfin-pointed face, at her green eyes, reddened lips, and waved auburn hair.

". . . and if there hadn't been a war on, I should have suggested France or Italy," he was saying. "But as I've no desire to meet Hitler or Mussolini, I think Scotland would be best."

"I think it's a splendid idea," said Charity. "You work far too hard. It must be a strain to return to the school again after you'd retired for three years. You deserve a rest."

"We do, you mean. You don't suppose I intend to go alone, surely?"

Charity looked bewildered.

"You don't mean . . . ?" she faltered. Then, seeing from his expression that she had indeed interpreted his unspoken meaning correctly, she blushed. "Have you gone mad?" she asked.

"Mad? Oh my God! That's rich!"

Mr. Hardstaffe rose to his feet, and strode across the room. Then, as if conscious that his height—he was barely five feet tall—might serve to render his behaviour ridiculous rather than impressive, he returned again to his chair.

"Mad? You know I am. Mad about you! I'm like a starving dog to whom you occasionally throw a crust. I want more, more! Why not face up to it, Charity? What's to be gained by being a hypocrite? What have we to lose, either of us? We love each other—surely that's what really counts. Oh God!" He beat his forehead with a clenched fist. "Am I never to know the joys of being loved for myself alone? Am I to remain bound to one woman in a living death until I die? Are you going to condemn me to that, Charity? Are you? Are you?"

He stretched out his hand, and stroked her knee. His voice grew soft and persuasive.

"My dear, I have never concealed from you the secrets of my heart. You know what my life is like. You know that at home I live in hell, tied to an old woman who is too utterly selfish to consider the welfare of anyone but herself: a hypochondriac, who is never happy unless she is ill. She always keeps a copy of "Medical Hints" under the Bible beside her bed, so that she can read up new symptoms at night, and awake in the morning to simulate a new complaint.

"You know me, a man of generous and passionate impulses, which are never allowed to blossom in my own home. You know the loneliness I shall face tonight and every other night, unless you give me the hope of something better. My dearest, you know that I love you."

"I'm sorry," said Charity, apparently unconscious of the inadequacy of her words. "I know it's simply awful for you, and whenever I see her long, white face, I could slap it with a wet rag. I only wish I could do something to help you: you know I'm very fond of you: but I can't. You know I can't."

"But you can." Mr. Hardstaffe leaned forward, and gazed more earnestly than before into her troubled eyes. "That's what I'm trying to tell you. Come to Scotland with me!"

"The village . . ." began Miss Fuller.

"Tcha! The village! What would they know? We need not travel together. We've been away at the same time before: everyone knows that our holidays coincide. How would they know that this was different? Besides, I've taught them all, man, woman, and child, all that they know. They respect me. No one would dream of tattling about me."

"Oh, but they would—they do!" exclaimed Charity. "They're talking all over the village already—about us, I mean, you and me. About the way I'm always staying behind after school, like this. And about you seeing me home in the black-out. Why, even the children . . ."

"The little bastards!" shouted the headmaster, an ugly vein pulsing in his scrawny neck. "I won't have it! I shall put a stop to it! They can't do that kind of thing to me!"

"That's what I thought," agreed Charity. "That's why I've sent in my application to be transferred to another district."

"You've—what?"

Charity looked at him with fear in her eyes. Then she looked down at her restless hands.

"Oh, I know you think I'm a coward," she said. "Don't think this has meant nothing to me. It's been marvellous to work here with you. I've admired you ever since I came to this school, and lately I—I've learned to love you. But I simply can't stand the idea of any scandal. I couldn't face it. It's better for me to go away where we can't meet. You'll forget me. There'll be other women in your life."

She pulled her skirt over her knees, and giving it a decisive pat, stood up.

Mr. Hardstaffe rose also, and put his arms round her.

"I'll never let you go, do you hear! Never! I forbid you to leave. I won't accept your resignation. I shall say that you're indispensable, and it's your duty to stay."

She did not resist him. She was head and shoulders taller than he, and knew from experience that his embrace, to be successful, needed co-operation from her.

"That won't stop me," she said coolly. "I'm not coming alone to your study again, either. I can't stand people's looks in this place. That caretaker, for instance. She's always waiting at the door when we go out. She looks at me as though I were—dirty. I can't stand it any longer."

"I'll dismiss her to-morrow!" he blustered.

"No, it would only make matters worse. Everyone is sorry for *her*."

He knew that this time she did not refer to the caretaker. He took her hands in his, and pleaded with her.

"Charity, have pity on me. Don't send me back without hope to my prison. If you do, I shall do something desperate. I know that all the little things you speak of seem important to you, but, darling, that's only because you're so young. I'm so much older than you, and when love comes to a man late in life, he has to snatch at the chance of happiness it offers to him, quickly and greedily. He knows that it is far more important than trying to build up a respectable life in the eyes of other people."

Charity shook her head sadly.

"We could be so happy, Charity, you and I. What does it matter what other people think? I'd do anything in the world for you. You don't realise how much you mean to me. Come away with me!"

"No."

Knowing that her lips were out of reach, he bent down, and covered her hands with kisses.

"My darling, come with me!"

But however much Mr. Hardstaffe might invite comparison with Faust, Charity had no intention of becoming another Marguerite.

"I can't," she said firmly. "Not as long as *she* is alive."

Hardstaffe dropped her hands, and moved away from her.

"I was afraid you would say that," he said. "Well, now I know what to do."

CHAPTER 2

WHILE all this was taking place, *she* was sitting alone in the drawing-room, frowning over a Service helmet, with earflaps, on which she had been engaged since the outbreak of war.

It was a long, graceful room, exquisitely furnished and decorated, for Mrs. Hardstaffe had excellent taste, and Mr. Hardstaffe believed in living up to his wife's income.

Although the day was mild and sunny, a huge fire burned in the grate, and Mrs. Hardstaffe shivered audibly as she sat as near to it as she felt she could do without appearing unladylike. Soon the door opened, and a rosy-cheeked maid in black uniform with white apron, cap, and cuffs, wheeled in the tea-trolley with an apologetic air.

Mrs. Hardstaffe looked up at her over the horn-rimmed spectacles she habitually wore when knitting or reading.

"Tea? Are you sure it's five o'clock, Briggs? You know the master doesn't like tea brought in a minute before five. He's never in to tea, I know, but that makes no difference. He would be most annoyed if I didn't wait until five."

"Yes madam." Briggs inclined a respectful, neat head. "But it's after five by the wireless. They'd started talking in Welsh when I wetted the tea."

Mrs. Hardstaffe brightened, and thrust her knitting down the side of the chair.

"Is it?" she smiled. "Well then, I can have a cup of tea. Not that I can say I enjoy it so much these days— you make it so weak now that it's rationed—but still, it will be hot, and I feel so cold to-day, so very cold."

She raised the heavy, hall-marked Georgian teapot over a pink-patterned Limoges cup, then hesitated.

"You're sure the master hasn't come in?" she asked.

"Quite sure, madam. There's a gentleman waiting for him in the morning-room. A Mr. Smith. He seemed a bit upset-like at not being expected, but I'm sure no one told me or Cook that he was coming, and I'd be obliged if you'd say as much to the master, madam, so that he won't be for putting it on to me."

Mrs. Hardstaffe frowned.

"Oh dear!" she exclaimed. "*Now* what ought I to do? I do wish they'd tell me when they're expecting people: it does look so bad when I don't know who is supposed to be coming to my own house—and at tea-time especially. It's really most inconsiderate of anyone to call at tea-time unless they've been asked. They know it means sharing other people's rations, and it isn't fair to expect it. Is he a gentleman?"

"Well—"

The girl hesitated, but her mistress answered the question herself.

"Of course, he's not likely to be, with a name like that; no hyphen, just plain Smith—no!"

"He's brought a suitcase with him," said Briggs, trying to be helpful.

Mrs. Hardstaffe turned with relief to her tea.

"Oh, then he's a commercial traveller. Something to do with school-books, or pencils, or perhaps chalk. In that case, I don't have to ask him to tea."

"I don't think so, madam. I think he's a visitor."

A look of consternation spread across Mrs. Hardstaffe's face.

"I do hope he's not been invited to *stay* here," she said. "I really don't feel able to cope with visitors. I feel so *ill* all the time, though no one believes me. Well, I'm not going into that cold morning-room. You'd better bring him in here, Briggs, and I can decide about tea then." Briggs went out quietly.

Mrs. Hardstaffe selected two cakes, placed them on her plate lest the unknown visitor might choose them, and began to eat a piece of bread-and-butter.

Just like *him*, she thought. He never considers me. I mean no more to him than a dog: far less: he's fond of dogs. The only time the house is free from the creatures is when he's out. It's the only chance I have of any peace at all, but then it's so lonely. Oh, he's a hard man and a cruel man, too. Well, if he's come to stay, I shan't let him have my best linen sheets.

Her thoughts were as inconsequent as her speech.

"Mr. Smith," announced Briggs' voice from the door, and Mrs. Hardstaffe looked up to see an insignificant-looking man coming towards her, wearing a burberry, and carrying a bowler hat in his hand.

She smiled frostily.

"I'm so sorry my husband is out, but he'll be back soon," she said. "I expect something has delayed him at the school."

Then, with more warmth in her voice, she exclaimed: "Why, you look cold! I feel cold to-day, too, but no one else has seemed to notice it. Sit down by the fire, and have a cup of tea; it's freshly made. Oh no, not in that chair, if you don't mind—that's Mr. Hardstaffe's chair. He'd be most annoyed if he came in and found someone sitting there. He won't use any other in this room, though I'm sure they're all comfortable. Sugar?"

"No, thanks. I never take it. Just a little milk."

Mrs. Hardstaffe beamed at him.

"Really! How very convenient that much be in wartime. One is allowed such a little bit—a quarter of a pound, or half, or is it a pound? I never can remember, but I know it isn't enough. For all I know, I may not have my full ration. My daughter *will* give sugar to the dogs, and she does all the catering. I haven't been able to do anything of that kind since my operation. It has left me very weak. Really, sometimes I feel so *ill* at night that I feel I shall never get out of my bed again alive. And however well I sleep, I always wake up tired."

Sounds like one of those pictorial advertisements they run in the daily papers, thought Smith, but he said sympathetically enough. "I'm very sorry. I hope it wasn't a very serious operation."

"Just one of those things we poor women have to bear. I've had three miscarriages, you see. But I won't go into details." (Thank God for that, thought Smith). "I have to take care of myself. My doctor insists that I should take very great care indeed. But how can I do that in these days, and in this house? I usually go abroad for the winter: I can't stand this climate, but what can I do? I don't want to go to a place where I shall be bombed, yet I feel I shall die if I stay here. Indeed, Mr. Smith, this war is very hard on us invalids."

She became quite animated. She so rarely found a new audience to listen to the recital of her troubles, or, having found one, was even more rarely allowed to monopolise its attention.

A tinge of colour came into her pale cheeks, and Smith, looking at her squarely for the first time, thought how pretty she must have looked in the befrilled skirts and bodices of the early Georgian days of his own youth.

Her hair, though nearly white, still curled about her head. Her eyebrows were delicately traced by Nature, her features small. But pale pouches, criss-crossed with fine lines, curved in baggy half-moons beneath her pale blue eyes, and there were deep lines from her nose to the corners of her down-turned mouth.

She was, reflected Smith, either a very ill, or a very ill-tempered woman.

He sat on the extreme edge of a low chair, cup balanced in hand, and plate on knee, scarcely knowing how to broach the purpose of his visit, when the sound of doors banging, of dogs barking, and of a loud, cheerful voice raised in greeting, came from the hall.

Mrs. Hardstaffe's face resumed its habitual aggrieved expression.

"Oh dear! That's Leda—my daughter, you know, though I never can think why we ever chose such a name for her, for I'm sure she isn't in the least swan-like, more's the pity. I think you'd better put your cup and plate on the table," she added, inconsequently, "I hope you like dogs."

Before Smith had time to assimilate the significance of these remarks, the door opened, and Leda Hardstaffe walked into the room, surrounded by a pack of delighted, yelping Sealyhams, whose squirming jumps left fine streaks of white hairs on the hem of her navy-blue uniform. Then, perceiving a stranger, they hurled themselves at Smith, knocking both cup and plate on to the carpet.

The bitches indulged in snarling matches for the cake Smith had been eating, while the dogs shared the spilled tea, licking cup, saucer, spoon, and carpet, with equal care. When the last crumb of cake and drop of tea had been consumed, the dogs dispersed to their several favourite chair-legs in order to dispose of other liquid previously imbibed.

Mrs. Hardstaffe threw her knitting at the nearest dog. "Leda! I will not have the dogs in here. It's positively disgusting—and with a visitor here, too. You must forgive us," she said, turning to Smith. "These are kennel dogs. Leda breeds them, and I have had the most beautiful kennels built for them outside, but she ** keep bringing them into the house."

"I've got to house-train them, Mother, if I'm to sell them," said Leda. "They only do this kind of thing when I've been out, and I've told you before that it's because you *will* shut them up as soon as my back's turned. If you'd only leave them alone, they'd be all right."

"Well, I don't like dogs in the house," replied Mrs. Hardstaffe. "I've never been used to it. Just look at them!" She pointed to the Sealyhams who now, with panting tongues, and paws draped over the edge of every available chair, were engaged in completing various stages of their toilet. "They'll ruin the covers, and these were expensive ones." She turned again to Smith. "Do *you* like dogs all over a room, like this?"

"I'm very fond of dogs," Smith replied, fondling the ears of a young puppy which had curled round on the chair, behind him, "especially Sealyhams."

"They are splendid little fellows, aren't they?" said Leda, smiling down at him from the corner of the hearth where she was standing. "They're easily the best of the terriers, in my opinion—such loyal chaps. These are very well-bred, as a matter of fact. I've two champions already in the kennels, and I was hoping that Cherub—that's the puppy you're stroking—would do well, too, but the war's knocked all the big shows on the head."

"I think that you ought to get rid of them, Leda," said Mrs. Hardstaffe, "With all this shortage of food, it's most unpatriotic, I think, to breed them. Don't you agree, Mr. Smith?"

"Well, I believe the question has been raised, and that the Government has asked breeders not to give up their stock," said Smith.

Leda regarded him with interest.

"That's quite true," she said, "although very few people seem to know it. I've done very well with my puppies since the war. My customers are mostly men in the forces who want to give their wives or sweethearts a present. Of course, they're fed on scraps. My Sealyhams will eat anything."

"Sugar," murmured her mother, but Leda ignored her, and went on.

"It's difficult to make people realise that if you've got valuable bitches, it's very bad for them not to be mated periodically."

Mrs. Hardstaffe shuddered.

"That word!" she exclaimed. "And the way you discuss their family affairs in public! It's coarse!"

Leda laughed.

"Well, I'm not going to call them lady-dogs, even to please you, Mother," she said. "You ought to be used to it by now."

"I shall never get used to it," replied Mrs. Hardstaffe, with dignity.

Leda turned to Smith.

"Are you waiting to see Daddy?" she asked.

Smith hesitated.

"Well, yes, in a way," he said, "although I believe I had all the correspondence with you. I'm Arnold Smith."

"Good Lord! You're our evacuee!" exclaimed Leda. "You must forgive me, but seeing you there, talking to Mother . . . It just didn't occur to me somehow. Do you mean to say you never even asked him to take off his coat, Mother?" she demanded.

"Evacuee?" murmured Mrs. Hardstaffe vaguely. "I'm sure he doesn't look in the least . . ."

"You mustn't mind my calling you that," laughed Leda. "It's only my fun. You must have thought us very rude not to make you more welcome."

"But Leda, you never said a word to me about an—about Mr. Smith. Briggs said he had brought a suitcase, but I never thought—"

"You never do," sighed Leda. "That's the trouble. You really are most exasperating."

"It's my head," moaned Mrs. Hardstaffe, "I don't remember things. I feel so *ill* all the time."

"You'd better go and lie down, or you won't be fit for dinner," returned her daughter, and Mrs. Hardstaffe, with an apologetic smile towards Smith, rose, and went out.

Leda seated herself in the chair just vacated by her mother, and, flinging off her black tin hat with the white- painted W. in front, began to run a small pocket-comb through the long bob of her waved, golden hair. Smith was old-fashioned enough to be irritated by this, for he considered that combs should be confined to use in dressing-rooms, but he admitted to himself that she looked much more youthful and attractive with her hair thus framing her face.

"I'm so tired of wearing that old tin hat," she exclaimed. "We've been having a full-dress A.R.P. practice, and I'm a warden, so I had to be there. I really can't afford to spend the time on it, but it's our duty to Do Our Bit, isn't it? And Mother, of course, never does a thing. Do take your coat off, and make yourself at home. Park it anywhere. You'll find cigarettes in the silver box on the mantelpiece. I can't tell you how sorry I am that Daddy or I weren't in to welcome you, but you didn't say what train you were coming on, and we didn't know of one that could get you here before seven."

"It's my fault," Smith assured her. "I came by car. I'd saved my coupons specially."

"Lucky creature! We've had to give our car up." She pulled at her cigarette, and exhaled the smoke down her long, thin nose. "Look here, Mr. Smith," she went on, "did you think it too awful of me to ask four guineas a week? If I could have my way, I'd have you here for nothing. I'd just love to throw the house open to all the people of our class who've been blitzed, but Mother wouldn't hear of it. She wouldn't have anyone in the house unless they paid their full share, and I couldn't possibly board you for less, with prices at their present height. We live very well here, and it includes drinks, of course. There's always whiskey on the dining-room sideboard."

"No, no, that's all arranged," returned Smith, in some embarrassment, "but I have been wondering whether it will be convenient for me to stay. It's lovely country, and a charming house, and I should think you never hear a night bomber, do you?"

"We had flares one night, and that was quite exciting," she replied, "but we haven't a siren or anything like that. Still, that's no reason why we shouldn't keep up our A.R.P. and Red Cross Lectures: we've all got to Be Prepared: that's what I say."

"Quite so. I quite agree," said Smith hastily. "It really does seem a perfect spot for an author trying to forget air raids, and if you've changed your mind about having me here, perhaps I could find another house in the district."

Leda jerked up her head in sudden suspicion.

"Changed my mind?" she exclaimed. "Why should I have gone to all the trouble of answering your advertisement and getting your room ready for you. Mother can't be trusted to do anything. She worries too much about herself. She's always like that. Thinks nothing but her inside, but there's really nothing the matter with her. Some damnfool of a doctor once told her to take care of herself, and she's been taking care ever since. Have a drink?"

CHAPTER 3

ARNOLD Smith, having wallowed in a hot bath in the Hard-staffe's super-appointed bathroom, was still attired in his dressing-gown when the sounding of a gong in the hall below warned him that dinner was served.

He arrived downstairs ten minutes late.

"I'm so sorry—" he began, as he entered the drawing-room.

His voice faltered into silence, and he fingered his polka-dot bow tie with increasing embarrassment, as he thought that he might as well have saved himself the trouble of dressing, and walked down in his dressing-gown. For Mrs. Hardstaffe, still shivering with cold, wore a mink cape over just such a frilled evening gown as his imagination had pictured earlier in the day. Leda wore a period frock of gold brocade, Mr. Hardstaffe's trousers wore the side braid of a discarded fashion, his dinner jacket barely buttoned across his U-shaped waistcoat, and his shirt was soft and tucked: nevertheless his attire was sufficient to make Smith's striped grey suit look out of place. His look of annoyance made Smith think at first that he had noted and disliked this. But his words soon dispelled this idea.

"When you've had time to get used to our ways, Smith," he said pompously, "you'll know that it's a fetish of mine to be punctual at meals. Eight o'clock breakfast, twelve-thirty lunch, five o'clock tea, and dinner at eight prompt."

"That's what comes of being a schoolmaster," smiled Leda. "It's my fault, Daddy. I forgot to tell him."

Mrs. Hardstaffe nodded sympathetically.

"Well, what are you waiting for?" demanded her husband. 'Why don't you go in?"

Mrs. Hardstaffe's face immediately assumed its look of mask-like petulance, as, shrugging her shoulders, she turned and walked through the opened folding-doors into the dining-room, followed in silence by the others.

Exhibition of Victorianism, thought Smith, in silent amusement.

Somehow, he had not, until then, thought of the schoolmaster as a Victorian. In the drawing-room, balancing a sherry glass in his hand, he had appeared to be too young, and Smith had estimated his age to be as near to the half-century as his own. But the low light from the glaring white electric bowl in the dining-room was less flattering than the rose-coloured shades of the room they had just left, and against the more solid background of walnut sideboard, high bookcases, and carved, plush-covered chairs, Mr. Hardstaffe looked a veritable Gladstone, albeit a diminutive and clean-shaven one.

Must be nearer seventy than fifty, thought Smith, He makes me feel quite a gay young spark.

And he winked at Leda, who responded with a girlish giggle.

"I can't think why you always give me ducks to carve when we have a visitor," grumbled Hardstaffe. "If we can't have clippers to use on them, the least you can do is to have them disjointed in the kitchen."

"It is just vat I say to Mees 'Ardstaffe—In Germany, I say to 'er, always ve . . ."

The carving knife clattered on the polished table as Mr. Hardstaffe jumped round.

"What on earth . . . ? Who's this? Where's Briggs?"

Leda, barely stifling her laughter, replied.

"This is Frieda, our new maid. You remember that Mary left last week, to go on munitions, and Briggs is expecting to be called up any day. It's her evening out tonight."

"Oh."

Mr. Hardstaffe looked with some disgust at the beaming, perspiring girl who stood at his left side.

She was dressed in a flowered cotton frock whose short sleeves exposed fat, hairy arms. On her frizzy, wiry hair was perched an absurd circle of frilled lace, which bore more resemblance to a pin-cushion cover than to a housemaid's cap. Swarthy skin, black hair and eyes, and curved nose pronounced her to be of Jewish descent.

The fact that she was the cynosure of all eyes in the room seemed to cause her more pleasure than embarrassment, and, with a broad smile which showed her strong, white teeth, she said gutturally,

"Me gut parlourmaid."

"Take this plate, and don't talk so much," said Mr. Hardstaffe. "No, not to the gentleman: to Mrs. Hardstaffe. *This* lady." Thumping the table in front of his wife until the trinity of silver condiments rang in their corner.

Why did you have to choose an untrained girl?" he demanded. "We seem to have had a procession of them all through the year."

Leda raised her eyebrows.

"Blame Hitler. I didn't start the war," she said. "You don't realise what a job it is to get anyone at all."

'No, indeed." Mrs. Hardstaffe smiled sociably at Smith. "Girls are quite above themselves nowadays, with all these uniforms and high wages. I shudder to think what they'll be like after this war. Our other maid was christened Victoria Alexandra. Did you ever hear of such names for a village girl? Of course, we call her Briggs. But still, Leda, I did say it would be a mistake to have a refugee, especially a German."

"She's Austrian," retorted Leda.

"That's no recommendation," said Hardstaffe. "So is Hitler."

"Me gut parlourmaid," repeated the maid, and the diners, exchanging glances, fell silent.

"You must forgive my not dressing for dinner," said Smith, rushing into speech, then wishing that he had not done so. "I somehow thought that, as it's wartime, you wouldn't bother."

He did not add that he had not anticipated that the family of a village schoolmaster would aspire to such social heights.

"I suppose I didn't mention it because we always do dress," replied Leda, "and even though it is wartime, we've got to keep things going, haven't we? Business As Usual, you know: If Invasion Comes, and all that."

"Yes, yes, certainly," agreed Smith. "I must say that I like to see it, but everyone has given it up in London. It's not much use in an air raid shelter: too uncomfortable for men, and too cold for women. No, thanks, no spinach," he said, as a proffered dish moved into view near his left shoulder.

"Go on, 'ave some! Ver' gut. I make eet," replied Frieda.

Mr. Hardstaffe leaped to his feet, and dashed his table napkin on to his chair.

"We can't have this sort of thing at meals," he said, pointing his finger at the amazed girl. "Go out! Go to the kitchen!"

Leda took the vegetable-dish from the maid.

"Go along," she said, giving her a little push. "Tell Cook to give you something to eat: that ought to please you. We'll wait on ourselves."

The girl stood obstinately still.

"Me no understand," she said, and her mouth quivered.

"Oh yes, you do," replied Leda, propelling her towards the door. "You told me you were fully trained, and you can't even wait at table."

"Me gut parlourmaid—" the girl said again.

"I won't have any more of this nonsense," stormed Hardstaffe. "Get out of this room, and don't come in again, do you hear? What do you think I am?"

"You bad man!" shouted the maid, and, bursting into a storm of weeping, she rushed out of the room.

Leda closed the door, then leaned against it, roaring with laughter, while Smith, who was hungry, wished she would return to her place at the table so that, he could sit down again.

"Do come and sit down, and let's get on with dinner," said her mother fretfully. "It's half cold already, and you know how it upsets me to eat stale food. Of course, we shall have to get rid of the girl. I've never seen such an exhibition in my life. I really couldn't sleep knowing that anyone like that was in the house. She's quite irresponsible. Why, she's capable of murdering anyone she takes a dislike to. Do come and sit down, Leda."

"We can't get rid of her, Mother," said Leda, striding to her chair. "Who do you think we can get in her place? She was the only one on the books, and if Briggs leaves us, we've got to have a maid. You know it's quite impossible to run this house without one. I'll train her, as I've trained all the others. As for being murdered, *I* shall have a say in that."

"I must say this is the first time I've felt any sympathy for 'That Man'," remarked Mrs. Hardstaffe, "but if all Jews are like her, I don't wonder he cleared them out of the country, do you?"

"Oh, I shouldn't be too hard on her," replied Smith. "She'll probably make a good maid in time. They've been through some terrible times, these refugees. I don't doubt that she's seen and heard things that no woman ought to do, and it may have unbalanced her a bit. We've most of us been through it, during the bad blitzes in the towns, and it makes one more sympathetic to those poor creatures who've had to face worse than that. It's bad enough to lose your home and possessions, but it's a great deal worse to have to pack your bag and flee for your life across Europe to a strange country where you don't understand their language or customs. Personally, I don't know how I should stand up to it: it must be much worse for a woman."

"You put it so well, Mr. Smith," smiled Mrs. Hardstaffe. "I'm sure I don't know what I should do if I were a healthy young girl in that position. But, of course, I do know what would happen to me as I am. My health would never stand it, and I should simply collapse."

"Oh, you're both Defeatists," said Leda. "I don't know what I should do, if it comes to that, but I'm quite sure I should make a better show of it than that wretched girl. What do you say, Daddy?"

"Aren't we going to have any sweet tonight?" growled the schoolmaster, as he tossed the bones off his plate to the dogs which had swarmed into the room with them, and then put his plate down on the floor for them to lick.

They finished the meal without further incident, then Smith rose to open the door for the ladies, while Hardstaffe, who had remained seated, busied himself with the decanter of port which Leda had placed in front of him.

Smith joined him with some reluctance, and the school-master, apparently sensing that he had made a bad impression on the guest, said, in his most ingratiating manner,

"You must forgive me if I'm not at my best to-day. I've been worried lately over a personal matter, and to-day has been particularly upsetting. Things go wrong at school some-times, and my wife is, of course, always an anxiety to me. I'm afraid I get short-tempered very often nowadays, but you mustn't take any notice of that. Leda would never forgive me if I frightened you away."

Under the mellifluous influence of his good Cockburn, Hardstaffe grew more jovial, and Smith noticed that his eyes looked more than ever "like fresh-blown thrush eggs on a thread, Faint-blue and loosely floating in his head."

They exchanged the jokes with which men are accustomed to entertain each other in the absence of their womenfolk, and decided, each for himself, that the other was not such a bad fellow after all.

When they got up to join the ladies, Hardstaffe playfully patted Smith's shoulder.

"I'm glad you've come," he said. "You'll be company for Leda."

CHAPTER 4

"BUT you haven't come here to be company for Leda," Smith reminded himself, a few weeks later. "You're supposed to be writing a book, blazing a new trail, striking out in a fresh line. You've no excuse: there's no blitz here."

No, there was no blitz in this peaceful corner of North-shire, although the inhabitants of Nether Naughton took their training as Wardens, Home Guards, A.F.S., and W.V.S. as seriously as if they expected invasion suddenly to be their lot, with squadrons of dive-bombers zooming down with every intention of exterminating the little village which sprawled so untidily over the very least of the Northdown Hills. Here was no ululating siren to disturb his work and shorten his temper; and only once had Smith heard the syncopated throbbing of a plane overhead at night, which, for all he knew, might have been British, though the villagers found it more exciting to believe that it was not.

Every night, he went to bed vowing that tomorrow he would begin to write his new book. Every morning, when he got out of bed to obey the call of a stuttering robin, drew back the patterned curtains, and raised the black linen blind to gaze across the misty-treed garden to the distant mountains and lake, he vowed that to-day he was going to begin it. Yet every day passed with his vow un-fulfilled, chiefly owing to his pursuit of Leda. For when she was so kind and jolly, how could he fail to offer to drive her to the nearest market town to do her shopping, to help her to exercise the dogs, or to give her a game of golf?

He sighed.

If only he could go on writing the kind of book he was accustomed to, it would be no trouble at all, he thought. He could hit off one of those almost without thinking about it. For many years now, he had been writing novels of weak adventure, sugared with ladylike romance, and for many years, they had supplied quite a comfortable income for a bachelor like himself, who had a simple taste for food and drink, and none whatever for women. Now, however, the sales of his books had dropped so low that he had had to consider turning his pen to a more modern style of fiction, for man cannot live by cheap editions alone.

"This is the Age of Youth," his literary agent had said, "and you must write for the young people of to-day if you want your books to become popular. Now you, Mr. Smith, if you'll forgive my saying so, never did write for young people even when you were young yourself, and when the last old lady who collects your books dies—and she can't be very far off it now—no one will read your books at all, let alone buy them."

"But what other kind of novel can I attempt?" asked Smith, running troubled fingers through his thinning hair.

The agent regarded him somewhat pityingly.

"Well," he said slowly, "unless you're related to a Personage, or have done something remarkable, such as travelling to Sardinia on a sardine, the only thing is to turn to murder. In other words, detective fiction."

"I don't like the idea at all," frowned Smith. "What about historical romance? I wrote a novel on those lines once. It was about the Queen of Sheba. Do you remember it?"

"Yes," replied the agent, suppressing a shudder.

In fact, he had never been able to forget it. It had lain in his office for years, until, in response to repeated inquiries from Smith, he had at length returned it with a softened paraphrase of his reader's very outspoken comments.

"That book illustrates what, to me, is the chief weakness of your books, Mr. Smith," he went on. "You have obviously never met a woman of that type—gold-diggers, I think they call them nowadays—and yet you go and write about one."

"I daresay you haven't met one, either," retorted Smith, who still thought it a good book.

"Perhaps not," replied the agent, with an air which seemed to convey the impression that, if he had done so, he would at least have known how to deal with her. "What I'm trying to say is that you must get into the atmosphere of your books more, if you want to become a successful author. And, mind you," he added, using in full the charm of manner which had gone far towards making him a successful literary agent, "there's no reason why you shouldn't make a name for yourself. No one can deny your ability to write."

"But—murder!" exclaimed Smith, now fully placated. "How can I possibly get into the atmosphere of crime? I know nothing about murder. I've never met a murderer."

"Well, go and meet one," was the agent's reply, as he rose to his feet and proffered his hand in the most genial manner to put an end to an interview which had already taken up too much of his valuable time. "And if you can't meet one, go and commit a murder yourself, because if you can't strike out in a new line, you might as well go sheep-farming in Australia. Good-bye."

And, since, at fifty, a man cannot summon up enough enthusiasm to go sheep-farming anywhere, Arnold Smith had decided, with many misgivings, to become a writer of crime stories.

That had been nearly two years ago, and he had spent the time in inventing excuses to account for the undisturbed pile of blank manuscript paper on his desk. At first, it had been the certainty of the blitz; then the uncertainty of it. Finally, his flat which had for so long remained intact, fell to the bomb of a lone raider, and he, who had been one of the faithful, at last turned his back on the dear, scarred face of London.

And now he had no excuse. And still he could not write.

And so it might have continued, had not Leda taken a hand in the matter, as, sooner or later, she took a hand in the affairs of every man, woman, and child in the village.

One evening, as she was on her way home from organising a committee to form a dance in aid of the local Spitfire Fund, she came upon him, glooming along the road.

"What's wrong, Arnold?" she asked, in her most cheerful voice. "Lost a bawbee and found saxpence—or have I got it the wrong way round?"

"Oh, nothing wrong," he assured her.

"I see. Famous author in the throes, eh?"

He matched his step to hers, and seemed slightly embarrassed by her words.

He rarely mentioned his books to anyone. In his experience, authors hardly ever did, possibly because the fact that they could write down their thoughts more easily than they could speak them, had first made them become authors.

Rather diffidently, he explained his difficulty to Leda.

"I see," she said, giving serious, and therefore, flattering consideration to his words. "But why don't you set the scene here? New type of book, new surroundings: it's too much of a coincidence to be ignored. Give us a murder in the village! We should all be thrilled to death. I've read somewhere that the plot of a book should grow out of the characters, so what about Mother, to begin with? I've often said she ought to be put into a book, though I daresay you'd have to tone her down a bit, for I'm sure none of your readers would ever believe that anyone so queer could exist in real life. Yes, I do think that if you murdered Mother, it would be a great success!"

At first they laughed, but suddenly Smith exclaimed, "By Jove, yes! I like the idea, Leda. I really think I could work something out on those lines. I should have to look around for a few more characters, you know. And, of course, I shall have to have a love affair."

"That ought to be easy," Leda replied archly.

CHAPTER 5

"How long is this evacuee fellow going to stay here, Leda?" her father asked her one morning, as the two of them were taking the dogs for their daily rabbiting expedition across the fields before breakfast.

"Why?" asked Leda.

"Why? Well, for one thing, I consider that in the country's present emergency, every able-bodied man ought to be doing his bit in his own locality. This evacuation is only intended for women and children—his being here is like his taking a woman's place in the life-boat when the ship's sinking. He's not even volunteered for the Home Guard. A bit of a coward, if you ask me, to say nothing of being a bomb-bore. What are a few bombs to any man worth his salt? Now, in the last war . . ."

"You sound very nautical this morning," returned Leda. "I seem to remember that you were not in the last war. Correct me if I'm wrong."

"Don't you take that tone of voice to me!" shouted Hard-staffe, then, taking her arm, he said more softly, "I'm sorry, Leda. I've got a touch of liver this morning. The fact is, the fellow's beginning to get on my nerves. He was two minutes late for breakfast yesterday, and you know how that upsets me. And he was having a bath in the afternoon and I couldn't get into the bathroom to wash. Whoever heard of a healthy man bathing at four o'clock? Besides, he was singing 'Waltzing with Matilda', or some such nonsense, and you know how I hate people who sing in their bath!"

"Well, he does sing in tune," was Leda's pointed reply. "I rather like it myself. He's what you'd call 'a pleasant baritone'. Anyhow, we can't very well turn him out for a reason like that."

"No. But you could invent a plausible excuse for asking him to cut his visit short. Tell him that you find the catering too difficult. I'm sure he'll believe it, after that skinny bit of meat you provided for dinner last night. And no savoury either."

"You had cold meat for lunch," retorted Leda. "You can't expect to have meat twice a day, every day, and we're all sick of rabbit. As for savoury, we can't get enough cheese or Tomatoes, or sardines. You might try to realise that there's a war on."

"Never mind that. The long and short of it is that I don't like having a stranger in the house, and if you don't tell him to go, I shall."

"Really!" exclaimed Leda. "The explaining I have to do to you and Mother about wartime conditions would fill a book. The point about Arnold is that he's a decent, presentable sort of man who isn't much trouble in the house, even if he does sing in his bath. Wouldn't you rather have him than two of your evacuee schoolboys from Liverpool?"

"Preposterous! As headmaster . . ."

"As headmaster you'd certainly have to take the first two of the next batch we're expecting," interrupted Leda. "The whole village looked down its nose when you didn't set them an example by having two of the first lot, and they'd never let you get away with it again. Then you'd have hobnail boots and swearing and free fights all over the house, and the servants would give notice, and Mother will take to her bed, prostrate with shock. You might as well make up your mind that we shall have to have someone billeted on us. It might even be one of the teachers prying into all our private affairs. And Arnold Smith pays."

"Of course, if you've made up your mind . . ." said Hard-staffe, and the subject was dropped.

So it was that this particular morning opened badly for the schoolmaster.

He was a man who expected always to be agreed with, and when anyone got the better of him in argument, as Leda frequently did, he was left with a sense of grievance which sometimes persisted for several days.

Smith added insult to injury by appearing in the breakfast room nearly five minutes before the gong sounded, and was as boisterously cheerful as a Master of Foxhounds before a promising day's run.

Hardstaffe growled a salutation at him, greeted the breakfast dish with a scornful "Sausage again!" and, with his meal half-finished, slammed down his napkin, pushed back his chair, and set off for the short walk to school half-an-hour before his usual starting-time, thereby missing his matutinal glimpse of Charity Fuller's shapely legs moving deliciously before him across the school yard. He meted out an aggregate of five thousand lines to the children who were playing five minutes too soon in the asphalt playground at the back of the school, reprimanded the caretaker for having allowed them to go in, and strode through the front door, to sulk in his study until the clock's fingers pointed to five minutes to nine.

As he mounted the rostrum to conduct the customary prayers, staff and pupils alike regarded his expression with dismay, knowing from experience, that the day was likely to be a difficult, if not a disastrous one.

A smile from Charity might have softened somewhat the gathering tempest of his mood, but, remaining true to the new standard of behaviour which she had set for herself, she resolutely averted her head.

"Everyone's hand is against me," he thought in some bitterness.

Even the Scriptures seemed to mock at him, for the reading for the day was the thirteenth Chapter of St. Paul's First Epistle to the Corinthians.

After this, only the slightest touch was needed to set his fury ablaze, but after the final prayer, he dismissed them without incident. The teachers marshalled their pupils out of the packed forms, their feet marking time with the beating of their hearts.

Half the children had dispersed to their various classrooms when it happened.

"You, boy!" shouted Hardstaffe, pointing his finger at a tall, ragged-looking boy in Charity's class. "Pick up your feet! Don't be slovenly!"

"Yessir. Nosir."

The child's bright, mischievous eyes gave the lie to his tone of respect.

The headmaster turned back to his desk. Then, thinking perhaps to catch Charity's belated smile, he turned, and saw instead, the boy whom he had just reprimanded sticking out a full tongue at him, while making an expressively suggestive gesture with his fingers.

Before any of them had realised what was happening, Hardstaffe, his face livid with rage, had flung himself forward, pounced on the boy, and dragged him by the back of his coat collar into the space in front of the desk.

"Come back, all of you!" he shouted. "Bring all the children back here! Come along, quickly now!"

He waited in silence while, with frightened faces, they obeyed.

"So! Now I will show you what happens to boys who make fun of me behind my back! This boy is an evacuee. He has come from one of the bombed areas, and we have taken him into our home and showed him every kindness. And this—this!—is how he repays our kindness." He took the cane from its hook on the wall over the desk. "I will teach you to be grateful to those who are kind to you!" he shouted at the panic-stricken boy.

The cane rose and fell, rose and fell, and fell, and fell, and fell . . . The boy, at first blubbering, began to scream, and, falling to his knees, tried to fend off the merciless strokes.

But it was too late. The schoolmaster was oblivious to boys, cane, school, teachers—to everything except that everyone's hand was against him, and that his own hand, of its own volition, was levelling the score.

The only other male teacher on the Staff, a man named Richards, looked intently at the Head's suffused face and staring eyes, then moved forward, wrenched the cane from his hand, and gave a quick order.

"Two of you take this boy to the caretaker. The rest of you get the children to their rooms. Hurry!"

Hardstaffe stood for a moment, arms and legs trembling. Then he jerked up his head.

"Richards! How dare . . . !"

"The boy's fainted," said Richards shortly. "You can thank your God that these town boys are tough. If he dies, it will be murder, and I'll see you hanged for it. If he doesn't, I'll finish you off myself, *Mr. Squeers*!"

He tossed the cane into the fire which burned brightly in the barred grate.

Hardstaffe took a menacing step forward, but all the bluster had gone out of him, and he compromised by a half-hearted attempt to regain his lost authority.

"You will take my Form with your own, Richards," he ordered. "I am going to my study to write my report upon this shocking incident. If there wasn't a war on, I should certainly demand your suspension."

He walked shakily to his study, and lighted a cigarette with trembling fingers. After a short time, he dozed in his armchair in front of the fire.

It was late afternoon before he saw Charity alone. To his eyes, she looked lovelier and more desirable than ever.

"How could you do such a thing?" she asked. "How could you lower yourself to do it?"

He gazed at her distressed face through the watering, blood-shot eyes of an old man.

"I lost my temper, my dear," he said slowly. "One day I shall lose it with my wife."

CHAPTER 6

A PICTURESQUE account of the caning reached Smith's ears the same afternoon, and he reflected that, in truth, "Walls have ears and country folk have tongues."

Leda made a point of referring to it openly.

"You mustn't believe all you hear in the village," she said. "There's so little excitement here apart from whist drives, dances, or a Ministry of Information film show, that they dramatise everything that happens. Poor Daddy! Of course he caned the boy, but he couldn't allow insolence, especially from an evacuee, and these town boys are so cheeky."

Smith, having had some experience of London gamins, was inclined to agree with her version of the incident. Nevertheless, he was relieved, after dinner, to find that Hardstaffe had to leave immediately to attend a Churchwarden's meeting so that he was spared the embarrassment of their usual tête-à-tête. Leda, too, was booked for one of her innumerable committees, and he found himself alone with Mrs. Hardstaffe for the first time since the day of his arrival.

He was genuinely pleased to be with her alone, for it gave him a chance to study her. And, ever since that little talk with Leda, he had not been able to make up his mind whether to murder her mother or not.

He wondered what Mrs. Hardstaffe would think if she could know what was in his thoughts.

Perhaps some inkling of it did reach her, for she seemed to feel uneasy in his presence, and continued to hover around the coffee table long after they had finished drinking.

At length, she must have realised that she was behaving in a strange manner, for she suddenly sat down on the chair nearest to him, and said with a smile,

"I'm afraid I'm very restless tonight: I do hope you'll forgive me. I'm worried about something, and don't know what to do about it."

Smith said the obvious thing.

"Can I help in any way?"

"No. Oh no, I don't think so, thank you. It's very kind of you to ask. You may think it's nothing to worry about, but it means a lot to me . . . It's my sleeping-draughts. They haven't come from the Dispensary yet, and I've none left to take tonight. I know I shan't sleep a wink."

"Perhaps an aspirin or two . . ." suggested Smith.

"Oh dear, no! They wouldn't be of the slightest use," she smiled. "Besides aspirins *do* something to me. They upset my stomach, and affect my heart. These are special powders which my doctor makes up for me. They contain morphia, I believe. Oh, you needn't look alarmed, Mr. Smith. I shan't take too many of them, though I believe it would be extremely dangerous to exceed the dose. I can tell that they are very strong. Indeed, I have sometimes felt the temptation to take too many, and remove myself out of *their* way!"

She leaned forward, and gazed earnestly at him, while slow tears welled into her eyes.

"I'm not wanted in this house, Mr. Smith. Even my own daughter hates me. You must have noticed it. No one could live here without seeing how much they both loathe me. They do everything they can to humiliate me in front of other people, and, when there's no one here . . . ! But it's no use talking about that. All they want from me is my money. If I were to die, they'd dance at my funeral!"

Smith felt uncomfortable.

If this is getting under the skin of my characters, he thought, I can't say that I like it.

He got up, and patted her shoulder.

"You mustn't talk like that, Mrs. Hardstaffe," he said. "I'm sure they're both very fond of you. They just pretend to belittle your bad health, to keep you from worrying about it too much. You see," he added helplessly, "I'm a guest in this house. It's—well—difficult to discuss them."

Mrs. Hardstaffe blinked away her tears, and nodded at him.

He walked across to the opposite side of the room and, without thinking, seated himself at the piano and let his fingers stray rather clumsily, into the melody of Mendelssohn's *Duetto*.

But if he had hoped to cheer his companion, he had failed, for he returned to find her weeping bitterly.

"I'm sorry," he faltered. "I'll go up to my room. You'd rather be alone."

"No, please don't go, Mr. Smith," she said. "I shall be all right again in a minute."

She dried her eyes, blew her nose noisily, and turned again to him.

"I must apologise," she said. "I feel that I owe you an explanation. That piano has not been played for years, although I have it tuned regularly. It belongs to my son. I gave it to him when he was twenty-one. We were the only musical ones in the family."

"It's I who must apologise," replied Arnold. "I had no idea you had a son. Of course, the grief of losing him . . ."

He left the sentence unfinished.

"Oh, but he's not dead," said Mrs. Hardstaffe with more animation than she had displayed throughout the evening. "He's alive, thank God, and as long as that is so, I have one person in the world to love me. That is one happiness left to me."

"Then . . . ?"

Smith looked puzzled.

"His father won't have his name mentioned. They quarrelled—terribly—about me. Mr. Hardstaffe turned him out of the house, and forbade me to see him again. But I'm not entirely without strength of mind, Mr. Smith, whatever *they* may think. He's married now and has a darling little son." A mischievous smile curved round the down-turned corners of her mouth for a second. "Oh yes, I've seen him several times. How *they* would hate to know that! . . . Well, no one has played on that piano since he left, but it's always been a whim of mine to leave it open. He used to play the *Songs Without Words* too, so I'm sure you'll forgive an old woman for behaving so foolishly. I'm sorry I have had to tell you all this, but I owed it to you. And, it would be dreadful if you were to start playing when Mr. Hardstaffe was here. I shudder to think what might have happened if he had walked in tonight!"

"I don't see what he could have done about it," remarked Smith, feeling not at all happy to receive these confidences.

"No, of course you don't," was her unsatisfactory reply, and their conversation moved on to less emotional topics.

Suddenly they were both startled by a prolonged banging on the door, then Frieda entered the room, carrying a small, sealed box in one hand, and a silver salver in the other.

"Oh dear, Frieda," sighed Mrs. Hardstaffe, "when will you learn how to do things properly? The box goes on the salver, so. Do you see? And you must walk in quietly without knocking."

"I see. Gut," grinned the maid. "Now I go to bed."

She trotted out of the room.

"Oh dear!" Mrs. Hardstaffe exclaimed again. "Now she's left the salver here. I really do think Leda ought to pay a little more attention to training her instead of going off to run something or other in the village every day. She neglects everything so. This house used to look so pretty when I arranged it all. I wish I could still look after it myself, but I always feel so *ill* and *tired*. Yet I don't sleep well. Isn't that strange?"

"Well, you have your sleeping-draughts now, haven't you? There's no need to worry about a sleepless night."

"No." She smiled. "I shall sleep soundly to-night."

CHAPTER 7

Nevertheless, it was Arnold who went to bed first. Mrs. Hardstaffe, who usually drifted palely to bed immediately after the nine o'clock News, showed an unwonted desire to sit up and talk—a desire which he did not share.

He felt strangely bewildered by this close contact with the woman whom he had every intention of making his chief character. It was as if he had put out a hand to touch a ghost, and had felt, instead, a creature of flesh and blood.

But although he went to bed early, he could not sleep.

At last, feeling hot and restless, he put on his dressing gown and slippers, and, lifting the blind in the darkness, went to smoke a cigarette in the cool air at the open window. When he first looked out, he thought that the moon was shining, but soon he realised that the broad beam of light which struck across the smooth lawn came from the uncurtained window of the study, the room immediately beneath his own.

His first reaction was a desire to yell, "Put that perishing light out!" But the night air was still and silent, free from the throb of aeroplane engines, and he resisted the impulse, and peered down over the low sill.

It must be burglars, he decided, and, having selected one of his steel-shafted golf clubs from the bag in a corner of the bedroom, he crept on to the landing, led by the light from his pocket torch which glimmered bravely through its regulation layers of tissue paper.

He leaned over the wide, carved balustrade outside the door of his room.

The hall was in darkness. He could hear no sound.

Strange that, in a house full of dogs, there should be this silence, if there were indeed burglars below, he thought. But here, of course, the dogs were always in the wrong place:

barking round your ankles during the day, and sleeping in the bedrooms at night.

Arnold descended the wide stairs, and halted outside the study door, holding his breath and the mashie, and wishing, for some inexplicable reason, that it was a Number 2 Iron.

No sound issued from the study, and he had just convinced himself that someone had accidentally left the light on, when an enraged voice bellowed through the door, "Sign, damn you, sign!"

Then came an ominous sound. Crack! Crack!

My God! He's shot him! thought Smith, with no idea of the persons whom the pronouns implied.

Well, he'd been endeavouring for weeks to feel the atmosphere which he hoped to create in his book: he was now being plunged into one so unbelievably like that of an old-time melodrama, that he would have some hesitation in describing it.

His instinct was to open the door, and bash the first head he could see with the mashie. He had, however, sufficient presence of mind to reflect that such a procedure might result in bashing the wrong person, and, as he paused, he tried to imagine what that gay, dashing, debonair, imperturbable, devil-may-care, amateur detective, Noel Delare (who, as yet, existed only in his imagination) would do. But he was able only to think of what that elegant theme-detective would not do, and this, as it happened, he found helpful. For Noel Delare made it a point of honour never to enter any room by means of the door.

There remained, then, the window.

Smith walked softly along to the front door, which he was not surprised to find unlocked, and made his way along the grassy edge of the herbaceous border flanking the house, to the study window. He peered in, cautiously, then quickly jerked himself back.

It needed only one glance to explain the whole pitiful story.

Seated at the opened roll-top desk at the far corner of the room was Mrs. Hardstaffe, holding a pen in her hand which trembled over the paper in front of her, while someone menaced her with a knotted horse-whip, cracking it expertly within a few inches of her cowering shoulders.

Unseen, the watcher walked softly back to bed, feeling a coward, and convinced that Noel Delare would most certainly have plunged through the closed window.

But how could Smith intervene between husband and wife? He had no right to do so, and, from what he knew of Hardstaffe, any intervention would serve only to increase his cruelty.

Hardstaffe!

For, of course, it was that man—bully and wife-beater—who was the only other occupant of the study.

That settles it, thought Smith savagely. He shall be murdered, even if I have to do it myself!

CHAPTER 8

THE following morning, Smith's fears that breakfast might prove to be an awkward meal were soon dispelled. It was, in fact, far less awkward than usual, for Mr. Hardstaffe, one of the wide circle of men who are not usually in control of their tempers before ten o'clock in the morning, was almost exuberant, and did not even glance at his watch when his guest came downstairs and found the others already eating porridge.

Mrs. Hardstaffe was unsmiling and monosyllabic, but this was not strange, since she commenced each day with the grievance that her husband would not allow her to have breakfast in bed.

As for Leda, she was her usual, imperturbable, cheerful self.

Really, no one can help admiring her, he thought. She takes everything in her stride. And a pretty hefty stride, too, he added, rather ruefully, as he remembered the pace she set for their walks together.

"Sorry to be late," he murmured. "I've been packing my case."

Mr. Hardstaffe looked up.

"You're not leaving us, are you?" he asked hopefully.

"Oh, no. I'm going to London for a few days on business."

"But I thought you were afraid of bombs," remarked Mrs. Hardstaffe.

"Mother!" protested Leda, turning to Arnold with a look which seemed to say, "What else can you expect from *her*!"

"Well, I'm sure your father told me . . ."

"Rubbish!" snapped her husband. "Besides there haven't been any in London for months. You'd better get back by Saturday," he went on, putting his porridge plate on to the floor for the dogs to fight over. "We have a charming young guest coming to dinner."

"That's the first I've heard of it," said Leda. "I think you might have asked me first. The food's difficult enough without anyone extra, what with a ration book and a pink ration book and a yellow ration book. Who is it?"

"Miss Fuller."

"Miss—?" Leda stared. "I thought you didn't like having any of the teachers here. What's the idea?"

"Don't ask me," replied her father. "Your mother invited her."

"Mother! You?"

Mrs. Hardstaffe moistened her dry, colourless lips.

"Yes. Your father—that is—I thought that as she is leaving soon . . ."

Leda smiled.

"Oh, if she's leaving . . ." she said, and left the sentence to hang in mid-air. "If you want to catch that train, Arnold," she went on, pushing back her chair, and moving from the table, "you'd better get a move on."

"Are you driving Mr. Smith to the station?" asked Mrs. Hardstaffe. "Can I do anything for you while you're away?"

"No, no," replied Leda hastily. "I'll see to everything when I get back. You know you always upset them in the kitchen."

"I hope I'm not taking you away from anything important by deciding to go so suddenly," said Arnold, when he was sitting beside Leda in his car, some minutes later. "I could easily have left the car at the station for you to pick up later."

"Nonsense!" laughed Leda. "You mustn't take any notice of Mother. Her one ambition is to go into the kitchen and tell the maids to stop doing one thing and go and do something else. She doesn't like to feel that I have the ordering of everything, but she's too bone-idle to do it herself. They simply dread her going into the kitchen. And anyway, I should be an ungrateful wretch if I couldn't spare half-an-hour with you. You're always doing things for me."

"Nonsense!" exclaimed Arnold, in his turn. "I shall miss you when I get up to Town."

"Splendid!" was Leda's gay reply. "There's no danger of your forgetting to come back to us, then."

"Rather not. Besides, I've got to finish my book, and you're my inspiration, you know."

Leda looked straight ahead without speaking, for a few seconds.

At length she said, quietly.

"I think that's quite the nicest thing any man has ever said to me."

"Oh, rot!" exclaimed Arnold in some embarrassment, for he had made the remark as a joke. "You must know dozens of people who pay you better compliments than that."

"I'm afraid I don't," she said, still serious. "Women don't like me, and I scarcely know a dozen men. It's quite true," she went on, cutting short his polite protest. "My people are so difficult. Daddy scowls if a man looks at me —he'd be so lost without me to look after him. And Mother! Well, you can see for yourself how helpless she is. I haven't had much chance to make many friends. You simply can't realise what it has meant to me to have you to go walks with, and talk to. Oh, I'm not being sloppy, or anything like that. You know I'm not that kind of girl. I've thought, once or twice, that your own life must have been almost as quiet, that is, unless you're married and want to keep it quiet for a bit."

Arnold laughed.

"No, I haven't got a wife up my sleeve," he said. "And, in a way, you're right about my life. I've certainly never met a woman I wanted to marry, and I'm afraid it's a bit too late now. For one thing, she'd have to have plenty of money, and rich women are a bit difficult to find nowadays."

Leda glanced at him quickly to see whether he was joking.

"You never know your luck," she said. "As for being too late—well, you know what the song says, 'When you fancy you are past love, it is then you meet your last love.'"

"'And you love her as you've never loved before! H'm, I wonder.'"

"Well, here we are!" exclaimed Leda, as she brought the car to a standstill outside the station. "No time to wonder now: you'll only just catch that train. You don't expect me to come onto the platform, I hope. I can't bear waving and shouting sweet nothings while the engine blows off steam. Good-bye. Take care of yourself, and come back soon."

She turned the car and drove off, leaving Arnold to wonder whether he had imagined that her eyes were wet.

He chose a compartment, and, having settled in a corner seat, glanced in desultory fashion at the morning paper.

But he soon grew tired of this.

Reading the papers wasn't much good nowadays, he thought. Once you'd listened to the wireless news, the printed words were just so much repetition, and the less official columns were given up to speculations about what Hitler might do next. As if everyone wasn't so sick of the little house-painter that they'd ceased to care what he did!

He gave the paper to a rather forlorn-looking man opposite, who received it avidly. Then he folded his arms and began to think about Leda.

The stay-at-home daughter was not so common now as in his younger days, and this, he felt, was as it should be. It was a shame that a young, capable girl like Leda should have so few chances. Young? Well, she must be about thirty-two, he supposed, but that was considered the most attractive age for a woman in these enlightened times. Women no longer lived in Quality Street.

Yes, he might have considered marrying Leda if she had had money of her own: they were good friends, and what with his books and her dogs, they might make a great success of life together. He might have considered it, even, if she had been in the least attractive physically. But, after all, he hadn't remained a bachelor for fifty years for the sake of a woman who hadn't a jot of feminine charm, or what was known in the language of to-day as "oomph." He wouldn't mind making a fool of himself over one of those "devastating redheads" about whom he heard a lot, but had as yet never seen. But . . . Leda . . . ! She wasn't the sloppy kind, as she often declared, but she would at least expect him to kiss her. . . .

No. Leda would have to have a good deal of money, he decided. . . .

His thoughts turned to the murder of Mr. Hardstaffe.

He smiled as he wondered how the other occupants of the railway carriage would have received the information that he was plotting to exterminate one of their fellow creatures.

"Impossible!" they would say. "Why, he's fifty if he's a day, and such a mild inoffensive-looking little man. I don't believe it!"

Oh, well! He was not the first mild little man of fifty to turn his hand to murder. There had been one, not so very long ago, named Dr. Crippen.

He had been studying the history of Crippen's crime for some weeks now, and Lord Birkenhead's words had seemed particularly applicable to himself.

"It seemed incredible," he had written, "that the little insignificant man should have been capable of such an unusually callous, calculated and cold-blooded murder."

For, allowing for the alliterative choice of words which he, as a writer, could fully appreciate, no better sentence could be composed to describe the murder which Arnold had planned in the early hours of this morning.

When the train drew slowly into Paddington Station, he had worked out the full details of that plan. It was so simple that he laughed aloud in the taxi which took him to his modest club.

But he was not the only man who planned murder that night.

He heard the sinister wail of sirens as he stepped into his bath, but with the deliberate bravado befitting a potential murderer, he continued his toilet as if unmoved by the sound. Then came the barrage of guns.

He was knotting his tie in front of the bedroom mirror when he heard the whistle of the first bomb, and was in the bathroom when he heard the second, with no recollection of how he had got there. He flung up his arms in an instinctive movement to shield his head, and yelled aloud as the third bomb struck the building with a devastating cataclysm of noise.

He felt himself lifted up and dashed against the hideously shuddering walls, and knew no more.

CHAPTER 9

TEN days later, Arnold Smith found himself returning to Nether Naughton in a first-class carriage filled with third-class passengers.

This time he was not thinking of murder. He was entirely absorbed in wishing that the other people in the compartment would stop talking, especially the sailor in the corner who appeared to be determined to indulge in Careless Talk.

Arnold leaned back in the corner seat which an exorbitant tip had procured for him, and closed his eyes. His head ached, and he still felt rather dazed and unsure of himself.

He had only a vague recollection of his experience in Town. He had been in a building which was hit by a bomb, he knew, but after that, he had seemed to be living in a dream, in which things were not quite real.

But somewhere in his mind he was conscious of something which he could not remember, although he felt that it was important for him to do so.

As the journey lengthened, the crowd in the carriage thinned, until he was left alone for a blissful half-hour, and dozed until the train drew up at the tiny station of Nether Naughton.

He had telephoned to Leda the previous evening, to tell her of his expected arrival, but she had been out, and he had left a message with a maid. He gave up his ticket, and walked out through the station gates, expecting to see her at the wheel of his car. There was no sign of her or of anyone who might have brought a message. The thought of walking was distasteful to him, for the station was situated a mile away from the village, presumably so that its inhabitants should not be disturbed by the noise of the main-line trains.

The train had been an hour late, so he returned to the station to ascertain if Leda had called for him on time, and intended to call again later.

"Who, sir? Miss Hardstaffe, sir?" asked the station-master-ticket-collector. "Oh no, not to-day she hasn't been. You wouldn't hardly expect it, would you?"

Arnold stared at him.

"Well, yes, I did expect her," he said abruptly. "She usually drives my car for me, and . . ."

The station-master looked at him more closely.

"Oh, it's you, sir," he said. "I didn't notice you properly. You'll be the gentleman who's staying at the Hardstaffes'. Well, you couldn't rightly blame her for not coming. Very sad, sir. Very sad. 'From battle, murder, and sudden death,' that's what we say on our knees of a Sunday, but it comes to us all just the same."

Arnold felt cold and apprehensive.

"Sudden death?" he asked. "At the Hardstaffe's? Sudden Death! Not . . . ?"

The station-master eyed him strangely, he thought.

"Why, haven't you heard, sir? I'm sure I wouldn't for the world have . . . but you being their friend . . . Yes, sudden death it was for sure. And," he moved his head confidentially forward, "if you was to say it was murder, sir, it's my notion you wouldn't be wrong. No, you wouldn't be wrong!"

It was then that Arnold remembered the elusive fact which he had felt to be so important.

He turned without another word, and made off as quickly as he could, leaving his suitcase standing on the ground, while the station-master lifted a bewildered forefinger and gave his forehead a significant tap.

CHAPTER 10

ARNOLD Smith passed the door of the constable's modern concrete bungalow several times before he finally summoned enough courage to walk along the narrow path between the cabbages and onions in the front garden up to the green-painted door itself. In response to his knock, it was opened by Constable Files, looking singularly undressed without his peaked, flat-crowned hat.

"Good-evening," he said in the cheerfully expectant voice which had sold many a ticket for Police Charity Concerts. "What can I do for you?"

"It's rather important," said Arnold, stammering a little. "Come in, sir." He ushered Smith into a small, barely-furnished, well-scrubbed room on the right of the tiny hall. "My Superintendent's here. You won't mind talking in front of him, I daresay. Superintendent Cheam. Mr. Smith. This is the gentleman who is staying with the Hardstaffes, sir," he explained, after having effected his introductions. "Glad to see you back again, sir. Miss Hardstaffe was quite worried at having no word from you."

"I was—detained," explained Arnold. "Well, as a matter of fact I bumped into the first raid London has had for some time. In a way, it has something to do with my visit to you now."

He paused for a moment, then,

"I've come to give myself up for murder!" he said.

The Superintendent and the Constable exchanged quick glances.

"Perhaps you'll sit down, Mr. Smith," said Files, pushing forward a hard, wooden chair. "Now, murder, you say. Was that in London?"

"In London?" repeated Arnold impatiently. "Of course not. It was here, in the village. At the Hardstaffe's."

The Superintendent leaned forward.

"And who told you that there had been a murder in the village?" he asked.

"The station-master," replied Arnold, adding in haste, "Of course, I knew about it before, or, at least I should have done if I hadn't happened to get a knock on the head in the raid. After that, I felt muzzy for days, and although I thought I remained in London all the time, there was something I knew I'd done that puzzled me. As soon as I heard that there'd been a—a murder at the Hardstaffe's I knew in a flash what had happened, so I came to give myself up at once. You ought to have no trouble in tracing my movements and getting the evidence you need to convict me."

The Constable nodded.

"I see, sir. A blow on the head, you said. You must have had a pretty narrow escape. Perhaps you'll tell us all you know about this murder."

Arnold ran a sweating finger round the inside of his starched collar, then played with the heavy, engraved ring through which his tie was threaded.

'It's all a dreadful shock," he said. "I'd made my plans for the murder and worked them out to the last detail; I admit that. But I never intended to murder Mr. Hardstaffe really. I only meant to write it all." He noticed that the two policemen exchanged glances again, and he hesitated. "I'm afraid I'm not being too clear about this," he said. "Perhaps you'd like to ask a few questions."

"No, that's all right," the Superintendent assured him. "Just tell us the story in your own way."

Arnold smiled ruefully.

"That's what I was afraid you'd say," he remarked. "I'm certainly getting some first-hand information for my book now, but I'm afraid it will be too late to be of any use to me. You see, it's like this. I'm writing a detective novel, and I'd cast old Hardstaffe as the victim and myself as the murderer. In it,

I am a writer who becomes so affected by the atmosphere of hatred in the house where I am staying that I become obsessed with the idea that it will make a perfect setting for a murder, and determine to commit one. It sounds a bit involved, I know, but there's no doubt whatever in my mind that when I got that bang on the head, I submerged myself in the character I had created, returned here to murder Mr. Hardstaffe, and somehow got back to London. My movements have all been rather hazy to me since I was in the raid, but as soon as I heard at the station what had happened, something clicked into place in my mind, and I said to myself, 'My God! I've murdered him!'"

There was a pause. Then the Superintendent said,

"You hadn't any real reason for killing him, then?"

Arnold hesitated.

"Well, I disliked him intensely," he said at length. "He was one of the worst-mannered men I've ever met, and he treated his wife abominably. There's absolutely no doubt in my mind that he would have murdered her if I hadn't disposed of him first."

For the first time, his audience showed signs of real interest.

"What makes you think that, sir?"

Arnold described the scene he had inadvertently witnessed in the study.

It could no longer hurt Mr. Hardstaffe, and it might count in his own favour if he related the incident, he thought.

"Most interesting," remarked the Superintendent.

"Most," agreed the Constable.

Arnold became annoyed.

"Look here!" he exclaimed. "You don't seem to believe a word I'm saying. Well, I'll prove it to you that I'm a murderer. I'll tell you exactly what I did, and exactly what Mr. Hardstaffe looked like after I'd—finished with him. The only thing I can't tell you is which night it took place, because . . ."

"Because it was after you'd had that knock on the head," the Constable suggested unnecessarily.

Superintendent frowned at him.

"Yes," agreed Arnold. "I know it sounds as if I'm joking, but you'll see . . . And, in any case, it doesn't make any difference to my story because they all do exactly the same things in that house every night of the year. Mrs. Hardstaffe goes to bed at half-past nine, Miss Hardstaffe goes at half-past ten, and Mr. Hardstaffe sits up with a tantalus of whiskey and a syphon of sodawater till after the midnight news."

"And who locks up the house for the night?" asked Cheam.

"Miss Hardstaffe," replied Arnold. "She puts the dogs outside, then goes to see that the kitchen quarters are safe— no fires burning or lights forgotten. She lets the dogs in again, locks and bolts the front door, takes the dogs to the bedrooms— yes, they all sleep upstairs—then goes to bed herself."

Arnold paused for a moment, and was pleased to see that Constable Files was apparently taking down his statement.

"I approach the house at about 11.15," he went on. "I enter through the open bay window of the drawing-room, knowing in advance that Mr. Hardstaffe is sure to have it opened, whatever the weather. (He's a fresh-air fiend). I stand for a few minutes behind the heavy plush curtain which blacks out the whole alcove. On the wall at my left hand hangs a meer-schaum pipe: on the right, a knobkerrie. I've often heard Mr. Hardstaffe's boast that he'd use the latter to split the skull of any parachutist who tried to force his way into the house. I take it, into my hand, and move silently through the curtains, blinking at first at the subdued light which comes from a standard lamp with a rose-coloured shade, which stands near the table at Mr. Hardstaffe's right. (Mr. Hardstaffe is partial to rose-coloured light: he thinks it makes him look young and handsome).

"I am not afraid that he will hear me, because he has now been alone for over an hour, and the tantalus is half-empty already. Besides, he is an old man, and his hearing is not as good as he likes to pretend.

"I am not afraid that he will see me, because the back of his chair is directly in front of the window through which I have just entered. And again, he is old, and is not likely to move out of his comfortable chair until he is ready to go to bed.

"I move across quietly to the chair. I steady myself. I lift the knobkerrie. I am too close to miss him. I bash his head in. I think of the cane beating a schoolboy to insensibility, and of the horsewhip cracking over his poor wife's head. And I *make quite sure* that he can't live!"

He shuddered.

"Then, sir," remarked the Superintendent, "he fell to the floor, and you dropped the weapon beside him, after wiping your fingerprints away?"

A cunning smile spread itself over Arnold's mild, round face.

"Oh, no. You'll find that you can't trip me up, Superintendent," he replied. "Hardstaffe didn't fall: he was held up by his own vanity! You see, although he was such a short, little man, he liked to pretend that he was really a Carnera. He took a large size in everything. Even collars, hats, and gloves were all a size too big for him—that's why he always looked so badly-dressed. His chair, too, was too large for him. It's one of those enormous, padded, enveloping ones with a low, inclined back. No one else is ever allowed to sit in it, and he never sits in any other, in that room. No. He just slumped in it, and his head rolled sideways towards the right arm. As for the knobkerrie, I threw it into the shrubbery on my way out of the grounds, and I had no need to wipe it because I was wearing gloves. Now do you believe me?"

He leaned back in his chair, and passed his hand over his eyes. The excitement which the telling of his story had aroused in him had suddenly passed away, leaving him very tired and dejected.

Constable Files completed his notes, then looked at Cheam.

"Thank you, sir, for coming along," said the Superintendent. "I expect you're feeling tired after your journey. We know where to find you if we should happen to need you for anything."

"But—but—" stammered Arnold. "Aren't you going to arrest me?"

"Not this time, sir," was the smiling reply.

"But—Mr. Hardstaffe? I—"

The Superintendent shook a weary head.

"He's not dead yet."

"Not dead?" Arnold stared unbelievingly. "Why, that's impossible! Those head injuries!"

The Constable shook his head. Superintendent Cheam had turned to look at some papers on the desk, as if to make it clear that he had no further interest in the interview.

"I'm afraid you're the only one whose head has been injured, sir," said Files patiently. "Nobody's even tried to murder Mr. Hardstaffe. I saw him walking down the village this morning."

Arnold looked utterly bewildered.

"But all that I've been telling you . . . ?"

"Ah! You've been letting your imagination run away with you a bit there. Been working a bit too hard on that book, I shouldn't wonder, and it's got on your nerves." Arnold rose to his feet, and swayed unsteadily. The Constable came across, and, taking him by the arm, propelled him gently through the door and out into the hall.

"If you take my advice, sir," he said, "you'll go and see the doctor in the morning. That knock on the head must have been worse than you imagined. You need a good long rest. Just you leave London alone for a bit, and stay up here in Nether Naughton: it's healthier."

"Then it's all nonsense?" demanded Arnold. "There isn't any tragedy at the Hardstaffes' after all?"

"Oh, I wouldn't go so far as to say that," remarked the Constable as he ushered him through the front door. *Mrs.* Hardstaffe was found dead in her bed on Sunday morning."

CHAPTER 11

THE inquest on Mrs. Hardstaffe was held on the following day.

Arnold, whose suggestion that he should move to the local inn had been waved aside by an indignant Leda, drove the bereaved daughter and husband to the large, bleak, single-storied building lent by the Women's Institute for the occasion. He sat with them in one of the small wooden chairs placed in rows, while the Coroner faced them over one of the green-baized card tables, and as many of the villagers as were not afraid of being dubbed "gawpers," crowded into the spaces behind them.

The doctor who had performed the post-mortem was called first.

The Coroner, a white-haired country lawyer, fidgetted as though his task was distasteful to him, and listened as though he did not in the least care how many grains of morphia had been found in the body of the schoolmaster's wife.

In fact, he did care very much.

He had lived in the village as long as he could recall—apart from such absences as were necessary for the purpose of education—and he had as a matter of course entered the legal firm in the nearby market town which bore his father's and grandfather's name. And so he remembered the time when Mrs. Hardstaffe had first come to live in Nether Naughton, a radiant little figure, suitably proud of being a headmaster's wife, and prouder still of the two children whom she adored.

To preside at an inquiry into the death of old Joe Latham who, too venturesome at ninety, had fallen downstairs and broken his neck, or to hold an inquest on Sally Mason's baby, left unattended in its gas-helmet during a mock attack by "invading forces;" such cases were part of his duty, and, legally, he found them a pleasant change from his routine work. But to inquire into the death of a woman with whom he had been friends as long as her husband permitted, and for whom he had remained a bachelor: a woman who, while appearing faded and nondescript to others, had remained radiant as a rose to him . . .

No, he did not like the task before him this morning.

He became aware that the young doctor had finished the medical discursion, and he hastily jerked himself into speech.

"There can be no doubt then, that Mrs. Hardstaffe died from an overdose of morphia. Did you at any time prescribe this drug for her, Dr. Lowell?"

The doctor hesitated.

"No, but I'm not Mrs. Hardstaffe's medical adviser. I am Dr. Macalistair's junior partner, as you probably know, but Macalistair always attended Mrs. Hardstaffe himself. She wouldn't have anyone else to advise her. But Dr. Macalistair happened to be away over the week-end, I answered Miss Hardstaffe's call, pronounced death extinct, and performed the post-mortem."

Superintendent Cheam leaned across from his own little cardtable, and whispered. The Coroner nodded, and was heard to say, "We'll call him later."

Dr. Lowell was waved away, and Leda called.

As she rose to her feet and seemed to steady herself for the ordeal, Arnold pressed her hand in sudden sympathy, an action which she seemed not to notice.

The Coroner regarded her without sympathy.

This was Emily Hardstaffe's daughter. A hard woman, competent, capable, and—to complete the alliteration, and only, he hoped, for that reason—callous. He'd like to bet that she'd led her poor mother the very devil of a life since her coming-of-age. And that had been a good many more years ago than Leda would care to admit.

Recollecting her as a pert, not unattractive, little girl, he reflected that, for her, the faery tale had been turned topsy-turvy: she was the Swan who had turned into the Ugly Duckling!

But he was not here to sit in judgment upon Emily's daughter. He could at least be thankful that she was not the kind of woman to faint or have hysterics.

"Dr. Lowell has told us that you telephoned him on Sunday morning. I take it, then, that you were the first one to find—er—Mrs. Hardstaffe."

"Yes," replied Leda.

Admirable witness, thought the coroner.

She's really marvellous, admired Arnold. Takes it all in her stride!

"Will you tell me about it—just in your own words?"

"Certainly," came Leda's calm words. "It was all very simple. We—that is, my father, mother, any guests we happen to have, and I—always breakfast together. Since rationing started, we've given up early cups of tea, so the maids don't go into the bedrooms before were up. We all rely on ourselves to wake on time: we're never called, like many people. On Sunday morning, Mother didn't come down at the usual time, and I thought it strange at once, because I've never known her late for a meal before."

I'll bet you haven't! thought Arnold grimly, as he pictured the scene: Mr. Hardstaffe, pulling out his watch, growing more testy every minute, and finally allowing his temper to flare out at the unfortunate culprit. Only, this time, the culprit had not appeared—would never do so again.

"After about ten minutes, my father and I felt uneasy," continued Leda, "so I went to find out why she did not come down." She paused, and for a second showed some sign of emotion. "She was quite dead. I went down to tell Daddy, and then rang up the doctor."

"It must have been a great shock," said the coroner.

"Yes. I thought at first that it was heart failure, but although Mother was always complaining about her health, I knew she was really as strong as a horse."

Poor Emily!

The Coroner restrained himself from any comment. He must, above all things, remain impartial, and remember that he was now the mouthpiece of Justice.

"I don't mean to sound unkind," said Leda hurriedly, as though she had sensed his antagonism, "but I once asked Dr. Macalistair if she had a weak heart, because if she had I knew she must be protected from all shocks, and he said that there was nothing wrong with it."

"I see. You've heard the evidence, now, that Mrs. Hardstaffe died from morphia poisoning. Have you any idea how she could have taken such a large dose?"

"Why, of course I have," replied Leda. "It's quite obvious that she took too many sleeping powders—the doctor had sent her a fresh supply a few days before. I've always been afraid that she might do so. She was always so careless over such things."

"Your mother took sleeping-draughts prescribed by Dr. Macalistair?"

"Yes. She's taken them for a year or more."

"And what makes you think that they contain morphia?"

"Oh, everybody knows that, even the servants," said Leda. "Mother liked to tell everyone that she slept badly and had to take morphia powders."

"Do you know how she knew they contained morphia?"

"I suppose Dr. Macalistair told her."

"So, in your opinion, Miss Hardstaffe, your mother accidentally took too many of the sleeping powders?"

"It's obvious, surely. What other explanation could there possibly be?"

The coroner glanced down at a pencilled note on the pad before him.

"When did you last see your mother alive?" he asked. "The night before she died. At about twenty-five minutes past nine when she said good-night before going upstairs to bed."

"You didn't go into her bedroom to see her?"

"No. I never did. She liked to read in bed, and didn't care to be disturbed."

"Did she seem any different from usual? Did she, for example, seem to be worried about anything?"

"No. She was worried about her health, of course, but there was nothing unusual in that."

"You didn't hear any sound from her room after you had gone to bed?"

"No. But my bedroom is on the opposite side of the house. Unless it was some loud noise, like a scream or a bang, I shouldn't hear it."

"Thank you, Miss Hardstaffe."

She was dismissed.

Hardstaffe gave a similar version of the breakfast scene, and he had last seen his wife alive a few seconds before Leda.

Arnold could picture the frail old lady bending down to drop a conventional kiss upon his half-averted brow, one over-ringed hand resting on his unresponsive shoulder. He had often wondered whether she still squeezed some sentimental pleasure from the habit, or whether it was merely a long-disused custom resuscitated for his own benefit. For Mrs. Hardstaffe's creed undoubtedly held the command, "Thou shalt always keep up appearances before strangers."

"You noticed nothing unusual about Mrs. Hardstaffe's manner that night?"

"Nothing whatever."

The coroner gritted his teeth before forcing himself to ask the next question.

"Miss Hardstaffe has said that you all met for the first time each day at breakfast. Am I correct in assuming that you and your wife did not occupy the same bedroom?"

"Quite right," came the bland reply, but Arnold saw the schoolmaster's hands clench until the knuckles were white.

He's having a job to control himself, he thought. I should think he's got a guilty conscience, too, after the way he treated that poor woman.

"You heard no sound during the night?"

"None whatever."

"Did you sleep near Mrs. Hardstaffe?"

Hardstaffe glared.

"We had adjoining rooms, if that's what you mean," he said.

"It is exactly what I do mean," returned the Coroner. "Are the two rooms connected or separate?"

"There is a communicating door which is always kept locked, but I don't see what . . ."

"And the key?"

"Oh, that was lost many, many years ago," replied Hardstaffe, whereat two of the men present were filled with a violent desire to punch his jaw.

"Have you any idea how your wife came to take an overdose of morphia?" persisted the coroner.

Hardstaffe relaxed his stance a little, and put his hands into his trousers pockets, jingling some loose coins.

"I see no reason to differ from my daughter's opinion," he said. "The first thing I noticed when I went into Mrs. Hardstaffe's bedroom was a number of wrapping papers from the powders scattered on the bedside table. Mrs. Hardstaffe had access to morphia through the powders, and evidently took an overdose by accident. I've told Dr. Macalistair dozens of times that it was dangerous to let her take these strong powders, but he simply took no notice. I hope that he will be publicly repri-manded for such gross carelessness."

"You don't think it possible that your wife deliberately took an overdose of morphia?"

"I can see no reason why she should have done such a thing," replied the schoolmaster.

Arnold could barely restrain his feelings. He could see nearly five feet of reason at present answering the coroner's questions.

CHAPTER 12

DR. MACALISTAIR next faced the bowling: a solid tower of a man with a wise face and brown, twinkling eyes.

"You have attended Mrs. Hardstaffe for many years, I believe, Doctor."

"Ever since she first came to the village some thirty years ago."

"For any particular ailment?"

"Apart from the usual bouts of bronchitis, influenza—that kind of thing—no."

"Your visits, then were not frequent?"

The doctor smiled.

"On the contrary. During the past few years or so, I have called regularly every month to see Mrs. Hardstaffe, and more often if she sent for me for any special reason.'

("My doctor's such a wonderful man," a quiet voice echoed in Arnold's mind. "I don't know what I should do if he didn't visit me regularly. I feel better as soon as he walks into the room. He's *so* sympathetic. I feel that he understands everything.")

"Professionally, of course?"

"Certainly."

"Perhaps it might be helpful if you enlarged on this a little," suggested the coroner.

The doctor smiled.

"With pleasure," he said, while his big burly figure seemed also to enlarge itself as if preparing to hold the audience. "Mrs. Hardstaffe was a highly-strung woman whose nerves were frequently upset. As a result, she suffered considerably from the little ills, such as indigestion, fatigue, palpitation, etc. which are produced by nervous strain. She was never in really good health, but there was nothing organically wrong with her . . ."

Leda and her father glanced at each other.

". . . Like most of us, she exaggerated her little ailments until they assumed important proportions in her own mind. It was all a part of the nervous trouble. Her insistence on her ill-health was a kind of escape-mechanism from certain personal troubles which—" He paused deliberately—"were real enough."

The coroner looked as if he were about to ask for yet more enlargement, made a note instead, then said,

"You prescribed sleeping draughts for her?"

"I sent powders from time to time for her to take with a little warm milk after she went to bed."

"Why did you prescribe them?"

Dr. Macalistair seemed to weigh the meaning of the question.

"Mrs. Hardstaffe complained of Insomnia," he said cautiously.

"Over a period of a year or more?"

The doctor shrugged his great shoulders.

"About that. It was all part of her nervous state."

"Did you specify that she should take only one powder each night?"

"The instructions would be on the box."

"And were the powders strictly supervised in the dispensary so that there could be no likelihood of a mistake being made in the prescription?"

"No. I should merely tell my partner, Dr. Lowell, who does the dispensing, that more powders were needed for Mrs. Hardstaffe, and they would be made up according to the prescription, and sent off."

"Surely that is a very dangerous procedure, Doctor." The doctor frowned.

"It is the usual thing."

"But suppose that a mistake had been made in this instance?"

"It is extremely unlikely."

The coroner leaned forward.

"It seems to me that it is very likely indeed," he remarked coldly. "In fact, it almost certainly has happened. You don't appear to understand the significance of this, yet, you know, I presume, that Mrs. Hardstaffe has died from an overdose of morphia?"

Macalistair jumped slightly.

"The devil she has!" he roared, to the joy of the congregated villagers.

Upon being called to order, the doctor lowered his voice slightly.

"I've come straight to this—this court," he explained, "by car from a short holiday in response to a wire from Superintendent Cheam. I arrived in time to take my stand here to answer your questions. I have not heard the testimony of the other witnesses, nor have I had a chance to pick up the local gossip. I knew that Mrs. Hardstaffe was dead, poor woman, and that there would be a post-mortem, but I knew Dr. Lowell would do it better even than myself, and didn't worry. If he says she died from morphia, you can take it that such is the case."

"Then surely you will agree that it is most probable that the morphia came from the sleeping powders."

"No!" roared Macalistair.

He moved the weight of his massive body from one foot to the other, and when he spoke again, his voice held a Scots accent which had not been perceptible before.

"It is not only improbable," he said. "It is an imposs-i-bil-ity!"

"But if we can establish the number of powders she swallowed . . ." persisted the coroner.

"Man!" roared Macalistair, "There was no morphia in those powders!"

The whole room gasped, and even the coroner was taken aback.

"But Miss Hardstaffe has told us that everyone in the house knew there was morphia in them."

"And who told them?" demanded the doctor. "Mrs. Hardstaffe, of course! And who told her? Did I? Certainly not! Nobody did tell her. She made it up so that she could impress her family and friends."

The coroner made a last effort.

"Both Mr. Hardstaffe and his daughter were considerably worried about your patient being constantly in possession of morphia. Mr. Hardstaffe has told us that he mentioned this to you several times. Didn't you explain that the powders contained none?"

"And have him go off and tell his wife?" demanded Macalistair. "No. As long as she thought the powders were doing her good, she could pretend that there was strychnine in them for all I cared."

"I see. And do you mind telling us what really was in the sleeping-powders?"

The doctor grinned like a happy schoolboy.

"Just powdered chalk with a pinch of sodium bicarbonate," he said.

CHAPTER 13

SUPERINTENDENT Cheam walked around the drawing-room in the Hardstaffe's house waiting for Leda.

The room reminded him of Mrs. Hardstaffe.

It was too fussy altogether for that horsey-faced daughter of hers, he decided. The old lady must have done quite a bit of travelling in her time, though, to judge from the many little ornaments scattered in glass-topped cases and over occasional tables. What if she had bought some morphia abroad, and concealed it in that Chinese ivory thing, probably bought in Cannes and made in Birmingham? . . . No, too much like a book: real life was less picturesque.

And, thinking of books, what a queer thing that confession of Mr. Smith's had been. Had the fellow been trying to collect authentic details of police procedure, or was it one of those Looking-Glass murders, confession first, crime afterwards? A bit of a loony, in his opinion. Must be, if he was keen on Miss Hardstaffe as they were saying in the village.

Well, there was the huge armchair with its back to the big bow window, and there the knobkerrie hanging on the left of the alcove. A nasty weapon. No man could recover from a blow on the head from that.

But, he reminded himself, he was not concerned with the murder of Mr. Hardstaffe with a knobkerrie; he was investigating the poisoning of Mrs. Hardstaffe by morphia.

And where the blazes had that daughter of theirs got to? Did she think he had nothing to do but wait here all day? Well, well, a man didn't become a Police Superintendent unless he had patience.

A few minutes later the door opened, and Briggs came in apologetically.

"I can't find Miss Hardstaffe anywhere," she said. "I think she must have gone out with the dogs."

"Oh well, perhaps I'd better . . ." began Cheam, then, looking at the girl, he went on, "I wonder whether I could go upstairs to Mrs. Hardstaffe's bedroom? You could come along too, to make sure that I don't pinch anything, you know. Not that I'm likely to, unless it's those nice pink cheeks of yours."

"Oh, Sup-er-in-ten-dent!" exclaimed Briggs in her high-pitched, off-duty voice. "And you with a daughter older'n me. Why, you're as bad as Mr. Hardstaffe, that you are!"

"Don't you be saucy, my girl, or I'll pinch something more than your cheeks," returned Cheam. "Come along now, unless you think Miss Hardstaffe will object to me seeing over the rooms?"

"Oh no, I'm sure she won't," said the maid, resuming her more serious manner. "How could anyone mind if it helps you to find out who murdered the poor mistress, and she such a kind, gentle lady who never harmed nobody."

"And who said she'd been murdered?"

"I did, and I'll say it again. Murdered. You'll never make me believe she killed herself. She wasn't that kind. She *enjoyed* life, did Mrs. Hardstaffe."

The Superintendent could think of no reason for such an extraordinary statement until he remembered that Briggs was one of those women whose chief pleasure is "a good cry." He assumed that she had placed her late mistress' enjoyment of ill-health in the same category of morbid pleasure.

By this time they had gone out into the wide, square hall, and were ascending the stairs to the balcony overhanging it, from which the bedrooms opened.

"It's the second of the doors from the left," Briggs explained. "The first one's the master's, the third one's the Best Spare, and the fourth is Mr. Smith's. Miss Leda's bedroom is round the corner, and so is mine and Cook's. But you'll know all about that, I expect: they've all been searched. My! but those men of yours are thorough, I will say. Cook says give them a vacuum cleaner and a few dusters and we'd have the spring-cleaning done in no time!"

Cheam unlocked the door of the second bedroom with a key he had taken from his pocket, and entered.

The bedroom still seemed to hold the pale, fleeting ghost of its late owner. Here, as in the room below, were the same scattered mementos of foreign countries, jostling alongside faded photographs of men and women, some of whom even Mrs. Hardstaffe must have forgotten.

"Why couldn't it have been suicide?" he asked suddenly.

Briggs started, then flushed.

"You fairly made me jump!" she exclaimed. 'Why? . . . Oh, you mean what I said? Because if she'd wanted to do away with herself, she'd have done it long ago. Stands to reason. A woman doesn't live with a man like the master for all them years and wait until she's sixty before she clears out of it. I shouldn't have stood the way he talked to her in front of us servants, and mind you, Miss Leda did her share of talking, too. She hasn't got her father's temper—not but what I think sometimes it's worse to be kind of cool and callous, the way she is."

The Superintendent did not seem to be listening. He walked across to the door connecting the two bedrooms and rubbed his little finger round the empty keyhole.

"What are you looking for?" asked Briggs suddenly suspicious.

"Grease," replied Cheam, regarding his finger thoughtfully. "I seem to have found it, too."

Briggs sniffed.

"Regular Mussolini, I shouldn't wonder," she remarked, tossing her 'permanent' curls. "I've got enough to do in this house as it is without cleaning keyholes out, and if you're looking for dirt, I can tell you right off that you'll find it. I've often told Miss Hardstaffe that she can't expect me to keep the place clean with only a half-daft German woman to help me. And those dogs!" She elevated a dainty nose. "They're always being sick or worse, on the carpets all over the house, making the place like a pigsty, and not healthy for decent folk to live in I say."

A distant wailing disturbed the Superintendent's delicately thorough examination of the room.

"What's that? An air raid siren?" he asked.

"You like your little joke, don't you?" said the maid, with pert assurance acquired from the knowledge that she was addressing the father of the girl friend with whom she "walked out of a Sunday." "You know as well as I do that we've got no sireens here. That's Mr. Stanton's little boy."

"Sez which?"

"Aren't you dense this morning, Mr. Cheam! Mr. Stanton is the master's son, and it's his baby boy crying. Mr. Stanton came for the funeral, of course, and I must say he's nice. Good-looking like his mother, not like *him*. It's like a book really, him coming back after all those years to his old home like the prodigal son after he'd quarrelled with his father. They still hate each other, though. I ve seen them looking at each other at dinner. They smile and talk as pleasant as you please, but there's murder in their eyes." She heaved a sentimental sigh. "Mr. Stanton's got such lovely eyes!"

Cheam turned on his heel, and walked out into the corridor, and into Mr. Hardstaffe's bedroom.

He walked round the room, noting the College Eleven photographs, the autographed oar suspended over the mantelpiece, the tasseled, moth-eaten cap.

Hardstaffe must have been Cox, with his build, thought Cheam. He must have been pretty fit for that. Perhaps it accounted for the old man's virility now, and his failure to take a degree then.

"Mrs. Hardstaffe must have been a very long-suffering woman," he murmured, forgetting that Briggs had followed him into the room.

"Oh, she was," said the non-stop maid. "It was anything for peace for her. She couldn't stand all the shouting and raving that went on when the master got really roused up about anything. He could always get his own way by smashing something, but it usually belonged to her, poor thing!"

"Did she ever stand up to him?"

"Oh yes, she did. She was proud, and there were certain things she wouldn't stand at all. I don't think you ought to touch any of the master's things, Mr. Cheam. I shall get into trouble if he finds out."

For the Superintendent was opening and searching the drawers of writing-table, tall-boy, and dressing-table.

"I'll deal with Mr. Hardstaffe," he replied. "What wouldn't the old lady stand for?"

"We-ll . . . Miss Fuller, for one thing. And a fair old row they had about her, I can tell you."

"When was this?"

"On Saturday night, the same night the poor mistress died."

"That's strange," remarked Cheam.

"I don't know that it was," replied Briggs. "It isn't the first time by a long chalk that the mistress has ticked him off about his girl-friends."

"I thought you said you weren't interested in keyholes," said Cheam, pointedly.

Briggs tossed an indignant head.

"Nor I'm not. I never was one to go peering about other folks' business. But it's like this: they've got such loud voices in this house that you can't help hearing what they say even when the door's shut, if you're passing. But on Saturday, the door was open. The master had just gone to bed, and the mistress must have been waiting for him, though she'd been in her room for some time. You see, Miss Fuller was here to dinner, and when she went, the master went with her."

"What time was all this?"

"Twelve o'clock or after. Miss Fuller went at about eleven o'clock. I'm usually in bed by ten o'clock, but when they have visitors, one of us has to stay up in case they ring for coffee or anything. It ought to have been Frieda's job but she doesn't seem able to keep awake after nine at night. Sleep and eat, that's all she does, the poor thing. So I sent her to bed and stayed up instead. I went along to see if the lights were switched off on the landing, and I saw the mistress standing in her dressing-gown and cap at the master's bedroom door."

"Go on," said Cheam.

"The door was open, and she was fairly giving it to him. She said she could see that he was up to his old tricks, and that she wouldn't have it. She said he'd had all her youth and he wasn't going to have any other woman's. She wouldn't have any more scandal in the village about his little ways. Everyone knew that he'd married her for money, she said, but if this affair with Miss Fuller went on, she'd take steps at once to see that he got none of it when she died. She said she'd go to see her lawyer on Monday. Then he must have laid hands on her, for she started to scream blue murder, and then I heard her go into her own room, and I went to bed."

"May I ask what all this is about?" asked a cold voice from the doorway.

CHAPTER 14

BRIGGS uttered a little squeal.

Cheam swung round to see Leda standing at the bedroom door wearing a holland overall over her black clothes, and muddied rubber Wellingtons. At her heel was the inevitable

Sealyham—a puppy which, not yet having reached the age of suspicion, ran forward in wriggling ecstasy to lick the Superintendent's regulation boots.

"I know you have certain inquiries to carry out, Superintendent Cheam," she said, pushing a grimy hand into her overall pocket to search for a cigarette, "but I think a certain politeness might be observed in the course of your duty. I should prefer you to ask for me personally whenever you wish to see anything in the house, rather than spend your time with this chattering girl."

"I'm sorry, Miss Hardstaffe," said Cheam. "Vicky did go to look for you, but she couldn't find you, so I took the liberty of asking her to let me come up to see the rooms. In a case of murder, you know, time is precious, and we have to come and go as we please."

Leda frowned at Briggs.

"Vicky" indeed! she thought. The girl will be getting quite above herself.

"Stupid girl!" she exclaimed aloud. "You know perfectly well that this is my day for doing out the kennels. Down, Cherub, down!"

The puppy, thus admonished, stopped making frenzied snaps at Cheam's hand, and squatted in an unmistakable attitude in the very centre of the carpet.

"Cherub!"

Leda glanced half-apologetically at the Superintendent.

"She's only a puppy: she doesn't know any better," she explained. Then, turning to Briggs, said, "Get something to clear it up."

Briggs cast a disdainful look at the offending carpet, and walked out.

"I've finished up here, Miss Hardstaffe," said Cheam, "but I should like to ask you a few questions if you can spare a few minutes. Perhaps you won't mind if I get one of my men to jot it down. It saves so much time."

Leda nodded, and led the way downstairs. She went into the morning-room, where after a few minutes, Cheam joined her, followed by a police constable.

"I really don't see what I can tell you that I haven't said already at the inquest," she said. "I'm still quite sure that there's been some ghastly mistake and that those powders did contain the morphia. I can't believe that anyone would want to murder Mother. She was really a very gentle woman."

"You never felt like murdering her yourself, Miss Hard-staffe?"

A startled look sprang into her pale, prominent eyes.

"No. Of course not. Oh, I suppose you've been listening to servants' gossip. I may have said I'd like to murder her, but I certainly never meant it. She was a very trying sort of person to live with, and got on my nerves sometimes, that's all. Do we have to go on with this?" she said suddenly. "She couldn't have been murdered. If it wasn't an accident, then it must have been suicide. It must!"

Cheam shook his head.

"I'm sorry," he said, "but you must try to realize that there is absolutely no doubt whatever that your mother was murdered. I ask you to face up to that, and give me all the help you can. I know it's hard for you to have to answer questions when you have had such a sad loss, and I sympathise very much. But the sooner we get at the truth the better."

"I realise that," replied Leda, once again in complete control of herself. "And don't worry too much about my feelings. I'm not very much upset at Mother's death. I should be a hypocrite if I said I was, and even my greatest enemy would tell you that I'm not. Mother and I never did get on very well. She consistently made my life a misery. She wouldn't do a thing in the house herself, but she never approved of anything that

I did. She used to drive me half crazy with all her imaginary ailments and worries, but I've never once known her ask whether I felt well. No, I can't pretend that I'm feeling much sorrow about her death, Superintendent. It's the way she died that seems so dreadful."

"You're afraid that someone in this house killed her?"

"No. Oh no. No," she protested. "And yet—" She walked across to her favourite corner of the mantelpiece, took a wooden spill from the container, and bent down to light it at the low fire. Then, as if she had forgotten why she had done so, she beat the flame out against the side of the grate. "And yet," she repeated, straightening herself, and turning to face Cheam, "who else could have done it? When I saw her that morning, she was lying peacefully in bed. And burglars don't use morphia."

"There's not much chance that it's an outside job," agreed Cheam. "I understand that all outside doors and windows were fastened that morning."

"Yes. The maids will confirm that. At least, Briggs will. The other one's a German Jewess and she's quite mad."

"Mad?"

"Not certifiable, I suppose, but next door to it. I've had stupid maids to train before, but she's quite in a class of her own in that direction."

"You don't think that she's capable of murder?"

"Oh, but I do," replied Leda. "She has the most violent temper, and flies into hysterics over nothing. If I'd been murdered, you wouldn't be far out in arresting her. She simply hates me, and often tells me so. I shouldn't dream of keeping her if I could possibly get anyone else, but every girl is doing war work now. I should be doing it myself, but I can't leave Daddy. But if I were called up, of course I should have to go."

Not very likely, Miss, thought Cheam. Your age group won't be reached in this little struggle—not unless it's going to be another Hundred Years War.

"Do you think she had any motive for murdering your mother?"

"Frankly I don't. But does a person of that mentality need one, do you think?"

"Everyone needs a motive for murder," stated Cheam, "But if she's a refugee, she's hardly likely to have got hold of any morphia."

Leda slapped her heavy thigh.

"But she *has* got some!" she exclaimed. "How stupid of me to forget. She carries a little packet of morphia about with her. She showed it to me when she first came, but I didn't believe then that it really could be the drug. I thought she was just romancing."

Cheam did not seem impressed by this information.

"You speak German then, Miss Hardstaffe?" he asked.

"Certainly not!" was Leda's indignant reply. "I wouldn't have it spoken in the house. I consider it most unpatriotic."

Yes, thought Cheam, you're the type of woman who thinks all foreign languages are unpatriotic. I wonder you don't breed bull-dogs!

"Yes, miss," he said, "but if you don't understand her language and she only understands a little English, you probably misunderstood her. 'Morphia' isn't a word she'd be likely to know in English."

"I'm quite sure that I'm not mistaken," said Leda in her haughtiest manner. "She dragged me into her bedroom one day, pulled a silk handkerchief from under her dress, showed me a little white packet wrapped inside it, and said, 'Morphia. Carry it always in Germany. Here I need it not'. Then she threw it into a drawer. I hate foreigners. They're always trying to impress you by being dramatic."

Cheam made no reply.

"Well!" Leda's voice sounded so hearty that the Superintendent braced his shoulder muscles for the slap on the back to which her tone seemed the prelude. "What are you waiting for? I've given you all the evidence you need. Frieda's the murderer obviously."

"Miss Hardstaffe," said Cheam, ignoring her words, "before you remembered about this girl having morphia in her possession, you were afraid of something. What was it?"

Leda looked at him as if wondering how much he knew.

"You're mistaken," she said. "I know it's that girl. Mother said she'd murder one of us if we kept her." Cheam waited silently, and, as silently, Leda watched him.

"I—oh—it has nothing to do with this, nothing," she said at length.

"Perhaps you would like me to repeat the question," said Cheam. "Or shall I put it more plainly and ask *whom* you were afraid for?"

Leda bit her lip, then said quietly,

"My father. Ever since the inquest I've been afraid that you would suspect him. That's why I wanted you to believe it was an accident or suicide. I'm afraid you, and everyone else too, will think he did it because he has more to gain by her death than any of us. You don't understand, as I do, that he's quite incapable of killing anyone. That's all."

Cheam nodded.

"Are you sure that really is all, Miss Hardstaffe?" he asked. "You're not trying to conceal anything from me?"

"No. No, of course not."

"Not a little thing like a key, for instance?"

The Superintendent, who had remained seated throughout the interview while Leda was standing, as if to indicate that social etiquette was not any affair of His Majesty's uniform, rose suddenly to his feet, and opened his right hand.

"You recognise this key?" he asked.

Leda stifled unsuccessfully a little gasp as she bent forward.

"Yes, I-I think so," she said. "It's the key to the door between Mother's and Daddy's bedrooms."

"I found it in your father's tall-boy, pushed underneath his socks," Cheam explained.

"I was afraid you would," whispered Leda.

CHAPTER 15

"AND now," said Cheam, after he had finished questioning Leda, "I should like to see Mr. Smith if he's in."

Leda raised surprised eyebrows.

"Arnold? He wasn't here when Mother was—died."

Strange, thought Cheam, how many people funk saying "murder."

"I would like to see him if I may, and the servants afterwards."

Leda, unused to being treated as if her opinion was of no value, turned away in some annoyance, and went out in finish cleaning the kennels.

Arnold had apparently caught a reflection of her mood, for he was frowning as he came rather fussily into the room.

"I understand that you wish to speak to me, Superintendent," he said. "I hope you won't keep me very long. I'm very busy this morning."

"Just a few questions, sir, if you don't mind."

"Well, if it's about Mrs. Hardstaffe's death," said Arnold, "I can tell you at once that I know nothing about it. I shouldn't dream of harming any woman, so it's no use trying to pin it on to me."

Cheam smiled.

"You seem to have some funny ideas about the police," he said. "We should get into trouble with the Chief Constable if we tried 'to pin' anything on to anyone. But a murder needs very careful investigation, and we need all the help we can get."

"I realise that, of course, but as I've already told you, I know nothing about it. I wasn't here at the time. I was in London, as I believe you know, and I can prove it."

Extraordinary! thought Cheam. A short time ago, he was doing his best to prove that he was a murderer, and almost imploring us to believe that his alibi in London was worthless. Now he's refusing to discuss the murder of Mrs. Hardstaffe, on the grounds that he was in London at the time.

"Well, sir," he said, "I thought that as you're a bit of an expert on crime, owing to your books, you might be able to put forward some theory about the murder. You may not have been here when Mrs. Hardstaffe was murdered, but you've had a front row seat at the theatre of the crime for some time now, and you must have ideas about it. Besides, if you could plan one murder so cleverly, there's no reason to suppose that you couldn't plan another."

"Tck, tck," clucked Arnold, "I hope you're not going to bring that foolish confession of mine against me. Of course it was all pure invention. I was still suffering from the effect of that bit of concussion, and I imagined things."

"Quite so, sir. But I hope that you won't mind if I ask you a few questions. Anyone as experienced as you in writing detective stories must have a good eye for details, and I'm sure your evidence will be most helpful." '

Arnold, flattered against his will by references to his writing which he knew to be undeserved, became less pugnacious.

"I'll certainly help you all I can, Superintendent," he replied. Whoever killed that poor lady deserves to be hanged."

"Amen," said Cheam. "Now there is one point on which I particularly need your help, Mr. Smith. I know all about your visit to London, of course, and have had the details checked as a matter of routine. And I may as well tell you that I'm satisfied about your alibi during that time. What I want you to do is to give me as many details as you can about the scene you witnessed through the study window on the night before you left for London." Arnold's apprehensive glance towards the door did not escape the Superintendent's notice. He interpreted it correctly.

"Don't worry, sir," he went on in reassuring tones, "if we have to inquire into that little affair from other sources, I promise that your name will not be mentioned. Now! When you looked through the window, you saw Mrs. Hardstaffe sitting at the desk?"

"Yes. It was impossible to mistake her for anyone, in spite of her unfamiliar attire."

"And you saw Mr. Hardstaffe standing behind her with a whip in his hand?"

Arnold hesitated.

"Er—no. Now you ask me, I can't say that I *saw* him," he said. "There's a short screen between the window and the fireplace which concealed half the room from me. The desk is on the farther side of the room so I saw that clearly. I could see the lash of the whip cracking over Mrs. Hardstaffe's head, but I never saw who was holding it."

"Why didn't you go and look through the other part of the window?" asked Cheam.

"I—I assumed that it was Hardstaffe. It's just the sort of thing he'd do. Oh, it's very much in character."

Cheam sighed.

"It may be," he remarked, "but it's evidence I want, not a character study. Let's try again. When you heard someone inside the room shout 'Sign, damn you, sign!' did you recognise the voice as Mr. Hardstaffe's?"

"N-no, not exactly," Arnold admitted. "It sounded like a man's voice, and as he was the only man in the house except myself, I assumed that it must be his."

"You told us that the front door was open, so presumably anyone could have walked into the house, and it might have been a stranger's voice?"

"I suppose so," replied Arnold with reluctance, "but I'm perfectly sure in my own mind that it was Hardstaffe. The words themselves have the genuine Hardstaffe ring about them."

"Could you swear on oath that it was Hardstaffe?"

"No."

"I see," said Cheam, with great restraint. "There's one other question. Do you know who benefits under Mrs. Hardstaffe's will? You probably know that she was a very rich woman, and anything you may have heard about her will may be important."

"Oh!" Arnold's exclamation expressed the utmost consternation. "Oh dear! This is very awkward," he said. "But I don't really know." He brightened at the thought. "No, I don't know any facts about it. I'm afraid I can't help you."

"I'm not asking you for facts," said Cheam patiently. "Has her will ever been mentioned to you?"

"It's extremely awkward," said Arnold again. "But—well—it's this way. Miss Hardstaffe, while not saying directly that she would benefit under her mother's will, gave me to understand that it's usual in the Hardstaffe family for the mother's money to be left to the daughters, and the father's money to the sons."

"A bit hard on the son, in this instance," remarked Cheam.

"Well—I'm not sure that it is," rejoined Arnold, still with the same reluctance. "I rather gathered from what Mrs. Hardstaffe remarked one day, that she intended to cut Leda out of her will. But I don't *know*."

"Thank you," said Cheam. "I hope that when you write that new book, Mr. Smith, you won't make your witnesses too glib at swearing to this and that. It's a rare thing to find a witness who can truthfully say anything except that they know a certain thing *must* be so, but no! they didn't see or hear it. You can see how difficult it is to piece evidence together that will stand the strain of cross-questioning."

Arnold nodded.

"About that will, though," he said. "Haven't you found it yet? Didn't she make one?"

"Oh yes, she made one, and we've found it," replied Cheam. "It's dated on the day that you saw someone threatening her with a horsewhip. And she left all her money unconditionally to her husband."

"By God!" exclaimed Arnold. "Then that's what he was forcing her to sign. The dirty swine!"

The Superintendent shook his head.

"Then how did he get it witnessed?" he asked.

"Oh, some trickery. Don't let a little detail like that worry you. I tell you that man would stop at nothing to get his own way. Do you mean to tell me that you're not going to arrest him?"

Cheam shrugged his shoulders.

"I've no evidence," he said. "Now, if you'd only looked through that window a bit more carefully—"

"Window be damned!" exclaimed Arnold with a violence which Cheam thought unjustified. "I tell you I *know* he was in that room. Of course he murdered her, and if you don't arrest him, I shall do something about it myself!"

CHAPTER 16

FROM the Cook, Cheam evoked nothing but a long eulogy on Mrs. Hardstaffe, to whom, rightly or wrongly, she ascribed all the virtues and none of the vices.

And what were things coming to, she'd like to know, when a nice, kind lady like the poor mistress was murdered in cold blood in her bed?

She supposed it was all on account of that there 'Itler and his New Order putting such ideas into people's minds, and it was a crying shame, for a better mistress than Mrs. 'Ardstaffe she'd never met with nor she wasn't likely to again.

She'd been in service for longer than she'd care to remember, and she'd known mistresses who'd spend their time in the kitchen pulling your Apple Amber to pieces, m a manner of speaking, and turning up their noses at your Rabbit Pie. But Mrs. Ardstaffe had never been like that. Not that she came into the kitchen much nowadays on account of Miss Leda not liking it, but in the old days she came in regular with always a kind word for your fish sauce, or a "however do you get the meringue on the Queen Pudding so crisp, Cook?" when she knew as well as yourself that it was the sprinkling of castor sugar on top before baking that did it.

Then she always remembered to ask after your sister Polly's little boy, who wasn't quite the same as other children, Polly having been frightened by a mad dog before he was born. But, there you were, it was all on account of the mistress being a Lady Born and she'd be sadly missed in Nether Naughton.

Not that you'd grudge the poor lady a rest from all the trouble she had for so many years, and she never being in good health neither, though there was few people in the house to believe it.

No, the old house wasn't the same nowadays. When the mistress had the running of it, there'd been fresh flowers in every room, not forgetting the kitchen, mind, and the drawing-room looked a fair treat with one set of covers for Winter and another for Summer.

But ever since Miss Leda had took to dogs, the place hadn't been the same, and the new covers were no sooner on than they were sprinkled with dog-hairs, and worse! As for carpets! There wasn't one in the whole house fit for the mistress to put her little shoes down on. It used to worry the mistress something dreadful. But Miss Leda was that strong-willed, there was no doing anything with her. Her father had spoiled her since she was a child, and he'd live to rue it to his dying day.

But there, talking of dying made her think of the poor mistress, and many a tear she'd shed over her, and that was more than the master or Miss Leda could say, she'd be bound.

Well, she was going to give in her notice at the end of the month. She wouldn't stay in a house where the cooking wouldn't be appreciated any more, and though she said as shouldn't, the way she managed with the rations was worth a bit of praise now and again. She'd only stayed on so long after the dogs came, to oblige the poor mistress who'd have starved if it hadn't been for her smuggling tasty little bits of food to her upstairs when she was feeling ill, poor dear. Miss Leda always seemed to delight in sending up sausages or kippers when she felt like that.

Besides . . . there had been Goings On.

"Well, if you insist, Mr. Cheam," she went on, "I must tell you, I suppose, but, mind, I'm not one to be gossiping about people's private affairs like some of them I could mention in this village; but there's no denying that there have been Goings On in this house on and off for years. Women, sir. The master couldn't leave a pretty girl alone and that's a fact. The first one I remember was a maid we had, called Lily. The mistress went into the study unbeknownst and found her sitting on the master's knee. That time it was the poor mistress who did the raving. Sacked the girl, and fair read the riot act to him. But she never put a stop to it, and well she knew it. Now it's that young Charity Fuller, and I wouldn't be prepared to say it's any better than the other Goings On. You'd think that any presentable girl'd have more sense than to take up with a man older than her own father, especially with all these different uniforms about, but I suppose there's something about him like that band leader who invented the trilby hat. Disraeli, I saw a play about him and it fair gave me the creeps."

The Superintendent, ignoring this libel on the worthy Prime Minister, interposed a question, and wondered whether he was likely to find any clue among the spate of words which inevitably must follow.

"When did I last see the mistress alive? On the Saturday morning it would be. Miss Leda was out with the dogs and she brought her morning coffee with her, and sat in the rocking chair in the kitchen as though she felt lonely-like. I tried to cheer her up reading out some of the Ministry of Food's hints, to make her laugh, but as I said, how can you expect a lot of men to know anything about food, except how to eat it? Very depressed she was because Miss Fuller was coming to dinner, and you'll never make me believe that the mistress had anything to do with inviting her. It was some monkey-trick of the master's more like.

"Frieda? Oh no, she never did it. A bit queer she is, right enough, but so'd we be if we'd been through half what she has. I never did hold with Jews, me being a good Church of England Christian, but I don't hold with torturing an animal, let alone a decent-living human-being, and the bits of tales that girl manages to tell you would fair make your hair curl. She hadn't had a good meal for months before she got to this country. As for murdering anyone, why, the girl's at her wits' end to stay here. She might kill herself if Miss Leda gave her the sack, but she was fond of the mistress like we all were in the kitchen. She's slow over her work, I'll admit, but she'd learn if Miss Leda would give over tormenting her: a fair down on her she has, her being a foreigner, but as I say, you might as well have a down on a sausage-dog for being a German. They can't neither of them help it. The girl's all nerves. And tired . . . ! She falls asleep whenever she sits down. It isn't fair the way Miss Leda goes on at her. She never calls her by her name in the kitchen. 'Jew', she calls her. 'Come here, Jew', and 'Go and do that, Jew'. It isn't right, sir."

"But what about these violent rages she flings herself into? Mightn't she do some harm to anyone then?"

"Bless you, no," was the comfortable reply. "They're no more than a child's tantrums. If she'd been going to murder anyone in this household, it would have been Miss Leda. It's my belief that she puts on these little ways just to annoy Miss Leda, and I don't blame her, though it's not my place to say so."

The Cook paused for breath.

"Did you hear anything strange on the night Mrs. Hardstaffe died?" asked Cheam.

"Me? Not a thing, nor likely to. Our bedrooms are over the kitchens and we go up by a different staircase. Vicky—that's Briggs, but you'll know that—did come into my bedroom when I was in bed reading 'Maria Marten or The Murder in the Red Barn'. A fair start she gave me, I can tell you. She said the mistress had been fair wiping the floor with the master, but I told her to get to bed and mind her own business."

"Have you any idea who killed your mistress?"

"No, nor nothing anyone says will make me believe she was murdered. She did it herself, the poor soul. Tired of struggling against them two and their Goings On, that's what it was, you can depend on it, sir. Why don't you let her be? She's happier now than she's been for years."

CHAPTER 17

THE little Jewish maid entered the room furtively, and stood with her back to the door. In her dark eyes was the kind of expression you see in the eyes of a back-alley cat, which wonders why any human being wearing boots refrains from kicking it, and, suspecting a trap, keeps its distance.

"Come over here," requested Cheam.

"Please?"

He beckoned, and pointed to the chair in front of his own.

The girl moved forward heavily on her black wardroom slippers, and stood, perspiring and afraid, before him.

"I want to ask you a few questions," he said.

Frieda clasped her hands together.

"But I know nothing," she said vehemently. "Nothing!"

"You know that Mrs. Hardstaffe is dead?"

She nodded.

"And you know that she did not die naturally. Someone has killed her."

"I know, I know. It is dreadful!"

"Do you know anything about it?"

The dark brown eyes dilated.

"Me? But I tell you I know nothing."

Cheam sighed. It was difficult to frame his questions within the three-hundred-word vocabulary of a two-year-old child.

"Did you like Mrs. Hardstaffe?"

For the first time since she had entered, the haunted look faded from her eyes.

"But yes. I like her so much. Very kind. Always I do things for her and she say 'tank you' so nice. Her voice soft not like that other. *She. . . .*"

Her gesture made her opinion of Leda quite clear, and Cheam, reflecting that such gestures seemed international and universal, wondered whether the British Navy was responsible for inventing them.

"Mrs. Hardstaffe was killed by morphia," he stated.

"I understand."

"You know what morphia is?"

She nodded.

"It is an unusual word in English. Where did you learn it?"

"Please?" She frowned in some perplexity, then her face cleared as his meaning became clear to her. "But it is German. In Germany we say always morphium."

"I see." (Must get hold of an English-German Dictionary, he thought). "And what do you know about—er —morphium?"

"I know. I have it," she replied eagerly.

"Where did you get it from?"

"But I bring it from Germany. My doctor, a friend, he give it."

"Why?" persisted Cheam.

"For me to eat." She became animated. "You do not understand? No. Because you are not German Jew. You say 'Itler is bad man, must be kill. But if you are not Jew, you do not know how bad. You understand bombs and Luftwaffe, but you do not understand Gestapo and torture if you are not Jew like me. I am told to get up from my bed one night. I must go to the frontier. If I do not go, I am sent to Poland in cattletruck or to concentration camp. I am not pretty enough to keep for Germans. But perhaps I do not get to frontier, and so I must have morphium. It is better then to die, being a Jew."

She gazed at his unaltered expression, and with a shrug of her shoulders, reverted to her former manner.

"You do not understand," she said. "You are not German Jew."

Cheam, feeling considerably shocked and endeavouring successfully to conceal it, continued with his questions.

"When did you last see Mrs. Hardstaffe?"

"Please?"

He repeated the question in altered form.

"Saturday night it is when I am in bed."

"In bed? She came to your bedroom?" asked Cheam, in some surprise.

"No. I go to her room. I am asleep. I hear voices. I awake.
Cook is talking to Briggs. They say he quarrel with her, so when
they are quiet, I go to see Mrs. 'Ardstaffe."

"Whatever for?"

"To see she is all right. I like her so much. She is so kind
to me."

"What an extraordinary thing to do!" exclaimed Cheam.
"Why did you do that?"

"She is kind. I have no friend but her. I am afraid the
Gestapo kill her."

Poor thing, thought Cheam. It's turned her brain.

Frieda achieved a smile.

"I make joke," she explained. "You not understand? Miss
'Ardstaffe I call Miss 'Itler: Mr. 'Ardstaffe is Gestapo."

"You don't like Mr. Hardstaffe?"

"Like him? I hate him! But she! She is worse." Her face
grew fiendish. "She is evil. One day I kill her!"

"With morphia?" asked Cheam.

"With morphia, no. With my hands—so!"

My God! she means it, thought Cheam. She's capable of
murder all right. Needs watching.

So you went to Mrs. Hardstaffe's bedroom. Did you see her?"

"I knock, but no answer. I open the door. It is dark. I go away.
In the morning, I know they have kill her, and I am afraid."

"Why?"

She shrugged her shoulders.

"I know Miss 'Itler will say it is me who kill her. 'The Jew is
not safe, she shall say, and she shall put me in concentration
camp or madhouse."

"That's nonsense!" exclaimed Cheam. "Why should she
want to do that?"

"You do not know her. She is not what you think. She is
evil. I know. I am young and she is old, but I know. I have
seen much evil."

Cheam rose to his feet.

"This morphia," he said. "Where do you keep it?"

"Upstairs: I shall show you."

He followed her up the main staircase and through the swing door into the servants' carpetless wing.

Her room was in quaint contrast to the more colourless bedrooms at the other end of the house. Cheam thought he had never seen so many pieces of embroidery collected into the space of four small walls. Embroidered hair tidies, brush-and-comb bags, and slipper bags; embroidered containers for umbrellas, spills, matches; embroidered boxes of all sizes and shapes; even embroidered panels and pictures.

She went across to a large box clamped with iron bands, and lifted the lid.

"This box only I can bring from my country. If you wish, I sell you some things—all embroidered—very cheap."

"No, thank you," replied Cheam. "I want the morphia."

"I get it."

She plunged her hand beneath the many articles which it still contained, then withdrew it, looking puzzled.

"I forget. It is the other side," she murmured, pushing her hand down again.

But again when she held her hand out, it was empty.

Cheam, who had wondered where she could have concealed the package to elude his searchers' experienced fingers, was silent.

Frieda tumbled to her knees beside the heavy box, while little beads of sweat gathered on her forehead and rolled down her face.

She took out sheets, cloths, corsets, shoes, a hat, beads, an umbrella, a pair of candlesticks, a case of spoons, and threw them in a heap on the floor, muttering in German.

At last she looked up at Cheam with terror in her eyes.

"It is gone," she exclaimed. "She has taken it. Now I know she will kill me!"

CHAPTER 18

AFTER an intensive search had failed to produce the missing morphia, Cheam detached himself from the hysterical clutches of the weeping maid, and went downstairs. As he entered the drawing-room for his hat, a tall, dapper man, dressed in immaculate town-cut black suit, rose from one of the chairs.

"Superintendent Cheam? May I have a few words with you? I'm Stanton Hardstaffe."

"Certainly, sir. Very pleased to have the opportunity. This must be a sad home-coming for you."

"Yes. It's terrible about my mother. I shall never forgive myself. I ought to have known it would happen one day if she stayed in this house. When are you going to arrest him?"

"Arrest whom, sir?"

Stanton tapped an impatient foot on the carpet.

"My father, of course. You must know that he did it."

"What makes you think that?" asked Cheam, glancing over his shoulder, and noting with satisfaction that the constable whom he had left in the room was already moving his pencil over his notebook.

"Good heavens, man!" exclaimed Stanton. "You must have been wasting your time if you haven't yet discovered that my father's whole married life has been dedicated to making my dear mother's very existence unbearable. If she'd been an American, she'd have got a divorce years ago, but you know what the laws in this country used to be like, dusty and logical, and after they were altered, she felt too old to bother. Oh, she did go to a lawyer for advice once, but all he could say was, 'I'm sorry but I'm afraid you've got no *case*.' Perhaps you haven't found out what a hypocrite my father is. He'd have gone into the witness-box with that bland, smiling, schoolmaster manner of his, and he would have killed her evidence flat, even if she had got together enough courage to give it. Then she would have been worse off than ever because he'd have taken an even greater delight in making her suffer in private as well as humiliating her in public. The Gestapo simply wouldn't be in it!"

Cheam blinked. This was the second time within the hour that Mr. Hardstaffe had been compared with this hated organisation.

"If you realised all this, Mr. Stanton," he said, "how is it that you were content to leave your mother here without even coming to see her?"

"Content!" said Stanton bitterly. "Of course I wasn't content, but what could I do? When I first left this house, we arranged to meet regularly at a friend's house, but of course he got to know about it and created a scene. So at last she refused to come."

"So you never saw her alive again?"

Stanton smiled.

"That's what my father thinks," he said. "But I loved my mother, and I'm not such a nit-wit that I couldn't think of some way of seeing her. We met every year. Doctor Macalistair was in the scheme—he used to paint the most lurid picture of what would happen if Mother didn't go abroad every year. She used to come to stay with us before getting the boat. One year, the three of us went for a cruise together, my wife, Mother, and me. I managed to get a long leave, and Mother paid for the trip. We had a heavenly time."

"I don't see why your father should have needed any persuasion to let her go abroad. If what you say is true, I should have thought he'd have been glad to get rid of her for a bit," remarked Cheam.

"He just didn't like her spending so much money."

"But it was her own money."

Stanton laughed.

"He didn't look at it like that. He'd married her, so he regarded her worldly goods as his."

"That's twisting the marriage service a bit, isn't it?" asked Cheam.

"He'd twist anything."

"H'm," said Cheam. "Then I can't understand why she left all her money to him."

"Oh, she didn't," returned Stanton. "She wasn't quite as simple as he thought. Those quiet women never are. She made a will in my favour, and my solicitor has the will, so that there's no chance of anyone having destroyed it."

Cheam sat up, and took notice.

"Really? When was it signed?"

Stanton looked mildly surprised.

"About three years ago, I think," he said. "It's all in order, I assure you. She told me she wanted me to inherit everything. She said Leda and my father had succeeded in making her life hell, and she'd make sure that neither of them had a penny of hers."

"H'm," said Cheam again. "I'm afraid that will isn't valid, sir," he said.

"Isn't valid? Rot! Why, I tell you . . ."

Cheam waved his hand in the air.

"Oh, I don't question that it was drawn up quite legally," he said. "But she made a later one a few days before she died. In it, she left everything unconditionally to your father."

Stanton's face grew fiendish in expression. He clenched his fists, and beat them against his temples.

"No," he shouted. "No, no, no!"

"Very disappointing for you, sir, I know."

Cheam sounded almost apologetic.

"It isn't that," said Stanton, when he had recovered himself a little. "It's the thought of what he must have done to her to force her to sign it. I tell you she wanted me to have that money. She didn't change her mind about that, I'm quite sure." He struck a clenched fist against the open palm of his other hand. "That's what she wanted to see me about, of course. And I failed her!"

"I don't understand, sir."

Stanton turned to him again, and spoke earnestly.

"She wrote to me—oh, I don't know whether she got the letter out of the house unnoticed, or whether someone read it first—asking me to come to the house on Saturday night."

"That was the night she was murdered."

"Do you think I don't remember that, Superintendent!" he returned savagely. "Don't you see that I might have saved her life if—if I'd come? She told me to wait outside, and she would come down to let me in."

"So you didn't come?"

"No!"

He flung himself into a chair, and shielded his face with his arm.

"I'm sorry," said Cheam, "but the only thing to be done now is to find her murderer and bring him to justice."

"It's up to you, Superintendent." Stanton passed a spotless handkerchief over his forehead, then stood up again. "It couldn't be anyone but my father. I'd give something to know what deviltry he used to make her sign that will."

Suddenly he moved forward and thrust a forefinger towards Cheam's astonished face.

"I know. Of course. The horse-whip!"

"Horse-whip?" gasped Cheam. "Why, what do you know about that?"

Stanton appeared not to have heard him.

"I ought to have guessed at once," he said. "You know I left home years ago owing to a serious quarrel with my father? It happened like this. I heard screams coming from their bedroom, and went in to find him thrashing her with a horsewhip. She was crouching on the bed with her clothes torn and her back lashed and bleeding. I'm a Hardstaffe, so I have a temper, too, and somehow I wrenched the damned thing out of his hand and gave him a dose of his own medicine. Like all bullies, he's a coward at heart, and I thrashed him till he crouched in a corner of the room blubbering for mercy. I moved Mother's things into the adjoining bedroom, locked the door, and took the key away, and I told him then that if he ever dared to lift a horsewhip to her again, I'd kill him.

"And, by God, I will!"

CHAPTER 19

SUPERINTENDENT Cheam, accompanied by a constable, crossed the ashphalt playground flanking the village school. They entered the front door, and saw on their right a green-painted door with the words "Head Master" stencilled in cream. Cheam knocked, and thinking that he heard a reply through the confused babel of voices issuing from the five separate classrooms, turned the knob and entered the study. Mr. Hardstaffe's arm slipped from Charity Fuller's slim waist as he swung round to face the intruders.

"What the devil do you mean by walking in without knocking?" he blazed.

"Good morning, Mr. Hardstaffe," was Cheam's affable reply. "I did knock, and thought I heard you say 'Come in', but I can see that I was mistaken. I'm sorry, sir, but there's a lot of noise outside in the corridor."

"Oh dear!" exclaimed Charity. "It must be my class. I'd better go back to them, that is, if you've quite finished with these papers, Mr. Hardstaffe."

"Yes, yes, go along. I'll see them some other time. I can't attend to figures while the Superintendent's here." No, that you can't, my lad, thought Cheam. Not to the kind of figure you've got your eyes on now, anyway. She's a good-looker this red head: plenty of "It", or whatever they call it nowadays. But it fair beats me what a girl like that can see in a wizened little fellow like you.

"Miss Fuller?" he asked aloud, as he opened the door for her. "I'm Superintendent Cheam. I'm investigating the murder of Mr. Hardstaffe's wife, and I should like to ask you a few questions."

Charity went very pale, and for a few seconds looked as if she were going to faint.

Hardstaffe lost his temper again.

"What's all this about?" he demanded. "I won't have this high-handed behaviour. Forcing your way into my private rooms, and throwing your weight about like this . . . What is it supposed to be—a hold-up?"

"It did look a bit like that, sir," returned Cheam gazing pointedly at Charity's waist. "Now there's no need to get nasty about it, sir. It's my duty to ask questions, and my time's limited. The inquest was only adjourned for a few weeks, and I've a lot of ground to cover."

"You're quite right, Superintendent," put in Charity, now fully recovered. "It's the duty of everyone to help the police, as I'm always telling my class."

"Thank you, Miss," said Cheam, opening the door significantly. "I won't detain you now, but you won't object if I see you later, I hope."

Charity flashed a smile at him: she had lovely teeth and knew it.

"Of course not. I've nothing to hide."

I'm not so sure of that, young lady, thought Cheam as he closed the door behind her. You're a bit of a dark filly if I know aught about women. And what policeman doesn't?

He turned to face the head master who, as he surmised, was getting "proper worked up."

"What's the idea, Cheam? What induced you to come here to ask your damned questions? Why couldn't you wait until I got home or ask for an appointment decently instead of butting in during school hours? You know what a place this village is for rumours and scandal, yet you deliberately march in without so much as a by-your-leave. I never heard of such damned impertinence in my life!"

"I knocked," said Cheam coolly. "If you were so busy that you didn't hear me, that's not my fault. And if I may be permitted to give you a little advice, Mr. Hardstaffe, I'll warn you that you'll do no good to yourself or to anyone else by shouting at me. I'm only doing my duty. I have to ask you and Miss Fuller a few routine questions, and as the school is on my way back home, I thought there'd be no harm in dropping in on you."

Hardstaffe fingered the heavy-linked, gold chain which he wore fastened across his waistcoat like a coronation decoration round a small bow window, and said more quietly.

"Yes, yes. I was perhaps a bit over-hasty, but you startled me. This affair of my wife's death has been a great shock, and no doubt I ought not to be at work so soon, but the school goes to the dogs when I don't put in an appearance. I once returned unexpectedly after a bout of 'flu and found my Chief Assistant telling the class a funny story. That sort of thing lowers the tone of the whole school. It's discipline that children need—discipline."

"Yes, sir. No doubt your wife's death upset you more than you realised at the time."

"That's it. That's it. Of course I always knew that her mind was unbalanced—all that nonsense about her health was a sign of that—but I never believed that she'd take her own life, or I should have taken steps to place her under some kind of restraint. All this publicity is very distasteful to me. I'm a man who is much in the public eye in Nether Naughton, and I've always kept my name away from scandal . . ."

That's what *you* think! said Cheam to himself.

"To have it dragged into a case of suicide is a very distasteful and bitter experience to me. And I must say I never thought she'd have the guts to do such a thing!"

Cheam frowned.

Mr. Hardstaffe," he said gravely, "I am investigating a case of murder."

The head master smiled.

'Oh, nonsense, my good man!" he exclaimed. "Who on earth would want to murder my wife? She was quite the most irritating woman I have ever known, but she was harmless. If it wasn't suicide, it was an accident, and that old fool Macalistair made a mistake in the prescription. When I think of the outlandish fees that fellow charges for his medicines, I don't know how he had the effrontery to stand up and admit in public that he puts nothing but chalk in them. I always did wonder whether he was a fool or a knave. Now I know he's a knave!"

"There was no mistake in the sleeping powders," replied Cheam. "All that has been investigated thoroughly. And if it was suicide, where did Mrs. Hardstaffe get the morphia from?"

"How the hell do I know? From that lunatic of a maid, I suppose."

"So you knew that she had some morphia?"

"Certainly. My daughter told me, and Mrs. Hardstaffe was there at the time. I said then that someone ought to take it away. The girl's not right in her head, and it wasn't safe to let her keep it."

"Do you happen to know exactly where she did keep it?" asked Cheam.

"Eh? Oh, in that enormous trunk-contraption of hers, I should think."

"You've been in her bedroom then?"

Mr. Hardstaffe looked up sharply as if he had every intention of denying this.

"As a matter of fact, I have," he admitted, however. "I needn't tell you that it's not a habit of mine to go into the maids' rooms, but my daughter said I really ought to have a look at this one. She said it was a regular Old Curiosity Shop, and I must say she was right. Fancy stopping to pack a huge box with all that junk when you're fleeing for your life half across Europe! But I believe these refugees are all the same."

It occurred to Cheam to wonder what Hardstaffe himself would choose to take, if forced to go on a similar expedition. But he denied himself the intriguing excursion into fancy which such a thought offered, and returned to his questioning.

"When did you last see your wife alive?"

"I've already given my answer to that question at the inquest. I've nothing to add to it now."

"I see," said Cheam thoughtfully. "You said, if I remember correctly, that that was downstairs just before she went to bed. I take it that it would be later than usual, as you had a visitor?"

Hardstaffe snorted.

"It was not," he said emphatically. "Mrs. Hardstaffe was a woman of fixed habits. She went to bed about half past nine every night whether we had visitors or not. It looked very rude, naturally, but Mrs. Hardstaffe *was* naturally rude."

"You're sure you didn't see her upstairs when you went to bed?"

"Sure? Of course I'm sure. Do you think I'd lie about a thing like that? I saw Miss Fuller home—you can't let a young girl like that go home alone in the dark—then I had my usual nightcap and went up to bed."

"I see, sir," said Cheam. "Now can you tell me what key this is, sir?"

He withdrew from his pocket the same key he had previously shown to Leda.

"Good God, no!" exclaimed Hardstaffe. "You might as well ask me to identify a pin."

"Then it would surprise you to be told that this is the key to the communicating door between your bedroom and your wife's?"

"Surprise me? I should think so! That key's been lost for years."

"So you say," returned Cheam. "But if that is so, perhaps you can tell me how it came to be in the drawer of your tall-boy under your socks."

Hardstaffe, his face suffused with anger, banged his fist against his heavy oak desk.

"What's this? Third degree?" he shouted. "The key to that door is lost, I tell you, lost! As for the one you're waggling at me, I know nothing about it, and if you found it in my drawer, someone must have planted it there. And what the hell do you mean by sneaking into my room while I'm away, eh? What else have you pilfered? You—"

"Now, now, Mr. Hardstaffe," said Cheam. "There's no need to upset yourself about it. I say I found the key in the drawer: you say you didn't put it there: that's all I want to know. Now, what about this will?"

"What will?" snapped the schoolmaster.

Cheam, feeling that the conversation might develop in these lines into the kind of cross-talk beloved of music-hall comedians, hastened to explain.

"Mrs. Hardstaffe's will, sir. I take it that you knew she had made one. We found it in her room."

"I've heard enough talk about it," said Hardstaffe more calmly, "so I always assumed she'd made one though I've never seen it. She was always threatening to alter it, whenever one of the family annoyed her, but I don't know whether she did. I lost count of the number of times she said she was going to cut me out of it altogether. If she really made as many new wills as she said, there must be enough to paper a room with."

"In that case," remarked the Superintendent, watching him carefully, "you'll be pleased to hear that she left all her money to you unconditionally."

Hardstaffe, whose body throughout the interview had been tensed like that of a pugnacious little dog scenting danger, relaxed, and sank back slowly into his swivel-chair.

"Did she now?" he exclaimed, smiling. "Did she really? Unconditionally? No, I certainly never expected that." His face gradually assumed the benevolent expression that he was wont to reserve for the annual visit of the School Governors. It just shows how one can misjudge those whom one knows best."

"Yes, sir. Of course you realise that no one can benefit by a will which is signed under coercion?"

"What do you mean?" Hardstaffe asked sharply, then, resuming his complacent smile, he went on, "This is part of your legal jargon, of course. I assure you that no one is likely to have coerced Mrs. Hardstaffe into signing anything. She was a damned obstinate woman in spite of her gentle appearance. I tell you that writing her will was a kind of hobby to her. It just happens that I'm the lucky one. She might have altered it by now if she hadn't happened to die when she did."

"Just so," agreed Cheam. "She might have altered it if she hadn't happened to—be murdered. There's a slight difference."

The smile faded from the headmaster's face.

What are you getting at?" he demanded. "Ever since you poked your nose into this place, you've been trying to cast suspicion on me. First it's that key, and now it's this will. I tell you I don't know anything about either of them."

"We have a sworn statement to the effect that on the same day on which this will was signed, someone was trying to force your wife to sign some paper."

"I know nothing about it."

"The whole scene was witnessed through the lighted window of your study at home."

"I know nothing about it."

"Someone of your own height, with a voice like yours, was threatening your wife with a horse-whip."

Hardstaffe half-rose from the chair, controlled himself with a super-human effort, and sat down again.

"It's a preposterous invention!"

Cheam, relentless, pursued the subject.

"You have never threatened your wife with a horsewhip?"

"Certainly not."

"Never?"

"No ne—" Perhaps aware of the Gilbertian savour of the conversation, he changed his reply to, "Never in my life."

"You won't deny that you recently thrashed a boy with a whip until he fainted?"

"That was different." Cheam could see him tensing the muscles over his heavy jaw. "It was a matter of school discipline, and it was a cane, not a whip. It is necessary to thrash boys occasionally. But I have never lifted my hand to a woman in my life. It is a malicious lie!"

"Very well. Just one more question. What are your relations with Miss Fuller?"

Hardstaffe leaped to his feet, and gripped the sides of his desk with fingers visibly twitching to be at the Superintendent's throat.

He looked like a small, malevolent devil.

"You leave her out of this!" he yelled. "Now get out, get out before I lose my temper. Get out, I say! Get *out!*"

CHAPTER 20

THE following week, Charity Fuller dined again at the Hardstaffe's. Stanton and his wife and son had returned home, so that it was an evenly-balanced foursome who sat down to dinner.

From the beginning, it was a distressing evening.

Last time I was here, thought Charity, we were three women to one man. Last time I was here, *she* was alive, and she was sitting . . . She shivered as she realised that for some reason, calculated or otherwise, she herself was seated in that place now, for Mrs. Hardstaffe used to sit at her husband's left, in defiance of all the rules of etiquette.

"Salt?"

Mr. Hardstaffe proffered the silver Georgian salt-cellar, contriving to brush his hand against hers as he did so.

Charity forced a smile to her lips.

I wish he wouldn't, she thought. He knows I don't like being touched in public, especially in this house. Miss Hardstaffe notices everything so quickly. I hadn't been in the drawing-room for five minutes before she saw that my belt was fastened with a safety pin instead of a patent fastener. She's not likely to miss seeing his hand touching me. I must refuse cigarettes: the way he lights mine is too demonstrative. I'm afraid he'll get worse now that *she* is dead.

Frieda, closely watched by Leda, created her usual diversion, by asking in her loudest voice, "I serve this woman first? No?"

"Yes, you fool," said Leda. "I told you about it before dinner."

Frieda made her perspiring way round the table, and thrust the vegetable-dish beneath Charity's nose.

"You like to sit in Mrs. 'Ardstaffe's chair? Yes?" she hissed.

Charity looked up in startled dismay, her cheeks white beneath their patches of evening rouge. Suddenly she covered her face with her hands, and sat there, trembling.

Hardstaffe's chair overturned with a crash as he moved to Charity's side.

"Get that Hun out of here, Leda, before I lay hands on her," he said grimly.

But it was on Charity that he laid his hands—gentle hands which moved caressingly over the rounded, white shoulders rising in tempting softness from the low-cut folds of the old chiffon gown which had dyed black so well.

"You mustn't take any notice of what she says, my dear," he said in playfully affectionate tones. "She's a lunatic."

"I'm sorry to be so silly," said Charity trying to smile, "but she startled me. I couldn't think what . . ."

"Of course, the girl's an absolute fool," remarked Leda. "I hope she hasn't put you off your dinner."

"Oh no, I'm quite all right really."

To her obvious relief, Mr. Hardstaffe removed his hands, and sat down once again in the chair which Smith had picked up.

Leda, who had driven the weeping girl out of the room, handed the vegetables, in her place.

"It's too bad of you to keep that dreadful girl here, Leda," said Hardstaffe. "She's worse than useless, and you know she's dangerous."

"I'm afraid our dear Superintendent might have something to say if we suddenly got rid of her," returned Leda. "I still have hopes that he will lock her up one day soon. If he doesn't, we shall have another m—" She broke off abruptly. "She's really not safe," she finished.

"Well, I wish you'd keep her out of the way when we have company," said Hardstaffe irritably. "Why didn't you arrange for Briggs to be in tonight?"

"Why didn't you arrange an evening when Briggs was in, if it comes to that?" Leda riposted. "You can't chop and change with maids in these days: they won't stand for it." Charity, feeling most uncomfortable, looked appealingly across the table at Arnold Smith, who smiled reassuringly at her.

Arnold thought that she looked very sweet and innocent. The curve of her lips, the rise and fall of her barely-discerned breasts fascinated him. He felt unreasonably infuriated that her white shoulders should be exposed to the touch of Hardstaffe's sensual fingers. He glanced down at his own well-manicured hands, as if comparing them with the schoolmaster's. Then, sensing Leda's mocking glance upon him, he jumped up.

'I'll collect the plates," he said gaily. "Might as well make myself useful."

And, as if glad of the chance to forget their several thoughts, they all began to help, and chattered again of pleasantly impersonal topics. For Charity was not the only one present who fancied she saw the frail ghost of Mrs. Hardstaffe walking behind her chair.

They had reached the final course of the inevitable sardines on toast ("and we shan't even get these if Hitler makes a grab at Portugal," Leda had remarked as her father stuck a reluctant fork into his portion), when they heard a furtive knock on the door. They all looked up with fearful expectancy, but no one entered.

Then Leda, murmuring "That daft Jewess," got up and strode across the room.

"How many times have I told you . . ." she began, then in softer tones, "Oh, it's you, Cook. I thought it was Frieda."

She stepped outside, whence came a sibilant whispering which the others strained their ears to hear.

"What is it?" asked Hardstaffe, as Leda returned. "Don't tell me that Cook has found some food in the larder. This meal isn't enough to feed a cat on."

Leda ignored his remark.

"Someone to see you, Daddy," she said.

Hardstaffe clicked his tongue impatiently against his false teeth.

"It's amazing how these villagers will call at dinnertime," he remarked. "I hope you said I couldn't see anyone tonight."

"I said you'd go at once," she replied calmly. "It isn't anyone from the village. It's a Mr. Ramsbottom and he's come from Westcastle to see you. I think you'd better go, too. He said that if you don't he'll come in here to see you, and Cook says she's sure he means it."

"Ay an' she's right!" said a loud voice from the door.

Hardstaffe jumped from his chair to confront the man who had entered through the door which Leda had left ajar.

He was a big, black-haired man, with unruly eyebrows which hung over his deep-set eyes, like black rocks over half-hidden ferns. His big-boned body towered over Hardstaffe, and his enormous, hairy hands were clenched impatiently at his sides.

A nasty customer, thought Arnold, watching him carefully. He means business.

"Ay, I'm a man o' my word," he said. "Five minutes I said I'd wait and five minutes I've waited. I've no time to waste on thee."

"How dare you walk into here like this?" blustered Hardstaffe, very conscious of his own lack of stature. "What do you mean by this intrusion? I've no time to deal with school matters in the evenings. You'll have to come again tomorrow. Are you going now, or shall I have you turned out?"

"Who's going to turn me out?" asked the man, looking from Hardstaffe to Smith, and back again. "Nay, it's no use coming across me wi' all that high-class talk, Mr. 'Ardstaffe. I've come all the way from Westcastle after my day's work to see thee, and see thee I will an' all. Name of Ramsbottom. I want to know what tha means by half murdering our little lad!"

"I don't know what you're talking about," retorted the schoolmaster, striving to gather about him some shreds of dignity. "Will you go or—"

"Nay I'll not go," returned Ramsbottom. "I'm talking about you half-murdering our little lad. Aye, and it's not the only bit of murder what's been going on round here seemingly. Nor it won't be the last if I don't get some satisfaction out of thee!"

"You must be mad to come here and talk to me like this," said Hardstaffe.

"Nay, I'm not. And I'm only talking like this because there's ladies present. If they weren't here, I shouldn't be talking, I'd be acting. Like this!" He thrust a huge fist forward a few inches away from Hardstaffe's chin. "Half- murdered our Alfie, you did—he's got bruises all over his body—and he's a good little lad, he never deserved that. I'd have you know, Mr. 'Ardstaffe, as I didn't send him away from the murdering Nazzies to have him killed by a murdering schoolmaster. There'd better be satisfaction, see, or else—"

Hardstaffe stepped away from the threatening fist.

Serve the rotten little coward right, thought Arnold. I'd just enjoy seeing that hefty docker's fist put our little Hardstaffe to sleep. Nevertheless he rose from his chair and came forward to assist his host.

"Look here, my man," he began.

But Hardstaffe seemed to gain courage from his support, and lifting his hand for silence, he assumed his most suave smile.

"There's no need for all this, you know," he said soothingly. "If you'd only waited in the study for a few minutes longer, we could have had the whole thing cleared up by now. You've had a long journey and you naturally feel a bit upset. And, of course, you don't know the facts of the case. Boys will be boys, and sometimes they have to be thrashed to maintain discipline. I daresay you've belted Alfie yourself before now. The discipline in our school may be a bit stricter than in most villages, but I can truthfully say that I've never been known to punish a boy unjustly. Now just come along to the study with me—we mustn't intrude on the ladies any longer—and I'll put the matter right in a few minutes."

"I hope so," returned Ramsbottom. "And I warn you that if I don't get some satisfaction, I'll take my own way of settling with you."

CHAPTER 21

"I THINK we all deserve a little drink after that," said Leda, putting all the plates on the dining-room floor for the dogs. "Bring the decanters into the drawing-room, Arnold. I'll take the glasses."

The three of them sat round the fire, each with a cigarette and a drink. Leda and Arnold did most of the talking, while Charity sat back silently in her chair watching them, and the dogs cracked the bones they had brought in from the dining-room.

At length, Arnold glanced at his watch.

"He's taking more than a few minutes to convince that fellow," he remarked. "Shall I go and see that he's all right? Those dock-workers are nasty customers to handle, and he was spoiling for a fight."

Leda laughed.

"Oh no, don't worry about Daddy," she said. "He's a regular Houdini for getting out of tight corners. He hasn't been a schoolmaster all his life for nothing. He'll talk him out of it all right." As if to prove her words, Mr. Hardstaffe opened the door and joined them.

"Have a drink, Daddy," said Leda. "I expect you need one."

"My God, yes!" he agreed, ignoring the port and sherry, and pouring out a generous double whiskey sprayed with soda water. "The nerve of that fellow, pushing his way into my house! But I got rid of him. All parents are queer creatures, you know, but one gets used to handling them. Oh, we've had worse than that one, haven't we, Leda?"

"Um," agreed Leda. "As bad, anyhow, though I don't remember having one in the dining-room before."

"You both talk as if they were wild animals," laughed Arnold.

"So they are, in a way," said Hardstaffe, perching himself on the arm of Charity's chair, and rubbing his hand along her bare arm. "They all think that their child is different from everyone else's—that is to say, superior, of course—and can't understand why he shouldn't have special treatment."

"Did Ramsbottom go quietly?" asked Leda.

"No, I can't say that he did," Hardstaffe admitted. "I believe that he threatened to murder me again, but I didn't listen very carefully, I'm afraid. He'll feel better tomorrow; they always do."

The conversation became more general until Charity rose to go. Hardstaffe went into the hall to put on his own hat and coat, obviously taking it for granted that she expected him to see her home.

"Really, there's no need for you to come," she said, as they walked down the drive together. "It's not far across the village, and I could easily go alone."

"Why, Charity, you used . . ." he began, then laughed, squeezing her arm. "You're teasing me, my sweet darling," he said, and began to sing softly in a highly unmusical voice the song of a past decade.

'Teasin', teasin', I was only teasin' you;

'Teasin', teasin', just to see what you would do.'

"To think," he went on, "that I used to listen to that song long before you were born. It makes me feel so proud, my love, to know that you chose me in spite of my age. Not that I *feel* any older than I did in the 'nineties'," he said hastily. "But when I look at your lovely young body, I feel that it must be a sacrifice for you to be seen out with a plain-looking old fellow like me."

"Oh no, I don't feel like that at all," said Charity. "But there's something I must say to you. I . . ."

"Have you laddered your new stockings?" he mocked. "I've still some coupons left. You shall have another pair, don't worry."

"No. Oh no! Nothing like that," protested Charity. "It's just that. . . ."

Again her courage failed.

They were some distance from the house now. Hardstaffe stopped, and drew her towards him.

"Kiss me," he commanded, and this time she could not withdraw from him in spite of her greater height.

She felt herself crushed downwards by his incredibly strong arms, felt his kisses on her mouth, throat, and shoulders, while his fingers fumbled, desirous, at her breasts.

At last he moved away, breathing heavily, while she pulled her coat closely around her again, and shuddered.

"To think that you'll soon be mine, dearest," he said. "You can't realise how much I've longed to fondle you all the evening. You're so tantalising and lovely in evening dress, and you look so cold and distant when other people are there. There'll soon be no need for that. Soon everyone will know that we love each other. I think Leda guessed tonight, but don't worry. She knows what a hell my life has been, and she will rejoice in my new happiness. To think that I've waited all these years for love to come to me. Some men never know it like this. For this, my dearest one, is love!"

"No, it isn't," gasped Charity unexpectedly. "That's what I've been trying to tell you. It's all a ghastly mistake. I can't go on with it."

"Charity! What do you mean, my love? Oh, you're upset this evening, and I don't wonder. I meant to make it such a happy time for you, but it all went wrong. First that wretched maid, and then that ridiculous parent. But I'll see that it won't happen again."

"Oh, it won't happen again!" exclaimed Charity. "It won't happen again because I shall never come again. I'm going away where you'll never be able to find me. Can't you see that it's all been a mistake? I don't love you, and you don't love me. You only want my body. That isn't love!"

Hardstaffe put his arms around her.

"My darling, you're overwrought. You don't know what you're saying."

"Don't I?" Charity's laugh was hysterical. "Oh yes, I do. I've just come to my senses and realised what kind of creatures we are, you and I, and I know that I don't love you and I never have. It's the truth. Why won't you believe me?"

In the silence of the night, she thought she could hear the beating of her heart.

"I—see." Hardstaffe's voice was hard. "And since when have you learned this—this truth?" he asked.

"Oh dear!" said Charity. "I don't mean to be unkind. I hate to feel that I'm hurting you. I did think I loved you. I wasn't pretending then, and I'm not pretending now."

"Would you mind answering my question?"

"It's—well, I don't know exactly, but it was after *she* was— after *she* died."

"I see," said the same cold voice again. "But I seem to remember that you used to say you couldn't belong to me as long as she was alive."

"Yes, but I didn't know—I didn't realise—"

"You didn't realise!" mimicked Hardstaffe. "You're not a baby. What didn't you realise? First you won't have me because my wife's alive, and then you won't have me because she's dead! What do you expect me to do? Walk gracefully out of your life with bowed head and tears in my eyes, saying 'It's a far, far better thing I do now'? Oh no, my girl. You might get away with this sort of thing with a younger man, but you won't get rid of me so easily. I've built everything on you. Every bit of life and happiness I have left, however short it may be, is wrapped up in you. I'm not going to give it up. Ever since I first kissed you, I made up my mind to possess you, and possess you I will, or die in the attempt! I'm not going to have my schemes mined just because you're wanton enough to change your mind. I've dreamed of you by night, and planned for you by day. Now that you're within reach at last, I'm not going to leave you for some other man to pick up and wear. No, by God! You're going to belong to me. You don't suppose I've planned all this for nothing, do you? You said you wouldn't be mine as long as *she* was alive. Now she's dead, and you've got to keep your bargain."

"Oh! Then you did—"

"Did what?"

"You did kill her!" she cried, and ran from him into the darkness.

CHAPTER 22

FRIEDA placed the last fork on the breakfast table, the following morning, and surveyed it with a scowl.

No, there's nothing wrong with it, she told herself in her own language. It is perfect. That won't do at all. She must have something to grumble at.

And she removed the spoon used for serving the porridge, from Mr. Hardstaffe's place.

There, that's good! she thought as she dropped it carelessly into the sideboard drawer. Now they will both have a good reason for being angry with this silly, mad Jewess!

She shivered as she walked out of the breakfast room.

It was cold to be out of your bed so early in the mornings, doing dirty housework for people such as, in the better days of her own country, she would have scorned to know. Their house was like them, too, always cold and unfriendly—not like the centrally-heated home she had known and loved, with its welcoming warmth and its lovely fuss of decoration.

She sighed.

I must learn not to think of these things, she admonished herself. They belong to a life which has passed away from Germany, perhaps for ever. I shouldn't find them if I went back.

If she went back!

If she went back now on a magic carpet, seeing, but herself unseen, would she find anything in her beloved Nürnberg unaltered? Was the flat where she had lived for so many years with her dear kind parents, still there? Was it occupied by some Storm Trooper and his wife? Were her parents—? No, no, not even in her thoughts dare she ask herself that question.

Did the swallows still go to Nürnberg in the Springtime, and fly through the open windows of the flat to build their nests high up in the cosy sitting room? Did old, fat Frau Bauer at the little confectioner's opposite still sell Lebküchen—those round, flat, rich cakes made from honey, ginger, and almonds, with a dozen different delicious coatings? Was the lovely old house of Hans Sachs still standing? Did friends still meet in the cafes to drink lager and listen to Chamber Music? Or had all those things which the word "Gemütlichkeit" implied, vanished from Germany for ever? Could she and the hundreds of thousands like her in exile ever again thrust the torn and bleeding roots of their lives into the soil whence they had sprung?

For Jewess as she was, she was also German, as her ancestors had been for hundreds of years.

But what did these English pigs understand of all this?

Nothing! They thought her dull, almost half-witted. And there were times when she did indeed feel crazed, when something within her made her feel that she must vent all her pent-up rage and suffering on these cold-blooded people to whom she was nothing but a slave. There were times when she came downstairs in the morning expecting to find that these two who made her life so unhappy were dead, coldly and horribly dead.

For, in this house, she had bad dreams . . .

She shivered again as she moved slowly about her various tasks in the kitchen quarters, then, on a sudden thought, she made her way into the large, warm kitchen where Cook was already preparing breakfast.

"I am hungry," she announced. "I will have my breakfast now."

"Ho, will you?" replied the cook placing a plump hand on her hip. "Have you laid the breakfast table?"

"Yes."

"And done the drawing-room?"

"The drawing-room? But yes."

"But no!" was the reply. "I know when you're telling lies, my girl, if no one else in this house does. Go on now, be off with you, and get that room finished or there'll be murder done. 'Ee well, it's bad luck to say that, but you're that aggravating."

"But that room—he is so cold," protested Frieda. "I am not use to work without breakfast."

The cook sniffed.

"Time you was then, lass. Go on. No drawing-room, no breakfast. And who do you reckon you are, coming into my kitchen and ordering your meals?" She eyed the tearful girl more softly, and took a tin out of the cupboard.

"Thinking about your home again, I suppose, and worriting over your ma. That'll get you nowhere. We all have our bits of troubles. Here's a cake for you. Now be off!"

Frieda's face lit up with pleasure, and she hurried off, munching the stale cake.

Like a child she is, thought Cook. A little kindness works wonders with her, the poor creature.

Frieda crammed the last bit of cake into her mouth as she reached the drawing-room door. She wiped her fingers down her apron, unlatched the door, then picked up dustpan, brush, and dusters, and shouldered herself into the room.

For a moment she did not notice anything out of order in the room, but when she had advanced as far as the hearth, she saw that the light was on.

She halted.

"Please?" she said.

For the room was not empty as it usually was at this early hour. The rose-coloured light from the huge standard lamp fell softly upon the figure of Mr. Hardstaffe seated in his favourite chair.

"Please?" repeated Frieda.

He did not stir, and, shrugging her shoulders, she dropped heavily on to her knees in front of the fire-place.

"You are asleep," she said aloud in English.

She spread a dust-sheet over the hearth-rug, and dropped the heavy brass fire-irons onto it with satisfying clangour.

"Asleep!" she repeated more loudly.

She glanced at the empty tantalus and glass on the table, and sniffed.

"No!" she exclaimed. "You are drunk. Like a pig!"

A little startled by her temerity, she looked sideways at the motionless form of the schoolmaster, but gaining courage from his immobility, she went on, "Always you are not drunk, but always you are a pig!"

She tinned to her task of cleaning the hearth, and picked up one of the andirons to polish its shining legs.

Miss Hardstaffe calls these the dogs just to make fun of me, she muttered to herself. I wonder that she thinks it so funny. She tells me to clean the dogs, and when I say it is not my place to do that—I am a parlourmaid, not a kennel-maid—she tells me not to be impertinent, for these are the dogs. As if I didn't know that dogs have four legs! But at least these are clean, not like her dogs!

She cleaned out the ashes, swept the hearth, and lit the fire. Then she replaced the "dogs" with their attendant brasses and went across to the window to jerk back the heavy velvet curtains.

She saw that the window was wide open, shivered again, and closed it with an emphatic bang.

These English! These Christians! Always trying to freeze themselves except at night when she had to fill bottles for their beds with hot, but not boiling, water. What people! What a climate!

She snapped out the light, replaced the stopper in the cutglass decanter, picked up an ashtray, scattering the ash and cigarette ends on the carpet, and walking round the back of the armchair, peered over it at the silent man.

"Pig!" she exclaimed, then started back.

For a second, she stood rocking on her feet as if she had just received a blow between the eyes. And in that fraction of time, a kaleidoscope of shifting horrors came to her mind. Rubber truncheons, screams of pain too horrible to bear, the sickening crunch of a crushed skull, sticky jags of broken bone, coagulated clots of blood . . .

But this man wasn't a Jew.

"You are not drunk. You are dead!" she said aloud.

At the sound of her own voice, she screamed, dropped tantalus and tray, and ran out of the room, making grotesque gurgling noises in her throat.

CHAPTER 23

CHIEF Inspector Alan Driver of New Scotland Yard placed his note-book on the square-topped oak table in the breakfast room, as if staking a claim, and looked up as Leda entered the room.

"Miss Hardstaffe?" he inquired, "I am chief inspector Driver. This is Lovely."

A look of supreme indignation spread over Leda's face.

"Really! I've no doubt that you have a certain interest in your work, Inspector," she said coldly, "but I hardly think that is a suitable way of describing the murder of my parents to me."

Driver apologised profusely.

"I'm extremely sorry, Miss Hardstaffe," he said. "I'm not very good at introductions. I should have said that this is my assistant, detective-sergeant Lovely."

Lovely, completely inured to the extraordinary situations in which his surname could place him, acknowledged Leda's frigid greeting with equanimity.

"I don't want to worry you with questions if it will upset you," went on Driver, "but if you could spare me a few minutes, I should be glad of your help."

Leda was silent for a moment, then,

"All this probing into things . . . can't it be stopped?" she burst out. "My mother's dead and Daddy's dead. What does it matter who killed them, to anyone except them?"

"There's such a thing as Justice," remarked the Inspector.

"But if Daddy murdered my mother, as you all seem to think, and someone killed him for that, isn't that justice?" Driver shook his head.

"It might do for the Frozen North," he said, "but it isn't good enough for Scotland Yard. And there's no proof yet that Mr. Hardstaffe did murder your mother. The inquiry must go on. But if you'd prefer me to interview the others in the house first, I will certainly do so. This affair has been very upsetting for you."

Leda was, indeed, a changed woman. She had none of the cheerful, arrogant manner so typical of her. She spoke quietly, and was not ashamed to show her grief. Her eyes were swollen with tears, and, in her dress of unrelieved black, she looked drab and lifeless, and plainer than ever.

"Thank you, Inspector," she replied, "but I'd rather get it over now. I believe in facing the unpleasant things in life. It isn't so much losing both my parents in this tragic way, it's— my father. We have always been such pals. He depended on me for everything. It's horrible to think that he had to be killed in that way."

Driver nodded his sympathy. There was nothing he could say to make things better. It was a most terrible thing for any woman to have to face, and although she was not a type whom a man wanted to try and comfort, he was none the less sorry for her.

Nevertheless he did not forget that although she had no apparent connection with the murders, she was not above suspicion, and his voice assumed a more official tone as he said, "Won't you sit down, Miss Hardstaffe?"

"I'd rather not, if you don't mind," replied Leda. "I'm not in the habit of sitting down much except for meals, and to-day I feel restless. But please don't stand yourself. You have your notes to write, I know. I suppose you won't smoke? Well, I will, if you don't mind. It may steady my nerves a bit. You see, I can't get used to the idea that Daddy isn't here. I keep expecting him to walk in through the door, and it's rather—upsetting."

She lit her cigarette, and inhaled deeply. Then, sensing the Inspector's hesitation, she said,

"Please don't take any notice of this. I'm all right really. If other women can stand up to incessant bombing, I guess I can stand a few questions. Go right ahead."

"I understand that you witnessed your mother's last will."

"Yes. I and the German maid, Frieda."

"Did you know the terms of that will at the time of witnessing it?"

"Yes."

"And did you ever mention them to your father?"

"Certainly not. I should never be guilty of such a breach of confidence," she replied indignantly.

Driver nodded his approval.

It was, he thought, just what you'd expect from Miss Hardstaffe.

"Did it occur to you as strange that she should make a will in which you and your brother were not mentioned?"

"I can't say that it did," said Leda. "She was always making new wills and cutting one of us out."

"Then you will be surprised to learn that, as far as we know, she made only that will and one other over a period of many years?"

Leda shrugged her shoulders.

"I'm afraid I ceased to be surprised at anything Mother did, years ago," she replied. "She certainly told us all enough times that she was making new wills, but I'm not surprised that she didn't. She told us all that there was morphia in her sleeping-draughts, and it wasn't true."

"Do you think it likely that your father murdered his wife, to get her money?"

"No. I don't believe he knew about it."

"I see," said Driver. "Then you believe he got rid of her, thinking it would never be found out, so that he would be free to marry Charity Fuller."

Leda gasped.

"I didn't say that. I don't know—"

"But that's what you think?"

She looked at him in sudden admiration.

"Yes. Now I understand why they sent you from Scotland Yard," she said. "Yes, that's what I do believe. I didn't realise that there was anything between them until the night she dined here when Daddy—" She broke off as if unable to pronounce the words, and looked at him appealingly. "It came as rather a shock to me. There was no mistaking the—the intimacy between them. Daddy seemed to be parading it for my benefit, and though I had no sympathy with Mother's behaviour when she was alive, I didn't like this. Daddy was too old for that kind of thing, but I suppose that's just when you begin to feel that way."

Driver paused for a moment.

"Do you know whether your father made a will?" he asked.

"No. I shouldn't be surprised if he didn't," she replied. "He was very rigid about school affairs, but rather careless over personal matters. Mother was far more business-like about money, though few people would believe it."

"I see," said Driver. "Now I must ask you about your father's murder. When did you first learn that he was dead?"

Leda put her hand over her eyes for a moment, as though she wished to blot out the memory of the last sight of her father, which Driver's words had revived.

"Before breakfast. I was just coming down stairs into the hall when Frieda ran out of the drawing-room and proceeded to have hysterics all over the house. I followed her into the kitchen, but she gabbled at me in German, and I couldn't make sense of what she was saying, so I went back to see if I could find out what had frightened her. I—found—him."

She described the scene accurately in a voice little louder than a whisper, while the Inspector listened, ignoring the several signs of her distress.

"Do you know of anyone who could have had a motive for murdering your father?" he asked.

"Yes, I—well, no, not exactly," she faltered. "That is, I know of several people who have threatened to murder him. He was a man whom you either liked or disliked very much, and he rather prided himself on this. There was a certain amount of jealousy at the school from the Staff. Then, he was a great disciplinarian, and the parents didn't like him for that. And, one way and another, people were always threatening to get even with him for some real or imaginary grievance."

She told him about Ramsbottom's threat in some detail. "Yes, we must certainly look into all that," agreed Driver. "But personal antipathy is scarcely enough motive for murder, and most people utter threats without any intention of carrying them out, I'm glad to say: otherwise we should be a much-overworked department at the Yard. There must have been a much stronger motive that induced someone to murder him so brutally. Something that affected the murderer deeply.

"If you, for instance, had been very fond of your mother, and believed that your father had killed her, you might have decided to take matters into your own hands and administer justice yourself. Especially if you knew that, as your father had left no will, both his money and that he'd inherited from your mother would be divided between your brother and yourself—"

Leda turned pale, and, forsaking the hearth in front of which she had been standing, stumbled to the chair she had previously refused, and rocked herself backwards and forwards, her face covered.

Driver jumped to his feet.

"I'm sorry," he said, "I forgot—I didn't mean—"

Leda shuddered, then looked up at him with frightened eyes.

"My brother," she whispered. "That's who you mean, isn't it? My brother! Oh no, I can't believe it!"

CHAPTER 24

INSPECTOR Driver's chief fault was an inclination to sum up people at a first meeting. He was well aware of this tendency, however, and although he could not prevent his mind from receiving and storing such impressions, he could and did avoid placing too much credence in them.

He thought Stanton Hardstaffe too suave in manner and in dress. There was too much accent on the accessories of his clothes, which made Driver over-conscious of the creased roll across his own waistcoat. Stanton's trousers were exquisitely creased, the bottom button of his coat carefully left undone, his handkerchief arranged with precision, his tie correctly askew. In Mr. Hardstaffe Senior's young days, he would have been dubbed a masher or la-di-da boy.

A bit of a wax-work, thought the Inspector, looking down at his own baggy-kneed trousers. Still, a man may be a man for a' that. Ay, and a murderer, too!

"This is a bad business, Mr. Hardstaffe," he said.

"A pretty bad show," agreed Stanton.

"I'm sorry to have to intrude my questions on you at this time, but you'll understand that it has to be done. Won't you sit down?"

"Thanks."

Stanton took each exquisite crease of his trousers in turn between a delicate thumb and finger, and sank back gracefully into the chair indicated.

Driver restrained a boyish impulse to shake his fountain pen over him, and said hastily,

"You'll appreciate that the sooner I can get together full details about your father's murder—"

Stanton raised a well-manicured hand.

"Don't apologise, please," he said, "I'll answer anything you like to ask. It won't upset me in the least, if that's what you're thinking, but why can't you drop the whole inquiry, and let murdering dogs lie?"

So both the brother and the sister want the case to be dropped, thought Driver. Queer! Now I wonder if—?

"You think that Mr. Hardstaffe murdered your mother?" he asked.

"Think? I'm sure of it, the damned swine! I told the Super-intendent so, but he took no notice. He made my mother's life hell, and did all he could to try and break her spirit. When he found that he couldn't do that, he murdered her instead. If you'd known him as well as I did, you wouldn't doubt it for a minute."

"I believe you left home years ago because of your father."

"That's quite true. I knew I should kill him one day if I stayed in the same house. I was young and impetuous then, of course. I don't suppose anyone would have blamed me for putting him away. Everyone hated the sight of him."

"Miss Hardstaffe seems very fond of him."

"Oh—Leda!"

Stanton dismissed her idiosyncrasy with a shrug of his well-padded shoulders.

"You left home because he ill-treated your mother. When you did return, you found that he had killed her," remarked Driver, striving to keep his dislike of this witness out of his voice. "Didn't you want to take matters into your own hands and kill him, too?"

"I'll say I did!" exclaimed Stanton. "It was as much as I could do to restrain myself from throttling the swine when I saw him strutting about the house with that sanctimonious, it-hurts-me-more-than-it-hurts-you expression on his face."

"Are you quite sure that you did in fact restrain yourself?" asked Driver. "Isn't it true that you lost control of yourself, and did murder your father?"

Stanton clenched his hands.

"No, it is not true!" he retorted. "I should have a greater respect for myself if I had bumped him off. If I'd seen him that night, I might have done it, but I didn't. Someone beat me to it. I tell you I'm sorry I hadn't the pluck to avenge my mother."

A strange affair, thought Driver. Both he and his sister feel upset about the murders, but for different reasons. Both are convinced that their father murdered their mother. The brother adored his mother; the sister loved her father. This, according to age-old beliefs was as it should be. Yet might there not be some Oedipus complex twining through these natural cross-currents of affection? He dismissed the idea at once.

In his long experience, he had found that murder usually had a more tangible motive—the acquisition of someone or something. Money, in most cases. Or a woman.

"Where were you, Mr. Hardstaffe, on the night of your father's murder?" he asked.

"At home. I live a good many miles away from here."

"So I understand. You are not in the Army or anything?"

Stanton looked at him coolly.

"No. I'm in a reserved occupation. Any objection?"

"Certainly not, sir. It all amounts, then, to this. You lacked the opportunity to kill your father that night, but admit motive and intention?"

Stanton looked a little perturbed.

"It sounds rather bad if you put it like that," he said, "but—well, that about expresses it."

The Inspector tapped his pencil on the table in front of him.

"You know, of course, that, so far as we can ascertain, Mr. Hardstaffe left no will, so that it is extremely probable that the money from him and your mother will be divided between you and your sister?"

"Yes." He laughed. "The old devil would be livid if he knew I should get any of it."

"I understand that you were disagreeably surprised to hear that your mother had cut you out of her will?"

"Surprised? I was dumbfounded!" exclaimed Stanton. "She meant me to have that money. I was the only one she cared about, and I know she would never have cut me out of her own free will. Oh, I say, that's rather good!" he said. "Of her own free will, do you see?"

The Inspector ignored the joke which he considered to be out of place.

"You had presumed, then, that her death would make you a rich man?"

The smile faded from Stanton's lips. He rose to his feet.

"If that remark is intended to mean what it suggests," he said savagely, "it's an insult, and I don't take insults well. I may be like my mother in looks, but I warn you that my temper is pure Hardstaffe. You'd better be careful."

"You've no need to adopt that tone with me," Driver replied calmly. "Even if you and Miss Hardstaffe aren't interested in finding out the truth about the murders, Scotland Yard is. You'll lose nothing by being civil, sir."

Stanton passed a hand over his shining brown hair.

"I'm sorry, Inspector," he said, "but I'm a bit on edge. First the sorrow of losing Mother, and now having to come over here at a minute's notice—People talk, and it's all most unpleasant."

Driver nodded.

"If I may say so, sir," he remarked, "you people never seem to realise that it's just as unpleasant for us to be prying into your private affairs, and if you'd only give us your full confidence straight away without holding anything back in the hope that we shan't find it out, we should get at the truth with less trouble."

"Look here!" Stanton thrust his head forward in a manner which, Driver thought, must have been characteristic of the murdered schoolmaster also. "Are you trying to hint that I'm not telling the truth?"

But the Inspector was spared the necessity of replying. At that moment, there came the sound of angry voices in the hall, and a knock on the door. A police constable entered, propelling an unwilling figure before him by means of a gruelling grip on his arm.

"Caught him in the shrubbery, sir," he explained in response to the Inspector's question. "He said he was looking for the instrument of murder."

"Have you all gone mad?" demanded Stanton. "That's our guest, Arnold Smith!"

CHAPTER 25

"I MUST apologize, Mr. Smith," said Driver after he had dismissed Stanton Hardstaffe and the misguided constable. "You have a perfect right to go anywhere in the house or grounds as long as you don't object to our men keeping you in view. I'm afraid the constable's enthusiasm exceeded his discretion. I'll see that it doesn't occur again."

"Oh, don't be too hard on him," replied Arnold. "He was only doing what he considered to be his duty. I suppose it must have looked suspicious." He rubbed his arm. "What a grip the fellow has!" he exclaimed.

The Inspector indicated the chair vacated by Stanton.

"Will you sit down," he said. "As you are here, I should like to ask you a few questions. First of all, do you mind telling me what kind of 'instrument' you were looking for?"

"The knobkerrie, of course," Arnold replied, sitting down. The Inspector stared at him for a few seconds.

"And would you mind explaining how you knew that Mr. Hardstaffe had been killed by a blow from a knobkerrie? I

understand that this fact has not been mentioned by Superintendent Cheam, and that no one else in the house has so far
thought of it."

"They must be blind then," retorted Arnold. "It was the
first thing I noticed when Leda—that is, when Miss Hardstaffe
called me into the drawing-room. I saw at once that it wasn't
in its usual place on the wall near the window."

"'There it was, gone,' in fact," remarked Driver with an
unbelieving air. "Surely the fact that you could no longer see
the knobkerrie in the room did not in itself prove that it had
been used to murder Mr. Hardstaffe?"

"No, perhaps not," admitted Arnold, "but it just had to be."

"Psychic?"

"No." Arnold looked down at his shoes, apparently intent
on examining the polish on their toes—or lack of it, since it was
one of Frieda's daily tasks to clean them. Then he looked up at
the Inspector, and said frankly, "It's this way. When I heard
that Mrs. Hardstaffe had been murdered, I rushed along to the
police station and gave myself up for murdering her husband."

"Extraordinary," murmured Driver.

"What? Oh, I see. Well, of course I didn't know at the time
that she had been murdered. I concluded that it must be him,
and as I'd had a crack on the head and was wandering a bit—"

"Excuse, Mr. Smith," Driver interrupted, "aren't you
wandering a bit now?"

"It's a little difficult to explain," said Arnold.

"Perhaps it will help you if I say that although I've not yet
had time to read the full statement you made on that occasion, I do know that you confessed to a murder which had not
then been committed, but which has since actually happened
in every detail."

"Yes, that's it. As all the other details have been exactly as I
described them, I thought I'd see whether I could find the knobkerrie in the shrubbery, too. It *was* the knobkerrie, wasn't it?"

"Yes," Driver said gravely. "It was the knobkerrie which bashed his head in. We found it in the shrubbery, with no finger prints on it, as you'd said, but plenty of other signs of the purpose for which it had been used. And doesn't it strike you as being strange that Mr. Hardstaffe's murder should have been carried out in exactly the way you had planned it?"

"Strange? Of course it's strange," retorted Arnold. "It's more than that. It's uncanny. It's—why damn it, Inspector, it's getting on my nerves."

"You're sure that it wasn't Mr. Hardstaffe who was getting on your nerves?" Driver persisted. "Mr. Hardstaffe whom you hated, whom you had planned to murder weeks before? You're sure that the blow on the head hadn't left you with any permanent injury, so that in a sudden fit of hatred, you crept downstairs from your room, entered the drawing-room through the window, and murdered Hardstaffe?"

Arnold looked startled, and sat blinking at him for a moment.

"Why, of course I'm sure!" he exclaimed at length, in a voice which expressed innocent astonishment. "I didn't murder him. I swear I didn't. Why, as soon as I thought there was even a possibility that I'd done it before, I went straight to the police constable."

"That might have been nothing more or less than a clever feint," replied Driver. "You might have staged the whole thing—yes, even to that blow on the head that seems to figure so largely in your conversation—in order to provide yourself with a kind of moral alibi, intending to murder Hardstaffe at a later date."

"But—but—" stammered Arnold. "What about Mrs. Hardstaffe's murder then?"

"I see no reason to suppose that you didn't commit that murder also."

"M-murder Mrs. Hardstaffe, me? Oh no!" exclaimed Arnold. "You must be joking. Mrs. Hardstaffe was a nice woman. I liked her immensely. Whatever motive could I have had?"

Driver stroked a reflective chin.

"I have always found that most crimes are committed for the sake of material gain of some sort or other. Shall we say you might have murdered her for her money?"

"But that's absurd," protested Arnold. "I haven't got any of her money—or any of his, for that matter."

"It might come to you less directly," said the Inspector.

Arnold gave a little jump in his chair, opened his mouth as if about to protest again, thought better of it, and relapsed into silence.

To his relief, Driver did not pursue the subject.

"Let's accumulate a few facts about your movements, Mr. Smith," he said. "Have you any idea at what time Mr. Hardstaffe was murdered?"

"Not really," replied Arnold, "but according to my imaginary plan, it should have been at about twelve minutes past midnight."

"That is the doctor's estimate approximately," confirmed Driver.

"Where were you at that time?"

"In bed."

"Alone?"

"Yes, of course."

Arnold looked shocked.

"That's very commendable from the moral point of view," remarked the Inspector, "but is much to be deprecated under the circumstances."

Arnold at last lost his temper.

"I strongly object to your tone, Inspector," he said, springing to his feet. "I refuse to sit here any longer and listen to your outrageous hints and flippancies. You're treating me as though I were a confirmed criminal. I demand an apology."

To his surprise, the Inspector gave it, and Arnold sat down again, feeling slightly mollified and very foolish.

"You really have only yourself to blame, Mr. Smith," remarked Driver. "You did tell the police you were a murderer. You can't blame us if we check up on you in any way which seems necessary. Now, let us assume for a moment that you are not guilty of murdering Hardstaffe. What is your explanation of the strange coincidence that in every detail the murder was carried out in the way which you yourself, on your own confession, had planned?"

"The only thing I can think of is that someone else copied my idea. I've thought about it till I'm dizzy, and that's the only explanation I can find," said Arnold.

"And who is this 'someone'? Did you tell anyone about your plan?"

"No, no one."

"Most interesting," remarked Driver. "So, unless the murder was committed by Constable Files or Superintendent Cheam, the murderer must be a thought-reader!"

"Oh no, no," protested Arnold. "I didn't tell anyone, but I've got it all written down. You see, it's in a book I'm writing and I described the murder in full detail, just as I did at the police-station."

Driver began to look interested.

"Did anyone know you were writing about a murder?" he asked.

"Oh, yes, I think so," said Arnold. "Miss Hardstaffe did, and I daresay I mentioned it to lots of people besides."

"Could anyone in the house get hold of the manuscript?"

"Well—yes—I suppose that anyone could read it if they wanted to. I keep it in my bedroom, and more often than not, I leave it lying on top of my writing table when I go out."

"I see," said Driver. "Now, Mr. Smith, if you didn't murder Mr. Hardstaffe, can you tell me who did?"

"Certainly I can," affirmed Arnold without hesitation. "It was that German girl, Frieda. She hated him more than I did. She used to call him 'The Gestapo,' and what German wouldn't put an end to that if he could?"

CHAPTER 26

DRIVER glanced up at the sullen, sweating, shrinking Jewess, and restrained a quotation.

The burly fifty-year-old chief-inspector (who had been educated at Oxford and was not ashamed of it) had learned to curb that habit of flinging into the air a sudden quotation whose very aptness had only served to irritate his critics. So, if the tortuous twists of Frieda's coarse hair recalled the locks of the Medusa, if her attitude might be likened to that of a creature whose nest had been turned up by a plough in the month of November, 1785, he gave no indication of such thoughts, but waved her silently to the chair in front of his desk.

"You are Frieda Braun?" he asked.

His question evoked neither movement nor reply.

"Come, come," he said gently, "surely you know your own name."

The girl remained standing before him. She did not speak.

"Gnädige Fraulein—" he began, but before he had time to say anything more, Frieda sat down in the chair, and, lifting her silly, befrilled apron to her eyes, burst into noisy weeping.

The constable, employed as a kind of human dictaphone by reason of his acute hearing and proficiency in shorthand, stirred uneasily in his chair in the corner, blew out his cheeks, and waggled his ears in a superhuman effort to concentrate on the Inspector's next words.

It had taken the constable many years to learn to write English as it is not spoken, and foreign languages were almost entirely unknown to him. For all the meaning conveyed to him by the last two words, the Inspector might as well have ejaculated "Abracadabra.'

And indeed, the words did appear to hold some magic, for Frieda's tears resolved themselves into tiny sniffs, while she put down her apron and regarded Driver with eager eyes, and the beginning of a smile curved round the corner of her mouth. Then, illustrated by waving expressive hands, she uttered a spate of words which left the constable gasping.

But at the Inspector's next words, he pulled himself together, and began to flick off lines of shorthand underneath the three-dots-and-a-dash which he had jotted down defiantly, at the top of the page.

"Ja," said Driver.

(Yah! wrote the constable.)

"Yes, yes, I understand, Miss Braun. But we must write down all that you say in English."

Frieda nodded.

"Ja, ja; me speak English very gut."

You're tellin' me, thought the constable, hastily amending the last word.

Sorry, continued Frieda, indicating her wet cheeks. "It is those words. Always it is 'Come here, Jew' in this bad house. You are so kind. I will tell you everything."

"And we won't go home till mornin'," sighed the constable.

Driver nodded encouragingly at her.

"Then it will be best if I ask you a few questions," he said.

God bless the bloomin' Inspector! the constable exclaimed to himself. What that man doesn't know about women—and him a bachelor! If I'd known as much about them ten years ago as he does, I shouldn't have to stand what I do from Aggie.

But perhaps the Inspector didn't know so much either, ten years ago . . .

The thought suggested such entrancing possibilities that he had to wrench his mind away to concentrate on his job.

"You are Frieda Braun. You are a refugee from Germany, born in Austria. The police have had no trouble with you. You have reported to them regularly and kept all the rules for aliens in this country. You have not tried to get married to any Englishman so that you would become naturalised . . ."

"But no," Frieda said indignantly. "Me engage to marry German."

"He is not in England?"

"He is in concentration camp in Poland—perhaps. But I wait for him," she replied with dignity.

Poor devil! thought Driver.

"You were the first one to find Mr. Hardstaffe dead," stated Driver.

"No."

"But—" He looked surprised. "You found him in the morning in the drawing-room?"

"But yes, I see him then. The one who kill him is first."

A gleam of suspicion kindled in the Inspector's eyes.

It was a nice point, he conceded to himself. But wasn't it rather too clever, too glib for one who professed to understand English "very gut"? If she were indeed pretending to have less knowledge of the language than she actually possessed, it would not have been so difficult for her to read Arnold's manuscript as he had imagined. And, for that matter, many people could read a foreign language quite well although their conversation in it was elementary.

Well, this was just another thing for him to find out.

"You had no doubt that he was dead?"

"Please?"

The constable was so delighted with the reply that he broke the point of his pencil on the word.

Driver swore, under his breath, and selected a fresh combination of words, which he pronounced with exasperated lucidity.

"When you saw Mr. Hardstaffe—he was dead?"

"Yes."

The dark eyes widened in an apparent endeavour to impress the Inspector with their owner's innocence.

"How did you know that he was dead?"

Frieda broke into the answer with a "pouf" of disdain.

"I see his head, no? It is enough. In Nürnberg I see many men with those heads. But," she added as an afterthought "they are Jews."

She spoke simply, without emotion, and Driver suppressed a shudder.

It offended his sense of propriety that any woman should have learned to accept such hideous sights as the normal happenings of life.

Could any woman, he asked himself, remain quite sane in such circumstances? Or would her mind gradually become so distorted that she would ultimately commit some such atrocity herself? Could it be that, in her changed sense of values, a human head had become a thing of blood and splintered bone, so that the sight of Mr. Hardstaffe's head above the low back of the chair, and the knobkerrie on the wall, had assumed some affinity in her mind, and provided a temptation too strong for her to resist?

"You hated Mr. Hardstaffe, didn't you, Frieda?"

"Yes, I hate him. He is bad man," she said.

"He was like the Gestapo, you said?"

"It is true. Always he tells tales to Miss 'Itler."

"You hate Hitler and the Gestapo. You would have killed them all if you could. But instead of doing that, you killed this Gestapo, didn't you? You killed Mr. Hardstaffe at midnight, and ran away leaving the light burning. In the morning, you were afraid to go into the room again. Cook has told me that you tried to keep out of the drawing-room. You wanted some-one else to find him first.' You murdered him, didn't you? Didn't you?"

"Please?" was Frieda's aggravating reply.

Driver jumped to his feet and, walking round the table, waggled his pencil in front of her eyes.

"I say you murdered Mr. Hardstaffe!"

"It is not. I do not. Me good girl," protested Frieda. "At night I go to bed. I am tired, but very tired. I am not use to work all day. I go to sleep. I do not kill him." Suddenly her self-control snapped. She flung herself at Driver's feet, clutching at his shoes. "No, no, I do not kill him," she cried. "Don't send me back to Germany. Me good girl." The Inspector shuffled his feet in embarrassment, and raised the weeping girl to her feet.

"If you didn't do it, you have nothing to be afraid of," he said somewhat sententiously. "But Miss Hardstaffe tells me that you hate her and her father, and often say you would like to murder them."

"She!" Frieda spat out the word venomously. "If she is dead one day, yes, I shall be murderer. But now it is she that is one. She kill her father and mother, I tell you. I know. I see much evil and murder in Nürnberg, and I know. And one day—" She moved closer to the Inspector and gazed at him with a look so malevolent that, involuntarily, he moved a step backwards . . . "One day, I kill her with my hands—like this!"

She twisted her hands in a sudden pressing, screwing move-ment, held the pose in silent hatred for a few seconds, then once more, she burst into uncontrollable, searing sobbing, and ran out of the room.

CHAPTER 27

"PHEW!" ejaculated Sergeant Lovely, pushing his fingers through his stiff brush of hair so that it looked like a corn field desecrated by hikers. "She's a queer customer and no mistake. A bit touched if you ask me. Do you think she did it?"

"I think she's capable of unpremeditated murder," was Driver's cautious reply. "I wish I knew how far her evidence is limited by her lack of proficiency in the English language. It might be worthwhile getting hold of an interpreter to find out."

"But you speak German yourself, sir," Sergeant Lovely pointed out.

The inspector laughed.

"Forget it!" he said. "That wasn't German, that was Psychology. I only know about a dozen words and three of them rang the bell, that's all. And by the way, Constable, you'd better forget them too."

The Constable ran a grateful pencil through the strokes and curves on his pad which combined themselves phonetically into a kind of Cockney-Australian sentence, "Garn a digger fer oi line," of which he could not even guess the meaning.

"Well," the Inspector went on, "I suppose I've seen nearly all the people who had cause to murder the old man."

"Bless you, no, sir," replied Lovely. "If you want to interview everyone who'd threatened to do him in, you'll have to see the whole village, I reckon. But I don't know that you'd get much out of them, being a stranger. They all seem to hang together."

"They will if they're guilty," replied Driver grimly. "What did they think of Mrs. Hardstaffe then?"

"Oh, the old lady was different, sir," the Sergeant replied. "They all respected her. They're old-fashioned in these Northshire villages. They hold that it's a woman's place to marry and keep house and bear children, whatever her station in life, and they judge her according to the way she does those things. As for a man: he's judged according to the way he treats his wife and children. If he sticks to them, and never looks at another woman, he's known as a good man. But if he lets his eye do a bit of roving now and again, they call him a bad kind of a man!"

"I see. So Mrs. Hardstaffe was a good woman, and her husband was a bad man. Simple enough. But they were both of them murdered; and the moral of that is— Who's there?"

He whipped round sharply with the sudden feeling that he was being watched, then relaxed as he met the gaze of two wondering blue eyes which regarded him steadily from a height of about two feet.

Resolutely banishing from his mind the jingle of words which reminded him that he could only stand and stare, Driver looked down at the solemn little face.

"Well?" he said.

Then feeling that his tone was too official for the occasion, he repeated the word in a voice pitched in the falsetto.

The child continued to regard him with an unwavering, concentrated gaze which made Driver conscious, for the second time that day, that his trousers were baggy at the knees and that he had outgrown the circumference of his waistcoat.

"Paul! Paul! Oh, he's here, Nanny. I'll bring him back myself."

The pretty, brown-haired girl smiled at the Inspector, as she came into the room and took the child's hand.

Driver, at first sight, thought of her as a girl in her teens, until the thin gold wedding ring on her finger made him think again.

"I hope Baby hasn't been a nuisance," she said, in an attractively husky voice. "He's just at the disappearing age, and doesn't understand that it's naughty to run away from Nanny."

"Oh no. We were just getting acquainted," replied Driver, clucking at the child as if it were a hen. "I'm Chief-Inspector Driver of New Scotland Yard. This is Lovely."

She blushed.

"Well, I—thank you," she murmured.

"Detective Sergeant Lovely," said Driver, firmly avoiding his assistant's gaze. "You, I take it, are Mrs. Hardstaffe."

"Yes. They all call me 'Mrs. Stan' or 'Mrs. Betty' in the village, but I suppose I'm really the only Mrs. Hardstaffe in the family now."

"Very sad, madam. We have some unhappy cases to investigate at times."

Mrs. Stanton smoothed her son's unruly hair.

"It must be a rotten job sometimes," she agreed. "Rather like having to censor other people's letters, but just as necessary, I suppose." She paused, then added, I know it's your duty to dig into people's private affairs, but all the same it does seem a pity, now that both Mr. and Mrs. Hardstaffe are dead, to disturb them. Couldn't the whole beastly affair be left alone?"

Here's another member of the family who wants me to drop the case, thought the Inspector. What's the big idea, I wonder?

"You believe it's a family affair then," he remarked, "You're afraid that one of the family murdered them?"

"No, no, of course not! I'm sure it isn't," she exclaimed.

Sergeant Lovely thought that she turned pale, but he couldn't be sure. You couldn't tell nowadays, he thought, when women covered their skin with all sorts of cosmetics in spite of the scarcity. Trust a woman not to have a shiny nose as long as a bag of flour remained in the war-time larder. He didn't doubt that they even put the yolk of their meagre egg ration into their stomachs, and saved the white for their faces. Silly creatures, women!

"You surely don't mean to suggest that it would be better to drop this inquiry, and allow the murderer to go free?"

"Oh no, Inspector. I realise it's impossible to do that. You've taken my remarks too seriously. I only mean that it's unpleasant to be mixed up in an affair of murder. I'm thinking about my baby. This may have some dreadful effect on his life when he's older."

Driver nodded sympathetically.

I sincerely hope it won't," he said. "Now have you any theory about the murders? Sometimes a woman's instinct jumps ahead to the truth without wasting time on the logical reasoning."

The Sergeant did a sudden imitation of Popeye.

The Inspector's belief is that a woman's instinct is a sixth sense that tells her she's right when she's really wrong, he thought. Now what is he getting at I wonder?

Mrs. Stanton seemed to be thinking along the same lines, for she surveyed Driver critically for a few seconds.

"That's very flattering, Inspector," she drawled in what her husband called her 'party voice,' "but I haven't the slightest idea."

The Inspector hardly appeared to notice her reply, for he went on, almost as though he were talking to himself.

There seems no doubt that Mrs. Hardstaffe was murdered for her money, and it looks as if the motive for murdering your husband's father was the same."

"Meaning that you suspect my husband?" she asked frigidly. "I find your method of saying so rather crude. I have always believed that a policeman's job—whatever his rank or department—is to find out the truth, and not to indulge in idle speculations. If you're determined to suspect anyone in the family, you shouldn't forget that if my father-in-law died without making a will, my husband is not the only one to benefit by his death. If anyone in this house is capable of murder, it's Leda. She's got her father's temper and her mother's cunning rolled into one. Don't leave her out of your calculations, Inspector."

Driver smiled to himself.

It's extraordinary what a bit of temper does to these society women, he thought. It sends 'em right back to the cavewoman age. If men saw women with their veneer off as often as I do, there'd be fewer marriages in the world.

"Was your husband at home on the night of his father's murder?" he asked suddenly.

"No. He was—"

Too late, she perceived the trap he had set for her.

"Well?"

"He wasn't at home," she said defiantly, "but he has a far better alibi than I can give him. He's in the Home Guard, and he was on duty all night."

"Thank you," said Driver. "I hope I haven't caused you any annoyance, Mrs. Hardstaffe."

She took the baby by the hand, and faced Driver with an expression of scorn on her pretty face.

"You haven't succeeded in annoying me, if that was your intention, Inspector," she said, and the slight tremor in her voice belied her words. "You have merely given me a most interesting insight into the way Scotland Yard conducts its inquiries. I read a lot of murder stories, and until now, I've always been amused at the character of the flat-footed police-man who stumbles about making a fool of himself. I really never believed before that such a man could exist in real life."

She held her head high, and turned to make a dignified exit.

But Hardstaffe Junior had other ideas.

Removing the thumb which he had surreptitiously slid into his mouth as soon as he had sensed his mother's preoccupation, he once again fixed the Inspector with a wide-eyed stare, and said emphatically,

"Daddy!"

The Constable and Sergeant Lovely exchanged glances.

They considered the honours even.

CHAPTER 28

THE following morning, Inspector Driver, Superintendent Cheam, Sergeant Lovely, and the "shorthand constable" approached the gates set in the tall iron railings surrounding the school playground, watched by curious eyes from cottage windows.

"This is about the last time we shall be able to go through these gates," remarked the Superintendent. "They're going for salvage. I don't know how we shall keep the children off the road once they're gone. There'll have to be an accident to one of 'em first, belike. That's the way things get done in this village and that's a fact."

The playground was unwontedly silent, although it was nearly nine o'clock. Superintendent Cheam, anticipating that Driver would wish to interview the School Staff, had demanded a holiday for the children, which the Vicar having certain qualms because it was not a Church Festival, had given with some reluctance, and with awful threats of dire penalties should any child be seen within the precincts of the school.

As they were about to pass the door of the caretaker's cottage which stood in the school grounds, Mrs. Burns, the caretaker, came out.

"Biggest busy-body in Nether Naughton," murmured Cheam for the Inspector's benefit.

Mrs. Burns, not at all daunted by the general air of official-dom which enfolded them, rested her hands on her hips, and looked directly at Driver.

"You'll be the gentleman from Scotland Yard, I reckon," she said. "Come to arrest that Miss Fuller I'll be bound."

"Why should I do that?" asked Driver.

"Because she's the murderer, of course," was the reply. "Who else in this village had as much to do with the old devil as she did? Carrying on something awful they were. I've seen the pair of them coming out of that there door arm-in-arm many a time. Always half-an-hour after the rest of the School had gone, mind you, and me waiting to go in and clean the floors. And a man can do a good many things with a girl in a half-hour."

"You're tellin' me!" murmured Cheam.

The woman, whose ears were evidently as sharp as her eyes, turned towards him.

"I don't need to tell you, Superintendent, and that's a fact," she said. "There's not a man, woman or child in this village as didn't know the sort of thing that was going on, but no one tried to stop it. I told the Vicar it was his place to do something about it, but he talked about throwing stones through glass, though I don't know what he meant by that. As I said to him, the children do enough damage what with their catapults and such-like without him encouraging them to break windows with stones. 'Very well, Vicar,' I says to him. 'If you won't do anything, I will.'"

"And did you?" asked Driver.

"Did I?" repeated Mrs. Burns. "Ho, yes I did. I told Miss Hardstaffe in this very yard when she called to see her father. 'The way that young girl runs after your poor old Dad, Miss,' I said, 'is a disgrace to the village,' I said, 'and it's about time someone did something to put a stop to it,' I said. And Miss Hardstaffe looked at me and said soft-like, 'All right, Mrs. Burns. I'll see to it.' But, you seer she didn't do anything after all, and now look what it's come to! He murdered his poor wife, did Mr. Hardstaffe, so's he could wed the girl, and she got sick of him and murdered him. Fair asked for it, too, he did, carrying on with a girl young enough to be his grand-daughter. Well, I've seen her come through that door, winter and summer, day in and day out, and I reckon that next time I see her she'll be wearing handcuffs."

She whisked herself back into the Cottage as quickly as a figure into a weather-house.

"Anything in it?" Driver asked the Superintendent.

"A good deal," was the reply, "but I don't see any motive. They were certainly 'carrying on' as Mrs. Burns says, but Miss Fuller swears that there was no intimacy between them, and who am I to doubt the lady's word?"

"Pretty, is she?" queried Driver.

"I resent that remark," retorted the Superintendent good-humouredly. "Yes, she's pretty. Rather a beauty in an exotic kind of way. Red hair, pale skin, bright makeup. If she'd been a village girl, she'd be reckoned the village belle. But she's always kept aloof from the local folk and gives you the impression that she considers herself above them. Stuck-up, they call her. She never bothered with anyone until she took up with the headmaster, and what she could see in a googley-eyed, wizened little fellow like him, I never could imagine. To my mind, she'd have been better off if she'd walked out with one of the local farmers. But there's no accounting for women. They all seem to fall for a fellow who hunts, and dresses for dinner. It don't seem to worry them at all what kind of man is inside the pink coat or dinner-jacket."

"Very descriptive," said Driver, "I've been trying for years to put all that into words. You don't happen to be attracted by the young lady yourself, by any chance?" The Superintendent laughed.

"Who? Me? Not on your life! She's very decorative and all that, but my old woman's a regular Old Dutch to me. She may not be much to look at, but she bakes the best pasty in Northshire, and what she doesn't know about a steak-and-kidney pudding isn't worth knowing."

Nevertheless, the Superintendent seemed disappointed to find, a little later, that Driver appeared to have little interest in Charity. It was, he thought, almost as though the Inspector had said when he first saw her, "Oh, it's you!" and had instantly made up his mind about her. Whether he thought her guilty or not, Cheam had no means of knowing.

Two of his questions only seemed to hold any significance.

"Have you any reason to believe, Miss Fuller, that Mr. Hardstaffe made a will in your favour?"

"He—he always intended to provide for me, but I—I don't know whether he did or not."

"If he had done so after his wife's death, was he likely to have destroyed it or to have wished to destroy it at the time of his death?"

"Yes. We—we quarrelled. He might have done."

"Thank you, Miss Fuller. I won't detain you any longer."

For all the world, thought Cheam, as though he were a Defending Counsel rather than a Public Prosecutor. Surely he couldn't have fallen under the spell of Miss Fuller's charm so suddenly?

The Inspector methodically interviewed the small wartime staff of the little school without eliciting any information beyond a general dislike of their late headmaster and all his ways.

His longest interview was with Mr. Richards who quite obviously enjoyed the experience of being questioned by a detective.

"I know why you're so interested in me, Inspector," he said. "It's because I'm one of the few people who have stated before witnesses that I should derive a considerable amount of pleasure from murdering Mr. Hardstaffe. In the world of fiction, this would quite exonerate me, for the real murderer would be far too clever to admit his dislike so openly. But the law, I know, likes witnessed statements, so carry on."

"Did you think you were really capable of murdering Hardstaffe?"

"No. I despised him too much. When he thrashed that boy, I was livid—well, you should have seen the fear in the child's eyes

. . . For two pins I'd have kicked him through the village and pitched him on a dunghill, but I wouldn't have crept up behind him and bashed his head in 'with a blunt instrument' in cold blood. One needs a certain sense of proportion in these things."

"One does," Driver agreed drily. "How do you know he was killed in that particular way?"

Richards grinned.

"This is the village of Nether Naughton, Inspector," he replied. "You're not in London now, you know. All the walls have eyes and ears which remain open all the year round."

Driver nodded.

"I understand, Mr. Richards, that you are a Conscientious Objector, or so the walls say. How is it, then, that you talk so easily of killing people?"

Richards bit his lip in annoyance.

"So that's what they say, is it?" he said. "Well, well."

"Healthy young men don't avoid serving their country without some reason of the sort, even if they are school teachers."

Richards looked up, with a wry smile.

"They do make artificial legs well nowadays, don't they?" he asked.

Driver nodded.

So that's it, is it?" he said. "All is not true that gossips?"

Lost my right leg in a motor accident when I was eighteen," Richards explained. "You don't need to stick a needle into me or slip a drawing pin onto the chair. I'll show you."

He bent down and began to untie his shoe-lace.

"Don't bother," said Driver. "I've already trodden on your foot!"

They both laughed.

"Of course I could join up for R.A.F. ground staff or something, even though I'm no Bader," Richards went on, "but they seem to think that, under all the circumstances, I'm being most useful where I am."

"Can you tell me anything about Mr. Hardstaffe's death?" asked Driver. "You must have thought about it a bit, and have some suspicions."

Richards shook his head.

"It's a pretty little problem right enough," he said, "but I really haven't thought about it very much. I can't say that I regret his departure or consider it inappropriate. He seemed to me to be the kind of man who is a blight upon the face of the earth, and it was about time someone bumped him off. As to who did it—well, almost everyone he knew hated the sight of him. Perhaps they all got together and drew lots."

"Do you think that boy's father might have done it?"

"Old Ramsbottom?" exclaimed Richards. "Oh, good Lord, no! A Westcastle stevedore doesn't commit a murder because his son's been given a beating. Why, most likely he belts the boy every Saturday night just for the principle of the thing. When the evacuee boys first came here, they couldn't understand why their foster-parents didn't thrash them once a week, whether they'd deserved it or not. To hear them talk, you'd have thought that they were sorry to miss it, but I don't know that they'd take so kindly to it again now.

"I don't think Ramsbottom's the type to murder anybody except, possibly, in the heat of the moment. Men like that have a great respect for the law although they're so free with their threats. What does he say about it?"

"I haven't seen him yet," said Driver. "He came down here on a day trip, and it means a special journey to Westcastle for me—"

"Special journey, my wooden leg!" interrupted Richards rudely. "The fellow's in Nether Naughton. I saw him this morning!"

CHAPTER 29

MR. RAMSBOTTOM heaved his cumbersome body out of a creaking wicker-chair, as Inspector Driver and Sergeant Lovely were ushered into the front parlour of old Mrs. Selby's little cottage next door to the village stores. His eyes were blood-shot, his gaze shifting.

Driver summed him up as a man with an uneasy conscience.

"I know what you've come about," he said in his broad northern accent. "I've been expecting ye ever since yon old devil was murdered. I tell you I didn't do it, so it's no good trying to make out that I did."

"Well, in that case, you won't mind answering a few questions, Ramsbottom," said Driver. "It's a case of murder as you know, and I've got to get all the evidence I can."

"Ay," agreed the stevedore cautiously. "I'll do my best."

"First of all, what are you doing here? I understand from Superintendent Cheam that you came down from Westcastle on a day trip."

"Ay, that's right." (He said "that's reet" and matched the rest of his pronunciation to those words). "But I changed my mind, like."

"You went to see Mr. Hardstaffe at his house, made a scene in the dining-room in front of his guests, and threatened him. He took you to his study. What happened there?"

Ramsbottom looked at Driver from beneath his thick black eyebrows.

"Nowt," he said shortly. "That was the trouble. He said nowt but a lot of claptrap that wouldn't fool a babby. But when he said it, see, it sounded sense. Yes, he fair put it across me, and I went out without getting owt out of him."

"What did you expect to get?"

"Satisfaction, sir, that's what! No one's going to treat our little lad that way without paying for it."

"Yes, I thought it was money you were trying to get out of him. Well, you didn't get it. What happened then?"

"I walked about a bit, then went into The Fox and Feathers for a drink. And I sat down with my mild and bitter and did a bit of thinking, see. And I had a few more drinks and thought that I ought to have stuck to him a bit longer. I'd got him shaking like a jelly inside of that dining-room, see, and what does he do but get round me with his well-off talk. 'And it won't do,' I says. My old woman'd never forgive me if I go back without satisfaction. Satisfaction's what I've come to get, and satisfaction's what I'll get, I say to myself. So I come back to supper and say I'm not going to catch the train after all. And I go upstairs after, and wait till Mrs. Selby's in bed, and then I come down again and let myself out and go back to see Mr. 'Ardstaffe."

"What for?"

"'Get some satisfaction out of him or murder him' was what I said to myself," replied Ramsbottom frankly. "But I never meant it. I'd had a few drinks too many, what with being worried and being a stranger in the village. On my way, I broke a stick off of one of the trees alongside the road, but I never used it on the old man. I'll swear to that. I only wanted to catch him alone and shake the stick at him."

"Well, what happened when you reached the house?"

"I walked round the garden and had a look at the windows. It was pitch black and I didn't like to use my torch. I'd forgotten about it being black-out. It must have been the beer."

"You'd be lucky to get into that state on war-time beer," remarked the Inspector. "You must have had a barrel full. Well, go on."

"When my eyes got kind of used to the dark, I did see a light in a room downstairs, but it was only a bit of a slit and I couldn't see inside but I felt the window was open. Then—then I came back here."

"Mr. Hardstaffe was in that room, and you know it!" exclaimed Driver. "You climbed through the window, crept up behind him, and murdered him!"

Ramsbottom look frightened.

"Nay, I did not. I swear I didn't do it. I never used the stick I tell you. I never meant to hurt him. I only wanted—"

"All right, we know," put in Driver. "You wanted to force Hardstaffe to give you a compensation for bruising your son. I've met fellows like you before. But if you're by any chance telling the truth, why didn't you try to see Hardstaffe? Having gone so far why didn't you climb through the window? And why did you wait here for us to come and question you? Why didn't you go home by the first train in the morning?"

Ramsbottom moved uneasily in the chair.

"I knew he'd tell you that he'd seen me," he said. "A bit of bad luck it were, that."

Driver looked puzzled.

"Who? Do you mean Mr. Richards?"

"Ay, happen that'll be his name. As soon as he flashed his torch on me I knew it was all up wi' me."

"Let's get this clear," said Driver. "What time was this?"

"I reckon it'd be as near half past eleven as makes no difference. Happen the bit of light caught his eye, and he was going to warn them at the house."

"You're not going to tell me that it was a police constable!" exclaimed the Inspector.

Mr. Ramsbottom looked surprised.

"Nay. I saw his uniform plain in the light. 'Twere one of them Home Guards!"

CHAPTER 30

ARNOLD was surprised to find that the present atmosphere in the Hardstaffe's house was not in the least conducive to the writing of a detective novel.

It had previously seemed an extraordinary thing that the author with whom he had a first name in common, if nothing else—a man named Bennett—had been able to picture so vividly the Siege of Paris although he had not been in the same country at the time. Now, however, he perceived that this admirably realistic description might have been less convincing, had the author of it actually been there.

Here I am, Arnold thought, living in a house in which two murders have been committed, a house overrun by the police who suspect me among others, yet if I were to describe it in a book exactly as I see it, everyone who reads it would say, 'It's evident that *he's* never had any first hand experience of murder!"

For after the second hurrying of police procedure, of photographing, sketching, searching, and questioning, the house had settled down again to a normal way of life.

Even the people within the house became quite natural. Leda, once again wearing her tweeds or uniforms by day, because she "didn't believe in mourning anyhow"; Stanton and his wife Betty, occupying the two recently-vacated seats at table, and their baby son darting about the house like a particularly plump butterfly; Cook carefully measuring a minimum of sugar for the apple tart; Frieda indulging in outbursts of temper and hysterical weeping, and so remaining normal in her very abnormality.

There were no outward signs of strained nerves or overwrought grief. There was no embarrassment between the members of the family. They spoke, ate, laughed, much as usual. They did not even avoid speaking of the two whom even murder had not put asunder, not, in speaking, did they lower their voices or utter hypocritical platitudes. They no longer used the drawing-room: that was all.

Arnold could not decide whether all this was due to the desire of the living Hardstaffes to maintain an air of serenity in front of their guest, or to a fanatical belief in the infallibility of Scotland Yard. But he reflected that it was a state of affairs which would have amazed his literary agent, if that suave, bald-headed gentleman were any longer capable of registering such an emotion.

Nevertheless, his book was progressing slowly.

One afternoon, he came down to tea in the breakfast-room, a little dazed from having concluded a new chapter in which his detective, Noel Delare, had become more than usually daring, and blinking because concentrated writing had made his eyes sore.

The dogs rushed towards him in ecstatic friendliness, and he stooped in an absent-minded way to pat the one nearest to his hand. They had become so much a part of his life that he no longer noticed the white hairs scattered over the legs of his trousers, nor worried that his bedroom smelled strongly of dog. At meal times now, he even threw bones under the dining-room table, and put down his empty plate to be licked.

He knew that such behaviour pleased Leda, and it had become a habit with him to try to please her.

He found that Betty Hardstaffe was holding out a cup of tea for him, and he stammered an apology. Leda chaffed him loudly about his preoccupation, then broke into a long account of her activities at a recent W.V.S. meeting, which enabled her sister-in-law and Arnold to enjoy their tea without the necessity of uttering a word.

When they had finished, Leda got up, gave Arnold a playful pinch on the ear, and said gaily, "Come on, Lazy bones, you haven't had any fresh air to-day. A walk will do you good."

She turned to Betty. "I have to look after him, otherwise he'd either kill himself with working on his old book, or else would suffocate to death."

She slipped her arm through his, and urged him into the hall, followed by the dogs, howling and snarling in their excitement at hearing one of the few words of the human language they cared to understand.

Once out of doors, Leda's animation left her, however, and she walked along in silence until they came to their favourite path through the wood beyond the paddock.

"Arnold, I've got a confession to make," she said.

Arnold turned to her with a startled look on his round, placid face.

To one whose mind was as engrossed with the intricacies of crime as his, the word 'confession' could convey only one meaning. For one brief second, he saw Leda as a murderess.

Then he as quickly shook the thought away.

"A confession?" he asked. "Do you think I'm the right person to tell it to? I mean, perhaps it would be better if you told—er—someone else."

Leda looked at him strangely for a moment.

"You sound as if you think I ought to go to the police," she said.

"No, no. That's not what I meant at all," he lied. "But I'm not much good at giving advice, that's all."

"I don't want advice," returned Leda. "I only want to tell you that I've done something which may offend you."

Arnold smiled in relief.

"That's quite impossible," he said.

"Is it?" Leda regarded him mischievously. "Would you mind being engaged to me?"

Arnold was so much taken by surprise that he could find no immediate reply. He wondered for a moment whether it was Leap Year, but a hasty division of the year by four reassured him.

Engaged to Leda? Engaged to be married? Married to Leda?

He was honest enough to admit to himself that the idea was not new to him. She had made him very comfortable since he had come to live in the village. She would soon be a rich woman, and she would be generous to him. They had become great friends and had much in common.

The lines of a once popular song recurred to his mind. "You like to tramp the hills and heather, and so do I. You like to stay in doors in stormy weather—"

or words to that effect.

But he had decided some time ago that this wasn't enough.

After all, he wasn't so old yet. At fifty, a man wasn't past feeling passion for a woman, and he found the idea of marrying just for a home and an insurance against old age irksome. And how could he feel passion for a woman who always looked lady-like, played a good game of golf and a good hand at bridge, was a thundering good sort, but had no—no 'oomph' whatever?

He was aware of Leda's clear eyes regarding him earnestly as these thoughts skimmed through his mind, and, anxious not to hurt her feelings, he answered her with another lie.

"I'm afraid I hadn't thought about it."

"Oh, that's all right," replied Leda. "You needn't be afraid that I want to try and hook you or anything. You know me better than that, I hope. I'll try to explain."

She paused, and appeared to be listening to the faint yapping of the dogs which told of their distant pursuit of conies.

"It's all Betty's fault," she went on. "She button-holed me this morning and asked me when you were going to leave."

"Well—yes—I—to tell you the truth, I was thinking about that myself," stammered Arnold.

"Liar!" exclaimed Leda. "Now, Arnold, do let me tell you about this in my own way. You know very well that I never hint at anything: I always say straight out what I mean and people can like it or lump it as far as I'm concerned. If I really thought you ought to leave here, I should tell you without all this rigmarole. Can't you see that what I'm trying to tell you is that I don't want you to go away? I've got used to seeing you around the place, and I don't see any earthly reason why you shouldn't stay if you want to."

She paused, obviously awaiting a reply, and Arnold, sighing for the glib tongue of Noel Delare, said awkwardly.

"Of course I do. I should be very sorry to go away. You've made me so welcome, and I'm comfortable—and—happy. We're such friends—"

"Well? there you are," smiled Leda. 'We're both agreed on that. But Stanton's wife is very strait-laced in some ways. Oh yes, she is—you'd be surprised," she went on as she sensed Arnold's disbelief. "I'm far less conventional than Betty, in spite of all her modern ways. I tell you she was quite horrified when I said that you and I had every intention of living in the same house together after she and Stan have left. 'What—alone?' she said, in a voice that would have done credit to Queen Victoria. Of course I laughed at her."

"But," protested Arnold, "it's a point of view that must be considered. I did mention it to you before, if you remember, but we decided that it would be more convenient for me to stay for a bit on account of the police always wanting me for questions. I'm so used to being here that I regard it as my home, and I haven't wanted to think about leaving. But if people are going to talk—"

"They're not," said Leda positively. "They wouldn't dare to talk about me in the village. Besides, I've arranged it all now. I just wanted to know how you felt about it. I did it on the spur of the moment, but of course I had to tell you about it."

"I don't quite understand," said Arnold.

"Well," explained Leda, "I just told Betty that you and I are engaged to be married. My dear, you should have seen her: she simply *crawled*! Oh, these conventions make me laugh. It always seems so much worse for two engaged people to be left alone together—but there you are. It's all right now."

But—but," spluttered Arnold, "you can't let people believe that we're engaged to be married. It isn't true."

"Of course it isn't," said Leda, "but they don't know that."

As if realising suddenly the reason for his embarrassment, Leda began to roar with laughter.

Oh, you poor dear!" she exclaimed, patting his shoulder. "You surely don't think that I mean to marry you, do you? I'm not quite so unconventional that I could propose to a man, and if I were, I do hope I should make a better job of it than this. I haven't any matrimonial designs on you, Arnold, I assure you, and I'm sure you haven't. But if people like Betty are going to be foolish over our being friends, the only sensible thing to do is to let them believe that it's quite proper according to their poor lights."

"Yes, but—"

Leda looked at him in sudden suspicion.

"You're not engaged to anyone else, are you?" she asked.

"No, no," replied Arnold. "You know I'm a confirmed bachelor."

"Sometimes they are the most susceptible," said Leda, "but I must say there's no one in this village likely to turn your head. But I can see that the idea of being engaged to me is hateful to you. We're such good friends that it didn't occur to me that you'd loathe it so much. I just thought it was the best way of avoiding an awkward situation. But, of course, if you feel like that about it—"

"Oh, it's not the idea of being engaged to you that worries me," Arnold hastened to explain. "It's just that I wonder if it's wise. But if you really think—"

"That's settled then," said Leda happily. "I'll try and ward off all the congratulations from you: people make such a fuss over an engagement. You don't need to bother about a pledge of our affection. I've plenty of rings, and of course I couldn't accept one from you as it's all a pretence. And now let's forget all about it. Where are those damned dogs?"

CHAPTER 31

"ARE you going to have any children?" asked Betty Hardstaffe. "I know it's awful of me to ask such a personal question, but after all, I'm one of the family, and I'm interested. It's seeing you with Paul like that, I suppose, that made me ask. I hope you don't mind."

She was sitting on the painted garden seat under the larch tree on the lawn, watching while Arnold played St. Bernard to her little son's Pomeranian. At her question, he rose to his feet, and dusted the knees of his trousers.

"No more," he said to the child. "Good dog, then. Kennel."

The child obediently backed on all fours under the seat, whence he uttered spasmodic growls and barks, until he forgot, and became a white rabbit instead.

"No, I don't mind," replied Arnold. "Why should I? I'm fond of children, always have been, but I don't imagine that I shall ever have any of my own now."

Betty looked puzzled.

"You mean—"

"I mean it's no use thinking about it until I'm married, and that may never happen."

"But Leda told me—" Betty hesitated. "That is, I thought that you and Leda would be getting married soon. There's no need for a long engagement, and neither of you is so very young, if you don't mind my saying so."

Arnold took a long time to walk the few paces to the seat.

Of course, the engagement! His engagement to Leda.

Somehow he could never remember it, and was always placing himself in some such awkward predicament as this. He wished he had never agreed to playing in this farce.

"Leda and I haven't discussed the subject," he said stiffly.

"Well, I think you ought to," said Betty, "for both your sake and hers. Leda may not be able to have children, though I believe there are cases where women of fifty have had babies quite safely, and she's not as old as that yet, of course. Perhaps she might not like to discuss it, though she's always boasting that she's very unconventional."

"And isn't she?" asked Arnold.

Betty raised her delicately pencilled eyebrows.

"Who? Leda? She's the most conventional woman I know, barring none. Why, old Mrs. Hardstaffe would have run away years ago if it hadn't been for Leda. That nice old lawyer who's the coroner for this district was in love with her for years, and they'd decided to elope and snatch a little happiness together. But Leda found out somehow and threatened to tell her father. Stan says that it finished his mother: she became an old woman overnight. She never tried to run away again."

"It's strange that the police don't seem to have discovered yet who the—about her death," said Arnold seizing the chance to turn the conversation as far as possible from its embarrassing beginning.

"Strange? It's dreadful!" replied Betty. "Sometimes I wake in the night and think about it until I feel I shall go mad. One murder in a family is bad enough, but two . . . ! It makes you wonder whether it's finished with yet. Most bad things go in three, don't they? And I'm so afraid for Stan or even the baby. If I wasn't quite sure that Stanton isn't in the least like his father, I should suspect some homicidal tendency in the family. But though he gets into a bit of a temper when I spend too much money on a hat, he's really got the sweetest disposition. He simply wouldn't hurt a fly."

Arnold, knowing her to be biased, murmured some non-committal reply.

Betty regarded him gravely for a moment, then put an impulsive hand on his arm.

"You'll think it dreadful of me," she said, "but I can't help saying this: I do wish you weren't going to marry my sister-in-law. You're far too nice, and you really don't know her as Stan and I do. I shouldn't be in the least surprised to hear that she did all the proposing, and you found yourself engaged to her before you knew what she was getting at. There!" she exclaimed. "I can see by your face that I'm right. I thought it the first time she told me about it."

She cut short Arnold's weak attempts at denial.

"Oh, don't worry," she went on. "I shan't say a word about it. But she'll never make you happy. You're not her sort. She's as much like her father as two peas are in a pod, and if Stan has all the good nature, she has all the bad." She gazed earnestly at him. "Take my advice, Arnold, and get out of it somehow. Go away from here— just disappear—anything—only don't let her spoil your life. I really do know what I'm talking about—"

"Well! And what *are* you talking about?"

They both swung round. To his startled dismay, Arnold saw Leda smiling at him.

"Vampires," said Betty calmly. "But I can't make Arnold believe in them."

CHAPTER 32

BETTY Hardstaffe cut across Leda's long-winded description of her latest cleverness in outwitting the local bore at the Woman's Comforts for the Troops knitting party, and said casually, but clearly, "By the way, I've invited Charity Fuller to dinner tomorrow night."

They were sitting alone in the dining-room with their inevitable knitting.

"—and you should have seen Mrs. Tyson's face when I said it, but, as everyone said to me afterwards, she really asked for it. 'My dear Mrs. Tyson', I said—You've *what*?"

Betty looked up.

"I presume that the last part of that sentence is meant for me," she remarked. "I said that I've—"

I heard what you said," Leda interrupted, "and if it's your idea of a joke, Betty, I can only say that it's in exceedingly bad taste."

Betty smiled.

"Bogey-bogey!" she jeered. "It certainly isn't a joke. I saw her in the village this afternoon and asked her. Stan rang up to ask if it was okay for him to bring a friend for the week-end, so I said of course it was."

"*You* said!" exclaimed Leda.

"Yes. Why not? You didn't happen to be in at the time so I couldn't ask you what you thought about it, and when I saw Miss Fuller a little while afterwards, I asked her to come, too. After all, nothing is more deadly than an odd number at dinner, and it will cheer us up to have a little company. This house is full of ghosts!"

She glanced round the room into which the evening shadows were already stretching their fingers, and shivered.

"If you had a clear conscience you wouldn't see ghosts," declared Leda. "I never do."

Betty flushed.

"What do you mean by that?" she demanded.

"Keep your perm on," laughed Leda. "I don't mean anything. It isn't my way to hint at things. I always say straight out what I have to say, as you should know by now. And I'm telling you that you have no right to ask people here without asking me first. When Stan comes, I shall tell him the same."

"Oh, don't be silly, Leda," said Betty. "What a fuss you make about two extra people! Why, at home, Stan brings back any of his friends he likes and I'm always having to open a tin of something for them."

Leda strode across to the silver cigarette box on the sideboard, and swore at finding it empty.

"Perhaps you've got more tins stored away than I have," she said. "Personally I consider it unpatriotic to hoard, and it's as much as I can do to make our rations go round as it is. In any case, I won't have that—that woman in my house."

"I think she's a nice little thing," replied Betty, speaking with the assured dignity of a young matron about a spinster as young as herself. "It isn't as if she'd never been here before. I'm sure all that gossip about her and your father was exaggerated."

"I refuse to discuss that with you," said Leda. "I've told you that I won't have her in the house, so you'll have to go and tell her so. I don't suppose she's on the 'phone."

"Being one of the lower-social animals!" murmured Betty. What a snob you are, Leda. Anyway, I shall do nothing of the kind. You seem to forget that this house is only half yours. You can't prevent Stan from bringing friends here if he wants to, and you can't prevent me inviting anyone into his half of the house. You're not afraid of her making eyes at Arnold, are you?"

Leda flushed angrily.

"Certainly not. He wouldn't take any notice of her if she did. You really do have some surprisingly—well, I can only say, *common* ideas sometimes, Betty."

"What can you expect from a grocer's daughter?" asked Betty, beginning to enjoy herself. "Oh, I know that Pa owns a whole chain of high-class stores now, and has a town house and all that, but you can't deny that he started by wearing a white apron and selling candles in his father's shop."

"Need we go into that?" asked Leda.

"I don't see why not," returned Betty. "I know you think that Stan married beneath him, but after all, your father was only a village school-master, and I never could see that that was anything to write home about. As for Arnold not noticing Charity Fuller, it would take a better man than him to avert his eyes when she pulls her skirt just a teeny-weeny bit above her knees, and looks meltingly at him. She'll pinch him from underneath your supercilious nose while you're sniffing at her. Red heads are notorious for doing that. I daresay you're wise to try and keep her out of his way. Once a man of Arnold's age starts looking twice at a pretty girl, he gets into trouble. I'd better write her a note putting her off!"

"No, you can't do that: it will look very rude," said Leda hurriedly. "I don't worry about her in that way at all, I can assure her. If Arnold met some woman he liked better than me, he would tell me so, and I should be sensible enough to understand. I'm not a child, and I daresay I know one or two things that even you have never experienced!"

She smiled suddenly.

"I'm sorry I sounded annoyed about dinner tomorrow," she said. "But it is a bit difficult to arrange meals at a minute's notice these days, and Cook gets upset. It isn't that I object to Charity Fuller personally, it's just that whenever she comes here to dine—"

She paused.

"Well?" prompted Betty.

"Things happen," replied Leda.

CHAPTER 33

SOME time later, Arnold was to wonder whether the solution of the Hardstaffe murders would ever have come to light if it had not been for Betty's sudden impulse to invite Charity Fuller to dine.

But that time was not to come for several weeks yet, and he had no premonition of it as he dressed for dinner that night.

He arrived downstairs a few minutes before Charity arrived, and it was with an unaccountable feeling of pleasure that he greeted her again.

She wore the same filmy black gown in which she had been dressed on her previous visit. It was, indeed, her only evening-gown, for in every other house in the district—even, it was said, up at the Castle—it was considered out of place to wear anything more elaborate than an afternoon frock even for dinner.

This was war-time, and you could not deal effectively with incendiary bombs, or stand by with a First Aid Party, in a gown which swirled around your ankles. There was, in fact, little scope at all for femininity in Total War, which for the time being, and possibly for all time, had destroyed the slogan that Woman's Place is in the Home.

Arnold thought it strange that Leda, who had always derided her father's insistence on dressing formally for dinner, should now be equally insistent on the habit although it could no longer concern him.

But tonight he was grateful for it, for the black dress fitted closely to Charity's lovely figure, framed her into the prettiest picture he had seen for some time.

Nor was he the only person thus affected.

Stanton Hardstaffe who, until that evening, had seemed little more than a stuffed shirt to Arnold, became imbued with a sudden animation which showed him to be a genial dinner-companion and something of a wit, as he leaned sideways and breathed on Charity's shoulder.

Yes, Charity certainly *did* something to a man, but whether she was aware of it or not, was a thing about which no woman knew and no man cared.

As the meal went on, and Stanton's jokes became slightly daring, the other two women fell silent, and Arnold, seated between them, grew uneasy. He wondered whether Betty was already regretting her invitation to Charity, wondered also, what impulse had prompted her to give it.

For Stanton had brought no friend with him, and they were five at dinner, with Leda seated in upright disapproval at the opposite end of the table to her brother.

When Stanton had arrived earlier in the evening, she had greeted him coldly as usual, offering a reluctant cheek to his equally reluctant lips. Then she had asked where his friend was.

Before he could reply, Betty had sailed into the conversation.

"Captain Homes had to put Stan off at the last minute—some Service duty, you know. Such a bore, because it completely ruins our numbers for dinner; and you've had all the trouble of getting a bedroom ready. I'm awfully sorry, but there it is!"

"But—well, it sounds funny to me," remarked Leda. "Of course I know he used to be Regular Army and got the M.C. in the last war, but he's only in the Home Guard now, isn't he? I don't see what duty could possibly crop up to keep him away like this."

"You'd be surprised," replied Stanton. "I know the Home Guard has become the lowest form of military life since the Observer Corps became Royal, but, strange to relate, we do have rules and we do have to obey them. Homes is a corporal like me, in spite of his retired rank, and he does what he's ordered to do. You wouldn't understand that though, would you, sister?"

"Of course I understand," said Leda irritably. "You forget that I'm entitled to wear three uniforms myself, if you include

The Girl Guides. And please don't call me 'Sister' as if I were something out of a hospital ward."

"Or a nunnery," suggested Betty spitefully.

But that had been some hours ago, and now, instead of being at loggerheads with each other, Leda and her sister-in-law seemed to be united in their disapproval of Charity.

Of this, Charity herself had no knowledge, for Stanton held her attention persistently, while, when she looked up-, Arnold was ready to return smiles and badinage from the side of the table opposite to her, and Leda and Betty were constantly jerking up from their chairs to collect plates or pass food around.

Frieda was still in the house and was now the only maid, since Briggs had left to carry out Mr. Ernest Bevin's admonition to Go To It. But Leda, mindful of her behaviour when Charity had dined before at the house, had ordered her to come no nearer to the dining-room than the dumb-waiter outside the door, and to remain equally dumb.

Arnold felt greatly relieved at Leda's decision to keep her out of sight, for one never knew what the girl might do or say. He had given up his study of her as a character, for although he had originally intended to put her into his hook, he had since decided that such a passionate creature could have no place in the world of unreality which housed the scintillating figure of Noel Delare. Besides, he doubted whether anyone would believe that such a person as the little Jewess could really exist in England, even during a war, which, proverbially makes strange bedfellows.

Not that 'bedfellow' was a word to use in connection with Frieda.

Never attractive, she had lately deteriorated in many ways. Although always clean in her person—for this was a matter of religion to her—she had grown careless about her dress and general appearance. Dirty collars and cuffs had been ripped off her once neat frocks and not replaced, her hair was unbrushed and tangled; her shoes were down at heel.

No. "Bedfellow" was certainly not the word to use. It had come unbidden into his mind for no reason that he could see. Unless—

He glanced up, and saw Charity smiling at him. His gaze lingered over the smooth, white skin above the heartshaped neckline of her low cut gown.

Unless—

The ladies rose, and he and Stanton raced for the door. Both reached for the knob at the same time, then stood side by side at the opened door, looking rather foolish.

They did not linger over the port, and when they joined the ladies, it was obvious that Stanton was again intent on monopolising Charity. Arnold felt unreasonably annoyed at this, until he remembered, with a new sense of shock, that everyone believed him to be Leda's fiancé.

Once settled round the breakfast-room fire with their coffee, however, their conversation became general, and after a scurry to find unsalvaged paper and blunt pencils, they finally settled down to a series of Parlour Games after the pattern of those brought back into fashion by the B.B.C. Arnold and Charity, having read more books in five years than the others had read in their lives, entered into a friendly rivalry which brought them into pleasant sympathy with each other.

When Charity said she had had a lovely evening but it must be getting late and she really must go, they discovered that it was pouring rain, and they all agreed that some one must drive her home.

"There's nothing I'd like better," said Stanton with obvious sincerity, "but I'm afraid it can't be done. I haven't got an ounce of petrol to spare. I really ought not to have driven over this week-end, but the trains are so crowded and so slow, and it's a wretched journey with so many stops, to say nothing of having no First Class passengers. With this new cut in the basic petrol ration I've only got enough petrol to get me home and I daren't risk an extra mile or two."

"If I could be of any use—" began Arnold, but Leda interrupted him.

"You'd be only too pleased, dear, of course," she said, playing ostentatiously with the solitaire diamond ring on the fourth finger of her left hand. "You see," she explained, turning to Charity, "he's taking me over to the one remaining dog show this month, and we shall only just do the double journey on his petrol ration. In the old days it would sound too mean for words to say this, but we've all got to Do Our Bit now, haven't we? I know that dogs sound rather a luxury these days but this show's rather an important one for Cherub." She picked up one of the many dogs which were lying on chairs and carpet, and held it near her face so that it could lick her mouth. "If ze 'ickle girlie wins a Savings Certificate for her Mummy, den Mummy can sell her wee bitchie for lots of doodledums!"

She kissed the Sealyham's wiry head, smacked it behind, and deposited it roughly on a chair, where it curled round and began to attend noisily to its toilet.

"Oh, please don't worry about me," said Charity. "There's no need really. I'm used to the rain, and I can easily walk."

"My dear girl, you can't go out in this," said Stanton. "It's raining cats and dogs. You'll have to wait a bit. Let's have another game."

"Oh, but I can't." Charity sounded upset. "I really must go. It's past eleven, and if I'm not in by twelve, I shall be locked out." She perceived their astonishment, and went on. "She'll think I'm in bed, you see—the old woman I lodge with. She's as deaf as a post, and once she's in bed, I shall never be able to rouse her. She won't think of me being out after twelve. I never am. I really shall have to go."

Betty glanced at Charity's little gold, high-heeled slippers.

"In those shoes? You can't!" she exclaimed. "And both mine and Leda's are sizes too large for you." She looked suddenly at Leda, and to Arnold it seemed as if she had asked a silent question, for Leda gave a quick nod. "What about that bedroom you got ready for Captain Homes?" she asked aloud. "Wouldn't that be the best solution? Miss Fuller doesn't have to go to school tomorrow, and we could send Frieda to fetch her shoes and a skirt or something. Anyway it will all be much easier in the morning."

"But I . . ." protested Charity.

"Of course you must stay," said Leda cheerfully. "It's no trouble. The bed's made up, and you'll even find a hot-water bottle in it. We were expecting a friend who didn't come."

"It's awfully kind of you," replied Charity, "but—"

"That's settled then," said Leda in tones with which Arnold had grown only too familiar.

If Leda said anything was settled, then settled it was.

"I can lend you anything you want for the night," said Betty. "Which bedroom is it, Leda?"

"Father's," she replied. "You'll like it, Miss Fuller."

CHAPTER 34

ARNOLD went to bed feeling, not for the first time or last time, that the ways of woman are incomprehensible.

After Leda's extraordinary remark, Charity had flashed an appealing look at him, and he had come gallantly to the rescue—or so he thought.

"Yes, it's a charming room," he had said. "Quite the prettiest in the house, and it's all been rearranged. I'm sure you'll sleep well there."

Charity had looked grateful. One of the most attractive things about her was, she thought, the expressiveness of her face. She did not need to put into words the emotion she was feeling, it was written in her lovely eyes and mobile mouth.

Then they had all had a drink together, and Betty had taken Charity up to her room. Stanton had followed, fifteen minutes afterwards, while Arnold, feeling that he had shown too little attention to Leda during the evening, stayed downstairs for a little longer and tried to make conversation. But Leda did not seem anxious for his company, and he soon said goodnight.

His bedroom lay beyond Stanton's and Betty's, and as he approached their room, he saw that the door was open.

"And now, young lady," Stanton was saying in his loud Hardstaffe voice, "perhaps you'll explain what all this lying is about. What on earth made you tell Leda that I was bringing old Homes here for the weekend? You know perfectly well that I never suggested such a thing when I phoned yesterday morning. What's the big idea?"

The door was slammed, and Arnold walked past it into his own room.

He switched on the light, then walked across to the window to make sure that the black-out was perfect. Frieda was often careless about it.

He took off coat, waistcoat, and trousers, then sat down on the edge of the bed to unfasten his sock suspenders which were garishly coloured in a riotous design of purple, red, and gold.

He could have sworn before tonight that there was nothing sinister about Betty Hardstaffe. But what possible reason could she have had for wanting to get Charity into the house tonight? It must have been a strong reason that made her plan it as far ahead as yesterday, when she had lied about her husband's visitor in order to provide an excuse for inviting Charity to dinner.

She could not have foreseen, of course, that the weather would provide her with the excuse she needed to keep Charity here overnight, but, no doubt, she had some other means of ensuring it, even if the rain had not proved such a good ally.

Wait a bit, though, he thought. Had it really been raining quite as hard as Stanton had said? He was the only one who had ventured outside.

But surely the words he had just heard showed that Stanton knew nothing about his wife's plan. Unless—unless they had heard him coming upstairs, and had staged the scene for his benefit.

It all seemed such a fuss about nothing. He could make no sense out of it at all.

And so he buttoned himself into his pyjama jacket, got into bed, and, still pondering on the inscrutable behaviour of women, fell asleep to dream that he was treating Charity in a way in which he had never before treated any woman throughout his life.

He thought that he had been awakened by a scream.

He lifted his head from the pillow, and listened.

It came again: a woman's scream, high pitched, terrified.

He leapt out of bed, struck his elbow against the bedside table, his chin against a chair, and stood in numbed agony for a second, before finding his dressing gown and torch, and making his way on to the landing.

He heard Charity's voice.

"If you don't let me go, I shall throw myself over this balcony!"

She screamed again, and Arnold forgetting the torch in his hand, fumbled, swearing, for the switch, and turned on the corridor light.

At the end of the corridor outside Mr. Hardstaffe's room stood Charity, clinging to the carved balustrade, and gazing with unseeing eyes down to the marble floor of the hall below.

She was clad in a pink night-gown of diaphanous material, which revealed details of a figure that was even more lovely than it had seemed to be in Arnold's dream.

With one bound, or so it seemed to him, he had reached her side, and had taken her into his arms as she stood there, shivering.

A moment afterwards, Leda came round the corner of the corridor from her bedroom, then Betty and Stanton joined them, while a sudden light illuminated the hall below and revealed Cook and Frieda staring up at them with frightened faces.

"It's all right. It's all right," Stanton reassured them, after he had counted them all. "We're all here. No one's hurt. Something scared her, that's all."

"Paul!" exclaimed Betty maternally. "I must go and see if he and Nanny are all right."

She slipped away in the direction from which Leda had come.

"Oh Lord!" said Leda loudly. "I forgot to tell her that Flurry sleeps in the wardrobe. She's Daddy's dog, you know. If she started pattering about in the middle of the night, it might have scared Miss Fuller. Flurry! Flurry!" she called, and one of the dogs came running up the stairs to her. "There she is!" she exclaimed. "Poor old bitchie, then, did 'oo scare ze pretty lady? Fancy being frightened of a dog!"

Arnold did not seem to hear what Leda was saying. He was patting Charity's soft shoulder, and murmured, "There, there, little girl. You're quite safe. No one is going to hurt you."

Leda stared at him in silence for a few seconds. Then she turned, and went into the bedroom, coming back again with a dressing-gown which she wrapped around Charity.

"Come along," she said. "You'll be frozen here. Come back to bed. There's nothing in the room to be scared of. I've just been to look."

Charity began to scream again.

"Let me alone!" she cried. "Don't touch me!"

Leda took one look at her, then slapped her face.

Arnold stepped forward to stop her, but Leda waved him away.

"Leave her to me!" she said. "She'll be in raving hysterics if you don't."

Charity stopped screaming, and held her hand against her face in a dazed way.

"You struck me!" she said. "How cruel you are!"

She began to cry.

"She'll be all right now," said Leda. "Bring me some brandy Cook, and a hot-water-bottle. Arnold and Stan go ahead into her room. Come along, Miss Fuller. You're all right."

Charity, still sobbing, allowed herself to be guided back to the bedroom. Once inside the door, she looked round wildly, but upon seeing the two men already there* she made no demur.

Leda half lifted her into bed, put the newly brought hot-water-bottle to her feet, and the glass of brandy to her lips. At length the colour came slowly back into her cheeks, and Leda nodding her satisfaction, said, "She'll do."

Charity leaned back against the pillow with her eyes closed. Then she suddenly looked up.

"I can't stay here," she said. "I must go. Please let me go!"

Leda's firm hand pressed against her shoulder.

"Now do stop worrying," she said. "Were all here with you, and no one can possibly do you any harm. It was all my fault. I forgot to tell you that Daddy's dog still sleeps in this room. She got out of her basket and scared you."

Charity regarded her with panic-stricken eyes.

"It might have been a dog that brushed against me when I ran out of the room," she said, "but it wasn't a dog that woke me up."

"What was it then?" asked Arnold. "What frightened you?"

"It was Mr. Hardstaffe," she whispered. "He was standing by the bed."

Stanton started forward.

"Here, I say!" he protested. "She's wandering in her mind. Why, Betty will tell you I've been with her all night."

"Do you really mean to tell us that my brother was in your bedroom?" demanded Leda.

Charity stared at her.

"Your brother?" she repeated. "Oh no. It was your father!"

CHAPTER 35

INSPECTOR Driver, cursing and shivering, tramped along the wet, muddy lane leading to the Hardstaffe's, just as the dawn was spreading its gentle fingers across the sky: a sign to many anxious eyes that those enemy bombers which had succeeded in eluding the warm attentions of Ack-Acks and Beer-Beers and had evaded the deadly pounce of the night-fighters, had now reached their bases.

"What do you think it is, sir?" Sergeant Lovely ventured to ask.

"God knows!" replied Driver. "It sounds as if someone has been trying to attack Miss Fuller, but you know how mysterious people are when telephoning to the police: they seem to think that the criminal must be lying in a ditch outside the house tapping the wires. It's all the fault of these crime-books you see on every library shelf. Now that every Tom, Dick, and Harriet has turned to writing about murder, the general public is as full of misleading ideas as old Lord Haw Haw himself."

"Yes, sir. But if Miss Fuller has been attacked at the Hardstaffe's, doesn't it show that someone in the house is the culprit? And, if the attack is connected with the murders, won't it help to prove that they weren't an outside job?"

"I never thought they were," growled Driver. "Outsiders like Richards and Ramsbottom are all very well, but, barring lunatics and rare cases, English people don't murder their fellow country men because they dislike them. Murders are committed for more sordid reasons than that, for money usually. Now Miss Fuller doesn't fit into that kind of motive, and if she really has been attacked by the murderer, I shouldn't be surprised to find that it's his first mistake."

When they had arrived at the house, they were shown into the breakfast-room, where they found the chief actors in the morning's drama grouped round a blazing fire, drinking hot coffee, and clad in an assortment of tweeds and woollens. Both men were wearing polo sweaters—Stanton's was yellow, and Arnold's royal blue—to avoid the tedious necessity of collar and tie.

Leda greeted Driver and his satellite as cheerfully as usual.

That one'd be cheerful at her own funeral, thought the sergeant, suddenly realising that "it was a queer saying and no mistake."

"Awfully sorry to drag you out of bed at this hour, Inspector," she said, "but we thought it advisable to send for you at once in case this is connected with the murders. Not that I think for a minute—" She checked herself and asked, "Coffee? It's hot. Or would you rather have whiskey?"

The Sergeant brightened at the thought of the alternative, but at his Superior's reply, he relapsed into gloom.

"Coffee, thanks."

Driver took the proffered cup, and having walked between the clustered chairs, took up his stand on the hearthrug, facing the five people.

"I didn't get a proper account of this new development," he said. "I understand that some attack was made on Miss Fuller in this house, but she looks little the worse for it. Perhaps one of you would be good enough to explain more fully. You were cautious over the 'phone— rightly so, of course: you never know who may be listening in."

A clever fellow, the Inspector, thought Sergeant Lovely. He's such a heavy-looking man that you'd expect him to go blundering about like a bull in a China shop, as the saying goes. Instead of that, he goes along gently, smoothing folk down, and feeling the atmosphere of the meeting. Then, before they realise it, he's got them exactly where he wants em. He's like one of those Negro preachers who gets his congregation alternately singing "Hallelujah," and groaning with the weight of their sins, until one of them can't stand it any longer, and makes a confession.

Not that anyone in the room at this moment looked in the least likely to give way to emotion of any kind, let alone confess to murder, but you couldn't always tell. And if, as Driver thought, the murderer of the Hardstaffes had made a mistake, you could trust the Inspector to have him neatly tied up in the bag.

In that case, thought the constable, I ought to be listening. No, by Jove! I ought to be taking it down!

He opened his book and plunged his pencil into the midst of Leda's brief account of the events of the early morning, and the reason why Charity had slept in the house.

"So you put Miss Fuller into your father's bedroom, and someone tried to murder her," remarked Driver.

Leda smiled up at him. She was standing at the small table, still busy with the coffee percolator, and Driver's bulky height accentuated the short stature of her stocky figure clad in a worn but well-cut tweed costume of a colour which must surely have been the least attractive of any woven by the islanders of Harris.

"Yes, she slept in Daddy's room, but I certainly don't believe that anyone tried to murder her."

The Inspector turned towards Charity, and earned the Sergeant's disapproval.

The Inspector's too unconventional by half, he told himself. One of these days he'll come unstuck. He's no business to be asking them questions in front of each other like this. One at a time's a good rule, whether you're dealing with murderers or women. If he's not careful, he'll get some fact from one of 'em that will incriminate the murderer. Then there'll be another murder—or have I been reading too many detective stories, like he said?

"Now, Miss Fuller, what do you think about it all?" asked Driver.

Charity shrank back into the shelter of the armchair in which she was sitting. Arnold had perched himself on its padded arm, and she clutched his arm, her limpid eyes looking up at him expressively. Arnold smiled, and patted her hand as if to give her courage.

The Inspector repeated the question.

"I—I don't know," replied Charity miserably.

"Well, just tell me what happened and we can help each other to decide," he said, with his most charming smile.

Charity withdrew her hand from Arnold's and leaned forward again.

"I was asleep," she said slowly. "Suddenly I woke with the feeling that something had brushed against my face. It was as if I had walked into a cobweb—nothing more."

"Did you hear any sound?"

"No. That is, not inside the bedroom. I could hear that it was still raining outside, and I was glad about that because I didn't want anyone to think that I was staying in the house under false pretenses."

Arnold thought this was a strange thing for her to say.

"But somehow I felt uneasy," Charity went on. "I didn't take any notice at first because you always do feel rather strange in a strange room, don't you? But I couldn't go to sleep again, and kept turning from side to side, so I switched on the bed-lamp, and—oh!"

She groaned, and put her hands over her face.

"Try to go on, my dear," said Arnold softly. "The Inspector must know the facts. Have a cigarette: that will help."

A smile struggled to Charity's lips as she accepted one from his case, lighted it from the match he held, and inhaled gratefully.

"I'm sorry," she said, "but it was horrible. Has anyone ever told you the shortest ghost story in the world? About the man who entered an empty room alone in the dark, and when he reached for the matches, they were put into his hand? It was like that. I'd been thinking about him, of course, because I knew I was in his room, and when I switched on the light, I saw him standing at the foot of the bed."

She shuddered.

"What makes you think it was Mr. Hardstaffe?" asked Driver.

"I recognised him, of course."

Driver looked puzzled.

"You mean that you saw his face and recognised his features?"

"No-o," said Charity slowly. "It's hard to remember. It was such a shock, and I only saw him for a second. But no, I didn't see his face. He had his back turned to me. Then when I screamed, he moved across the room and went through the communicating door."

That door again! thought Driver. And a ghost in the house now!

"But if you couldn't see his face, how did you 'know' it was Mr. Hardstaffe?"

"I knew him so well," replied Charity. "His height—the way he held himself—his shoulders—his clothes."

"What clothes was he wearing?"

"A dark overcoat and hat, just as he was the last time I saw him."

"It might have been someone else dressed in his clothes."

"No, no. I'm sure it was *him*," asserted Charity.

Leda could restrain herself no longer.

"There you are, Inspector, it's all nonsense. She was over-wrought, and imagined it all. I'll admit that I did think at first that it might have been my brother or Arnold, though I thought it extremely unlikely. But no man who wanted to become a woman's bedfellow would go and put on a hat and overcoat first. The whole thing's ridiculous! I blame myself for the whole affair. I ought never to have allowed my sister-in-law to persuade me to put her into that bedroom. Miss Fuller knew Daddy well through being one of his Staff at the School, and the idea that she was sleeping in a murdered man's bed got on her nerves. We all know that the dead don't walk, and the idea of anyone dressing up like that—! It's obvious that she imagined it all, so for goodness' sake don't let's make a mystery of it."

She finished by explaining her theory about the dog, Flurry.

"No, no, it isn't true," protested Charity. "I tell you I—"

The Inspector interrupted her.

"I'm afraid it's only too true that Mr. Hardstaffe is dead," he said gently. "You yourself went to the funeral."

"Funerals can be faked," said Charity stubbornly.

"This one was not," he assured her. "Mr. Hardstaffe was murdered in a very horrible way. There are four people in this room who can swear to that. I am one of them and I give you my word that he was very dead indeed, begging your pardon, Miss Hardstaffe. Also, his wound was such that although it disfigured him, it did not obscure his features. Is that quite clear?"

"Yes," whispered Charity. "Horribly, horribly clear!"

"Good. Now his death has preyed on your mind a great deal, and the idea that you were actually in the room of a dead man got on your nerves, just as Miss Hardstaffe has said. I must ask you to believe that it is extremely probable that you have indeed imagined the whole thing, and that in all probability this dog which, Miss Hardstaffe tells us, slept in the bedroom in the wardrobe, awoke you by jumping on or off the bed, and followed you out of the room when you screamed again."

Leda smiled.

"But," went on the Inspector, "there is a possibility also, that some person, as yet unknown, did plan the scene exactly as you have described it, hoping that in your terror, you would not be responsible for your actions, and would rush out of the room and throw yourself over the balcony into the hall below. And so it is my duty to investigate the matter more thoroughly. Shall we all go upstairs?"

Before they could recover from their surprise, Driver had ushered them out of the room and across the hall. Then, taking Charity's arm, he went up the stairs, bidding the others to follow.

He paused at the door of the late Mr. Hardstaffe's bedroom, and listened, while the others exchanged deprecating smiles.

But as he put out a gentle hand and turned the knob, their smiles changed to expressions of apprehension and fear, as they heard from within the room the sound of a cracked, unmusical voice singing, "Teasin', teasin', I was only teasin' you—"

At Charity's scream of terror, Driver flung open the door.

A short figure, wearing a man's dark overcoat with up-turned collar, and a trilby hat was strutting up and down in front of the long wardrobe mirror.

As they rushed into the room, the figure turned, and they looked into the startled face of Frieda Braun!

CHAPTER 36

AFTER Frieda had been dispatched to the kitchen and placed under the care of the cook, the others returned to the breakfast-room.

Leda went up to Charity.

"I owe you an apology," she said. "I honestly thought you'd made it all up, and if I think a thing like that, I can't pretend that I don't. I know it offends a lot of people, but that's my way, and I don't suppose I shall ever alter it now. You see I know that Daddy's dead, and I don't believe in ghosts, so I thought you'd got a touch of indigestion or something and had a nightmare that made you hysterical. I'm never hysterical myself but I know the symptoms when I see them. I've not taken First Aid, and Warden's courses, and Life-saving for nothing. That's why I had to slap your face. I don't suppose you remember anything about it, but if you do, I want to say I'm sorry."

She insisted on taking Charity's cold, inert hand in her own firm grasp as if to prove her sincerity.

"Well, it seems fairly clear what happened," said the Inspector. "I shall have to ask you all a few more questions just to clear it up, if you don't object."

"Do you want us all to go out of the room, and come in again separately, as in 'Postman's Knock?" asked Betty facetiously.

Driver shook his head.

"No, we'll keep it informal if you don't mind," he said, "and of course, you needn't answer any question if you prefer not to."

He turned to Charity, and, noting the signs of strain visible in her face, said gently, "Was it just the idea of someone being in the bedroom just now that made you scream?"

Charity clenched her hands as if to keep a hold on herself.

"No," she said, "It was the song. I'd heard Mr. Hardstaffe sing it the last time I saw him, when he was walking home with me. I'd never heard it before in my life."

"Good heavens!" exclaimed Leda. "I thought everyone knew that old song."

"I don't suppose Miss Fuller does," remarked Arnold. "'It was in fashion a good many years before she was born."

And he doesn't realise what he's said, thought Sergeant Lovely, glancing at Leda's face. The man's a fool!

"And when you saw Frieda dressed in that overcoat did you recognise her as the same person you saw in the night?" asked Driver.

"No. She didn't look the same at all. I tell you it was him," she cried hysterically.

Driver shrugged his shoulders and turned to Arnold.

"You were the first person to reach Miss Fuller when she screamed," he said. "What were you doing when you heard her?"

"I wasn't sure I had heard a scream at first," replied Arnold. "I was dreaming."

"Dreaming, my darling of thee," thought the irrepressible Sergeant. The fellow looks embarrassed, too. Funny that he should feel that way about Miss Hardstaffe. She's not my idea of a dream, but there's no accounting for tastes, and it takes all sorts to make a world, as the saying goes.

"It seems a little strange," remarked Driver, "that although you and Miss Hardstaffe both have the bedrooms farthest away from Miss Fuller's, you both reached her first. I should like to know what you, Mr. Stanton, and your wife were doing when you heard the screams."

Betty and Stanton exchanged stealthy glances.

It was Betty who replied.

"We—we were in bed, weren't we, Stan?" she said, and her husband nodded.

"Did the screams wake you?"

"Yes, that is—no," replied Stanton. "We were awake already."

"Both of you?"

"Yes."

"It took you rather a long time to decide to investigate."

Again that stealthy glance. Again Betty was the first to reply.

"I suppose it took us some time to find our dressing-gowns and things," she said.

"That's about it," agreed Stanton.

To their evident relief, the Inspector did not pursue the subject.

"Now then, Miss Hardstaffe," he said, "whose idea was it that Miss Fuller should sleep in your father's room?"

Leda stared at him.

"I've explained all that to you," she said. "Don't you remember what I told you—"

"About Mr. Stanton's friend? Yes. But surely you don't expect me to believe that. Isn't it a fact that the friend was never invited at all? That he was, in fact, an excuse to get that room ready? I know more about it than you think."

The Sergeant looked up in surprise, glanced at the faces of the others, and whistled softly.

I believe you've got something there, Baby, he thought disrespectfully. Now whatever put him on to that track, the old fox?

Leda looked completely bewildered.

"I don't know what you're talking about," she said. "The bedroom was prepared for a friend, exactly as I told you. Stan rang up Betty and asked—Oh, you tell him, Stan."

"It's just as she says," Stanton said awkwardly.

Leda looked steadily at her brother, but he did riot raise his eyes.

Arnold stood up suddenly.

"You'd better tell the truth, Hardstaffe," he advised. "If you don't, I shall have to. I overheard you and Betty talking about it last night. You'd left the door open, and I couldn't help hearing. What's the sense of telling lies about it?"

Stanton made no reply.

Leda turned to her sister-in-law.

"Betty!" she appealed.

But Betty merely compressed her lips and looked obstinate.

"Very touching," remarked Driver. "You know, of course, that husband and wife need not testify against each other. I don't know what your little game is, but I suppose I shall have to justify my title of detective, as meaning 'one engaged in detecting, uncovering, discovering, or finding out.'" He turned to Leda. "The truth is, Miss Hardstaffe," he said, "that your brother made no suggestion that he should bring a friend this week-end. Mrs. Hardstaffe, for some reason, invented the story. We can only guess that it was an excuse to get Miss Fuller into the house. When her husband arrived, she evidently explained things in such a way that he decided to back up her lie."

Charity sat up, rigid, in her chair.

"You mean that it was Mrs. Stanton who—oh, no! I don't believe it," she said. "This dreadful house has bewitched us all!"

Leda's face was suffused with anger.

"Stan! to abuse my hospitality and lie to me! How could you do such a thing? How dare you! I always knew you were a weakling and a liar. That's why we never got on well together when you were at home. You were always poisoning Mother's mind against me. But after you were married, I thought you'd improved. I never really liked Betty, but I've always given her credit for turning you into a decent human being. Now I can see that you're both as bad as each other. Well, thank goodness, I've found it out in time. At least I don't need to shield you any longer."

Stanton took a step towards her.

"What are you saying, Leda?" he demanded. "Don't do anything you'll be sorry for later. I can explain—"

"Explain!"

She turned to the Inspector.

"You've heard him tell you one lie to-day," she said. "It isn't the first one he's told you. He lied when he said that he'd never been near this house since his quarrel with Daddy. He was here on the night that Mother was murdered!"

CHAPTER 37

IT WAS Inspector Driver's turn to stare in astonishment.

"Do you realise what you are saying?" he asked. "This is a very serious matter."

Leda laughed.

"I certainly do realise it, Inspector," she replied. "Doesn't the fact that I've kept it to myself for so long prove that?"

"You might have had some other reason," returned Driver. "Now perhaps you'll tell me exactly what happened."

"I shouldn't have known anything about it if one of the dogs hadn't started heaving on my bed," said Leda, without expressing any distaste for this circumstance. "I knew there'd be an unholy row if she was sick there, so I pushed her off, and rushed her out of the door, and along to the stairs, without even waiting to put my dressing-gown on. When we got into the hall, I bumped into somebody in the dark. No, I didn't scream," she smiled. "I called out 'Who's there?'

"It was my mother.

"I switched on the light, and asked her what on earth she was doing there. At first she told me some rigmarole about looking for a book, but I soon got the truth out of her. She told me that Stanton had written asking her to let him into the house after we were all in bed, because he wanted to see her about something important. She was on her way to the front door when I came downstairs. I told her that she couldn't possibly let him in at that hour, because if Daddy happened to hear of it, he'd half kill Stan, and after a bit, she agreed that I was right, and she went back to bed."

"Did you go outside the house then?"

"In a pair of shell-pink pyjamas on a frosty night?" exclaimed Leda archly. "Have a heart, Inspector."

"So you didn't see your brother?"

"No, I didn't see why I should risk catching cold on his account. He ought to have had more sense than to expect to see her at that hour. He could have met her somewhere in the daytime if he'd wanted to see her so badly. Or he could have told her about it in a letter. I've no sympathy with people who try to make mysteries over everything, and I thought it would do him good to kick his heels outside in the cold."

"Have you any idea what he wanted to see her about?"

"I just thought it was another of his attempts to borrow money from her," she said coldly.

"That's a lie!" shouted Stanton. "I've never borrowed money from her in my life."

"Her cheque books are full of counterfoils made out to you," replied Leda. "You must have had hundreds of pounds from her."

"They were gifts. I never asked her for money."

Leda shrugged her shoulders.

"That's what you say," she returned.

The Inspector interrupted them.

"Miss Hardstaffe," he said in grave tones, "you don't seem to realise that you've deliberately hindered the police in the execution of their duty by withholding vital information. That is a punishable offence."

Pompous ass! thought Lovely, and was delighted to hear Leda say, "Oh rats! You never asked me about my brother's movements that night. I should have told you if you had. I never believed that he'd had anything to do with my mother's death, so I decided to keep quiet about it. But if he's going to tell more and more lies, I'm not keeping quiet any longer. I've no intention of landing myself into trouble for his sweet sake, I assure you."

"The fact remains that you lied about the time when you last saw your mother alive," said Driver. "You gave Superintendent Cheam to understand that you did not see her after she went up to bed at about nine-thirty. Yet all the time you knew that she was alive at—what time was it?"

"Somewhere about half-past twelve, I suppose. I don't know the time more accurately than that. But I knew it made no difference: you knew the time of her death by the post-mortem. I was so sure then that her death was an accident that I didn't see the point of involving any of the family."

"It didn't seem to occur to you that you might be involving yourself by keeping silent," remarked Driver. "We always find these things out, sooner or later, and we naturally suspect anyone who withholds information for any reason whatever."

"Nonsense!" laughed Leda. "You know I had nothing to do with it."

"Did you go upstairs with your mother or see her again alive?"

"No. I waited for her to go upstairs again before I switched off the hall light. You must think it ridiculous that there's no two-way switch in a house of this size, but Mother was awfully mean over little extras like that. Then I went up to bed myself."

Driver regarded her seriously.

"I find it difficult to believe that you could let a dog out of the house at that hour without attracting the attention of anyone who was in the grounds, or without his attracting the dog's attention," he remarked.

"But I didn't let her out," explained Leda. "I didn't go as far as the front door. By the time that I'd finished talking to Mother, poor old Ming had been well and truly sick in the corner of the hall near the grand-father clock, so there wasn't any need to let her out."

"So you don't know whether the front door was locked or not?"

"No. I'd locked it before going to bed the first time, of course, but for all I know, Mother might have unlocked it to let Stanton in, although she said she hadn't."

"Then you went to bed and didn't know until after breakfast that your mother was dead?"

Leda nodded.

Betty grasped her husband's arm.

"Stan darling! It isn't true, is it? Leda's making it up because she hates us both so much. I've felt it ever since we came to stay in this horrible house. I won't stay here a day longer. I'd rather go somewhere to be bombed than breathe the same air as Leda. Tell the Inspector it isn't true, Stan."

"I'm afraid I can't do that," replied Stanton. "He knows it's nearly all true."

Betty turned away, with a sob.

"You swore you'd never been near the house," she said. "I never believed you'd lie to me like that."

Stanton shrugged his shoulders.

"You're a nice one to talk about telling lies!" he replied.

"Then you admit that you were here on the night that your mother was murdered?" Driver asked him.

"Yes. I was a fool not to tell you, I suppose, but I never thought it would come to this."

"Perhaps you'll tell me just how much of the statement you made to the Superintendent was true."

"Yes," Stanton agreed. "Well, it was all true except for one thing. I told the Superintendent that Mother had written a letter to me asking me to see her that night. And so she had, in spite of what my charming sister has just said. Nothing else would have induced me to come near the house, but her letter sounded so worried that I could tell she was very much upset about something. So of course I came. I came by car in the dark. I don't know whether you'll be able to verify it, but I stopped on the way at a road-house called The Golden Fleece and had dinner. I took my time over it because I knew that my father wouldn't go to bed till after the midnight news."

"So you knew that, even though you hadn't visited the house for years?"

Stanton did not choose to explain.

"Yes," he said.

"And what happened?"

"Nothing. I arrived at about a quarter past twelve, but couldn't see whether there were any lights on in the house, because of the black-out curtains. I waited until nearly two o'clock, then I called it a day, drove back to the inn, and spent the night there. They were expecting me, and I had no difficulty in getting in. They're used to people going in and out at all times of the day and night since the war started."

"You didn't try to get into the house or to attract your mother's attention?"

"By throwing handfuls of gravel up at her windows?" Stanton laughed. "No, I did not. You simply can't have a ghost of an idea of the relations which existed between my mother and father if you can ask such a question. My father was always on the look-out for a new excuse for inflicting some new indignity upon Mother. If he'd known that I was outside trying to see her, he would have flung himself into one of his rages with God knows what consequences to her."

"And you really expect me to believe that you drove away quite happily?"

"Believe it or not, Mr. Ripley," he said, indifferently. "I knew it wouldn't be easy for Mother to get downstairs to the door without being spotted. The dogs sleep upstairs: she didn't like them, and they didn't like her: one of them was quite likely to give an alarm. I knew she daren't risk calling through her window. So I went away expecting to have another letter later."

"H'm," said Driver. "Now you say Miss Hardstaffe is lying when she says your mother told her that it was you who had suggested meeting her after midnight. Have you got that letter you say your mother wrote?"

"No. I put it in the salvage sack."

"That's a pity. It would help to clear up that point," said Driver. "I can't see, myself, why you said anything about that letter in the first place. Surely it would have been better not to mention it to the Superintendent."

"Possibly so," agreed Stanton, "but I happen to be a truthful kind of fellow, though I don't expect you to believe it. I mentioned my mother's letter because I intended to say that I had done what it asked. But when he asked outright if I'd come to the house that night, my courage gave out, and I funked telling him."

"And that's the only other lie you've told us, Mr. Hardstaffe?"

"Yes."

"H'm," said Driver again.

There was a pause.

"Don't you believe me?" demanded Stanton.

"Well, sir," said the Inspector slowly. "There's that little matter of your presence here on the night of your father's murder. I don't so much mind you telling lies to other people, but when it comes to telling them to me, I take it as a personal matter. And you must admit that it does look a bit more than a coincidence that you were standing outside this house on the two nights when your parents were murdered."

"Stan! Oh Stan! What have you done?" wailed Betty. "Oh, poor little Paul. What will become of us all?"

She flung herself into a chair, and wept as wholeheartedly as her baby when bereft by a callous adult hand of some beloved toy.

"You told your wife that you would be on Home Guard duty all night," said the relentless detective-inspector. "You put on your uniform and she believed you implicitly."

Cue for song, thought the Sergeant, and hummed under his breath,

"Pom. Pompom. Pompompompompom. Pom. Pompompom. Pom. Pompom,

A fact that I counted upon, when I first put this uniform on!"

"*And* a member of the Home Guard was seen outside this house before Mr. Hardstaffe was murdered. *And* the local village Home Guards all have unbreakable alibis for that night. *And* it happened that you asked and received permission to change duty with another Guard on that particular night, saying that your father had been taken ill and had telephoned to ask you to see him!"

Leda, white with emotion, was gazing at her brother.

"Stanton! Is this true?"

It was the truth about my father," Stanton replied, ignoring her.

Yes," agreed the Inspector. "That was true all right. He was ill, very ill. Sick unto death!"

"No, no. I mean that he did 'phone me. Oh, I know you'll never believe it, but it's true, I tell you, true! He 'phoned to my office and said he was in a terrible predicament. He'd learned something about Mother's death, he said, but he felt he couldn't go to the police about it. He wanted me to advise him I know it sounds impossible, but it's true. I didn't know what to do. It was so queer for him to ring me at all that I at once thought it must be some kind of plot, and I decided not to go."

"You must have changed your mind suddenly."

The Inspector's voice was charged with disbelief, but Stanton went on as if determined to finish his story in his own way.

"That's exactly what I did do. I went eventually, not to keep the appointment, but to try and find out what was going on. I frankly thought that he wanted to frame me for my mother's murder. Instead of that, he seems to have framed me for his. If he wasn't dead already, he'd die with laughing at that."

The room was silent for a minute.

"Well," said Driver at length, "I can understand your going back without seeing your father, but I still don't see why you didn't try to see your mother."

Stanton suddenly lost his suave self-possession.

"Oh God!" he cried, "Have you no pity? Have you no mothers, no wives, no children, you detectives? Can't you understand that I've been tormented day and night, night and day, by the thought that while I was standing there in the darkness, my mother was slowly dying?"

He buried his face in his hands and began to cry—long, slow sobs that brought Betty to her feet.

"No one's going to touch you, Stan," she said. "If they don't believe you, I do."

She turned on Leda with the ferocity of a wild cat with young, "This is your fault, you—you vampire!" she cried. "And now I'll tell you all about why I wanted Miss Fuller to come here. I'll explain your old mystery. Mystery? It was nothing but fun. I—"

"It's no use, Mrs. Hardstaffe," Driver interrupted. "No jury would believe a word of it. They'd say you'd made it up to help your husband."

Betty stared at him wildly.

"Jury? No—jury—" she repeated. "You can't mean—"

"Stop it, all of you! I can't stand it!"

Charity's voice cut across the emotionally-charged atmosphere of the room. She sprang to her feet, her eyes feverishly a-glitter, and for a moment her tall figure dominated them all.

"You're driving me mad; I can't stand it any longer!" she cried. "*I* did it, if you want to know. He pestered me with his attentions and I couldn't stand it any longer. I wanted to be free, and he wouldn't let me go. So I killed him! And now, for God's sake, let me go home!"

CHAPTER 38

ARNOLD was beginning to think that, as far as he was concerned, the murders of Mr. and Mrs. Hardstaffe had been so much waste of time.

Any writer worthy of a crime club would, he felt sure, have completed his book while the murders were still front page news, would have cashed in on the publicity, and would have been well on the way to solving the crimes, over the Inspector's head.

Instead of that, he had been unable to write a word in the three weeks which followed Charity's dramatic confession, and the recollection of the primitive emotions exhibited that same morning still caused him the acutest embarrassment. To describe any of them in his book was unthinkable.

And so page after page of manuscript paper was filled, not with Noel Delare's picturesque appearances on the scene of the crime, nor his careless perception of carefully dropped clues, but with scribbled calculations upon the state of Arnold's dwindling bank balance.

One afternoon, after yet another fruitless attempt to complete Chapter Twenty, he threw down his fountain pen and faced the fact that he must either starve or marry Leda.

Neither of these alternatives held any attraction for him.

He did not doubt that Leda would marry him if he asked her. She might laugh at him and call him a silly old fool, but she would accept. He had little to offer her except the honest name of Smith, which had earned as much respect in London town as that of Brown, and was many hundreds of years older than the more elaborate surnames of those who professed to despise it. But Leda was in need of a husband, not of money, home, or position, and although she might insist on being known as Hardstaffe-Smith, she would not refuse him.

If he could have dismissed from his mind the romantic episode with Charity Fuller which seemed each day to assume a more colourful place in his life, he would have proposed to Leda that very day. But the thought of Charity wearing the black evening frock which so cleverly concealed her figure, and the even sharper thought of her wearing the night attire which as carelessly revealed it, made him hesitate to commit himself to an alliance with Leda whose figure promised no such delights.

A silly old fool? Perhaps so. But surely it was no unusual thing for a man to fall in love at fifty, particularly if he had had no previous sexual experience. No one could call him a *roué* and that should count for something with a woman nowadays.

It wasn't as if he were over sixty, like old Hardstaffe, he thought. There had been something indecent in the idea of *his* possessing a young girl like Charity. But if old age were a second childhood, then, at fifty, a man was back again in his twenties!

But, even if she would consider his advances, Charity had no money. And Leda was now a rich woman—

Having thus worked himself into a Hamlet-like mood of indecision, Arnold decided to give up all pretense at work, and go out in the hazy sunshine to think things over again. Leda, he knew, was presiding at the monthly meeting of The Women's Rustic Arts and Crafts Society, so that he was absolved from the polite necessity of asking her to accompany him.

With some idea of imposing a little self-discipline upon himself, he avoided walking towards the house where Charity lodged, and turned in the opposite direction. As far as he could see, the road was deserted, but when he turned along the narrow lane leading to the path through the woods, he caught sight of Charity's tall figure ahead, and invested the chance encounter with all the romantic significance he might have given to it, had he indeed been twenty instead of fifty.

Charity walked quickly, and she was deep in the woods before he caught up with her.

"Miss Fuller!" he exclaimed. "What a pleasant surprise! I heard that you were coming back again this week. Are you sure you're strong enough to walk as far as this?"

"Oh, I'm all right now," replied Charity. "Walking is good for nervous complaints, you know, and I've been told to get out-of-doors as much as possible."

Her voice was impersonal. It chilled Arnold, and seemed to be telling him to mind his own business.

"Forgive me if I seem curious," he said. "It isn't the curiosity of the villagers, I assure you. I've felt anxious about you ever since they took you away."

"It's very kind of you, Mr. Smith," she said, still in the same cold tones. "I must thank you, too, for inquiring about me when I was in the nursing-home. The flowers you sent were lovely, but you shouldn't have bothered about me." She paused, then added, "I'm not worth it." Arnold's impulse was to raise his cap and walk away in the opposite direction, but suddenly he grasped her arm, and turned her towards him.

"Why, you're crying!" he said. "Whatever is the matter? If I've said anything to upset you—"

Womanlike, she cried more bitterly at his evident sympathy, and he put an arm round her shoulders and waited for her to stop.

"Here. Let's sit down," said Arnold.

He drew her towards a tiny clearing which might have provided a faery bower for Titania, and they sat down together on a felled tree, their feet rustling among dead leaves and beech mast.

"Now tell me all about it," he said gently. "I know that you couldn't have killed old Hardstaffe, though I'll admit you scared me a bit when you confessed that you had."

"Of course I didn't!" she said indignantly. "It was just nerves. I'm not usually given to making scenes, but all that sob-stuff from Stanton and his wife fairly finished me after the awful time I'd had that morning. I felt I must do something to stop all those questions and arguments or I should go mad."

"Yes, I can understand that," replied Arnold. "It was lucky that the Inspector had the sense to send for the doctor. When he arrived he couldn't tell us whether you'd recover or not. He just bundled you into his car and insisted on taking you to a nursing-home, and said he'd have to keep you doped for a few days to give your brain a chance to recover from the shock. I wonder he let you out so soon really."

"Oh, I'm as strong as a horse," said Charity. "I feel that I owe you all an apology, though, for making an exhibition of myself."

"You didn't," Arnold smiled. "You looked—magnificent. Really, I mean it. We ought to do the apologising, not you. We ought to have had more sense than to subject you to such an interview after the shock you'd had. So, if that's all you were crying about—"

"No, it isn't." She sat quite still for a minute, then looked at him in that heart-piercing way of hers. "Mr. Smith, you've always been kind and understanding to me," she said. "I'm so alone in the world, and everyone in the village dislikes me. I suppose it's because I never mix with them, and they think I'm a snob."

"They probably envy you," returned Smith. "They're none of 'em noted for their looks, and you are beautiful."

"No!" cried Charity. "They've no reason to envy me. They say that good looks are the snares of the devil. If I have any, that's what they are. If I'd been ugly, I shouldn't have attracted *him*, and I shouldn't need to feel so wretchedly miserable now."

Arnold stared at her in amazement.

"You mean—you're still in love with Leda's father?" he asked.

Charity's laugh was full of bitterness.

"In love? No! I hated him! I'm glad he's dead, though it was my fault, I know, that he died. All those rumours about us were quite true. He was in love with me—at least he was crazy about me, if that's the same thing. He wanted to marry me. No, that's not the truth. He wanted to make me his mistress." Arnold winced at the word. "When I refused, he said he would marry me even if he had to kill his wife first. I don't know whether he did it or not, but I think he was capable of it.

"But it isn't that. It's my own part in it that makes me feel so unhappy. He flattered me, and gave me lovely presents. I ought not to have accepted them, but I did. I was so lonely here and he was unhappy at home, and I thought I was in love with him. It all seemed so natural at the time, then I suddenly came to my senses, and realised that I didn't love him and never had. I knew that he was just a dirty old man and I was pandering to him. Oh, I'm not shirking ugly words," she went on. "It was just like that. It must have been a kind of Svengali attraction, for, until then, I'd seen it as a great romance. That night when I came to dinner and met you, he tried to kiss me when he took me home. I told him how I felt, and I'd have killed him if he'd tried to touch me again."

Arnold did not perceive her reason for telling him all this, and said with some diffidence, "But you found it all out in time. I don't see why you're letting it worry you so much."

Charity looked at him, her lips trembling, and he saw that her lovely green eyes were filled with tears.

"Can't you understand how ashamed I feel?" she asked earnestly. "I felt ashamed that you should have seen Mr. Hardstaffe treating me as though I belonged to him. I still feel dreadful when I think of it."

Arnold took her hand in his.

"My dear, you have no cause to feel like that," he said. "However foolish you may have been, that's all over. I don't believe all the awful things you've been saying about yourself. To me, you are quite lovely."

Charity squeezed his hand.

"You do say the sweetest things," she said, smiling through her tears. "I've wanted so much to be friends with you, but I felt that I couldn't until I'd told you the truth about *him*."

One of the woodcutters passed them, his footsteps deadened by the soft mossy ground. He whistled as he went on his way, hoping to convince them, perhaps, that they had not been observed.

First old Mr. Hardstaffe and now old Mr. Smith, he thought. Well, they do say Charity always begins at home!

Charity withdrew her hand and got up hurriedly.

"It's getting late. I must go," she said in the old, impersonal voice.

Arnold, finding the sudden change in her manner disconcerting, got up, and turned to accompany her.

"No, don't come with me," she said, "You'd better go back the short way. Your fiancée will be waiting for you," and, waving a slender hand, she walked quickly away through the wood.

Arnold turned back thoughtfully.

Before he had reached the house, he had resolved to break his non-existent engagement with Leda.

CHAPTER 39

HE HEARD Leda's voice calling to him as soon as he entered the hall, and, disturbed by its unfamiliar urgency, he hastened forward.

The hall, like many others in old houses, lacked adequate windows, and he could see her indistinctly among die shadows.

"Oh Arnold, I'm so glad you've come!" she exclaimed. "I'm in such trouble."

He stretched out a hand, but she drew back.

"Don't touch me," she said quickly. "I'm—wet."

"Wet?" repeated Arnold. "On a lovely evening like this? What on earth have you been doing? Falling into the river?"

He switched on the light.

"Good Lord!" he exclaimed. "What have you done? What is it—oil?"

He streaked a finger across the front of her coat, then looked at it, and gasped.

"It's blood," he said. "Blood!" He looked at the wide smears on the sleeves of her coat, at the great, spreading blotch across the waist and breast, at her bloody hands, and his voice grew urgent.

"Has there been an accident? Are you hurt?"

"No. *I'm* all right, Arnold."

He gazed at her agitated face and frightened eyes.

"Then, what is it? You don't mean—?"

Leda gulped.

"It's Cherub," she said, "my little darling Cherub. I was coming back from the meeting and she must have heard my step. She ran right across the road. A motor-bike—the man couldn't help it. No one could have avoided her. It caught her with some sharp part. She's—terribly injured, Arnold. Oh, why didn't I come home five minutes earlier? Why did it have to be Cherub?"

"I'm sorry, Leda. Is there anything I can do?"

In his relief, Arnold found it difficult to express his sympathy, though he knew that the puppy was as dear to Leda's heart as Paul was to Betty's. But, standing there motionless, her hands stained with blood, and that look of horror in her eyes, she had looked a veritable Lady Macbeth, and he had imagined a tragedy much greater.

"Yes. Ring up the vet for me—you'll find his number on the telephone pad. I've put her in one of the kennels. She's bleeding so terribly."

"Right," replied Arnold. "Vincent's the name, isn't it? Perhaps it isn't as bad as it looks. It isn't always a bad thing for a wound to bleed at first."

"You haven't seen it," Leda replied in dull tones. "I want him to put her to sleep at once. She's in no pain yet, but there's absolutely no hope of saving her."

"I'm sorry," he said again. "I know how you feel. You can't do anything for a few minutes, though, so how about mixing yourself a drink and then taking that coat off? You must be sensible, dear."

As he spoke, it occurred to him that this was probably the first time in her life that anyone had ever had to tell Leda to be sensible.

She fumbled with the belt of her coat, but before she could take it off, Arnold was put through to the vet's number, and she waited while he took the call.

At last, he put down the receiver and turned to answer her unspoken question.

"He can't come," he said. "He's out on an emergency call some miles away. Sir Andrew Carnford's brood mare. He isn't expected back for hours. Isn't there anyone else we can get?"

Leda shook her head.

"No," she said. "He's the only vet within miles. I shall have to do it myself."

Arnold stared.

"Your favourite puppy? You can't, Leda."

"I can. I've got to. When the first numbness wears off, she'll be in agony. You'll help me, won't you, Arnold? I can't do it alone."

"Of course," replied Arnold, "but wouldn't it be better to wait for a bit? Vincent might get back earlier than they expect."

"I don't relish it any more than you do," said Leda, "but it's just got to be done. When you see her you'll understand."

In the last few minutes, she had contrived to regain her self-control and once again seemed her usual calm self. Arnold, much relieved by her manner, followed her out of the house and across the yard to the kennels, where they entered the large central wooden building.

It was about the size of a large hen-house and smelled of saw-dust, creosote, and dog. Leda could walk about on the raised wooden floor in comfort, but Arnold had to duck his head except in the very middle of the little hut, under the apex of the roof.

The puppy lay on its side on a bed of straw. It raised its head slowly from its front paws, and uttered little whimpers of welcome as Leda knelt down beside it, but its eyes were dazed.

Arnold saw with some surprise that Leda had brought some food in a dish which she offered to Cherub.

"Is that wise?" he asked. "I thought they were supposed not to have it when . . ."

"I always give them a good meal before they go to the vet for this kind of thing," Leda replied, "but she doesn't seem able to eat it."

Arnold felt the pathos of the scene. But one glance at the puppy's injuries assured him that Leda was right about them. The dog could not live long, but it might feel pain again. You couldn't take that chance with any living creature you loved. He admired Leda for her courage.

"I'll get you to hold the lamp up, if you don't mind, Arnold," she said. "It will be dark before we've finished, and I must be able to see what I'm doing. It's one of those patent A.R.P. lamps that throw the light downwards, and I'm afraid there's no nail to hang it on. When I come here in the dark, I just put it down on the floor, but that will hardly do for this job. I'll be as quick as I can."

Arnold held the lamp obediently, as she took some small bottles, cotton wool, a cardboard funnel, and finally ampoules and a hypodermic syringe from a tin case originally designed to hold some long-forgotten Christmas gift.

"Morphia?" he asked.

Leda looked up quickly.

"No," she replied. "I can't get that, you know. This is a new drug—I forget the name—but it doesn't kill. It temporarily paralyses the motor nerves and eventually induces sleep. She might not need it, but I couldn't bear it if she started to struggle when she smells the chloroform. If she did, I don't think I could go on with it."

"I shouldn't think she could do much struggling with a wound like that," remarked Arnold.

"No, I don't suppose she can, but I'm taking no risks. If a thing has to be done I believe in doing it properly. It causes less heart-ache in the long run."

Arnold watched her pinch together a fold of the dog's skin, and make a gentle injection. Then she stroked its head with a slow rhythmic movement.

"The stuff takes a little time to take effect," she said, "I usually give it in their food when I have to use it at all, but an injection is quicker."

They watched the dog blink drowsily until, after some minutes, its head dropped on to its front paws, and it breathed deeply in sleep.

Leda's hand did not falter as she packed some cotton wool loosely into the narrow end of the funnel, and sprinkled a few drops of chloroform on to it.

"It looks strange to see you doing this sort of thing," said Arnold, finding the silence oppressive.

"I daresay it does," replied Leda. "You don't often see me in the kennels, though, do you? I've done quite a few first aid jobs since you've been here, all the same. When you breed dogs, you have to be prepared for things like this, though I always get the vet, if I can."

She placed the wide end of the funnel over the dog's nose and held it lightly with one hand while she sprinkled more chloroform on to the cotton wool at the other end, from time to time.

Arnold never saw her hand tremble.

Hours seemed to pass, and still the puppy breathed.

Arnold's head began to ache and he felt slightly dizzy standing there, with the lamp hanging from his out-stretched hand.

At length Leda said, "She's gone," and laid the funnel on the floor. Then she looked up at Arnold and said with tears glinting in her eyes, "I did it for the best."

Arnold shook off his lethargy and forced himself to speak.

"I know you did," he said, and his voice seemed to mock at him from a great distance. He swayed a little, and would have dropped the lamp if Leda had not taken it from him.

The next moment, as it seemed, he found himself outside, shivering in the cold wind, and asked, "What happened? What am I doing?"

"The chloroform made you a bit dizzy," said Leda. "I hadn't realised that you were standing right over it in the heat of the lamp, and the kennel is so stuffy with the windows closed. I'm so sorry, Arnold. It was selfish of me."

They walked back in silence to the house, where Leda insisted on his sitting down just as he was, while she took off her coat, and went to wash her hands.

"Are you sure you're all right?" she asked when she came back.

"Quite," smiled Arnold. "It was silly of me to feel like that, but it was the fumes rising up in the heat that knocked me over. If you want to bump me off at any time you'll have to think of a better way than that though. Here, what's wrong?"

For Leda suddenly looked as pale as a ghost.

"I—I'm all in," she said.

Arnold pushed her gently into the nearest chair. "Stay there!" he ordered, and went out of the room, returning a few minutes later with a half-bottle of brandy, a syphon of soda, and two glasses.

He poured out two stiff drinks and placed one in her hand.

"There you are," he said, "drink that, and be grateful that your father kept a well-stocked cellar! I'm a selfish brute. I ought to have known that you'd have some reaction after this unfortunate affair, and instead of that, I go around trying to get sympathy for myself. It seems to me that we both need a keeper."

"You know," he went on after he had finished his drink, "you really are a marvel, Leda. I don't know any other woman who would have had the courage to do what you have done tonight."

The brandy which Leda had drunk with the grimacing gulps that are usually reserved for a particularly evil-flavoured medicine, had speedily brought back the colour to her cheeks.

"I don't deserve all those compliments," she protested. 'If I make up my mind to do something unpleasant, I can usually make myself go through with it, that's all."

Arnold took the empty glasses, and began to fill them again.

"No more for me, Arnold. No really. I shall be drunk!"

"Do you good," he replied with some ambiguity. "Go on. I haven't made it quite so strong this time. You need a pick-me-up tonight. Uncle Arnold says so."

He placed a cigarette in her mouth and held a match for her, and they sat for a little while in silence, warming themselves at the fire.

At length Leda got up.

"It must be awfully late," she said. "I must go and change for dinner."

She moved forward unsteadily, and would have fallen if Arnold had not put his arm round her.

She startled him by flinging her arms around his neck, and bursting into tears.

'Oh, Arnold! Whatever should I do without you?" she cried.

CHAPTER 40

A FEW weeks later, Arnold walked into the breakfast room at tea-time to find Leda, surrounded as usual by her dogs, already pouring out tea.

"Hallo," she said. "Better late than never! My goodness! You do look pleased with yourself."

"Ah!" he exclaimed, rubbing his hands together. "This is my lucky day."

"It must be," laughed Leda. "You look just like a schoolboy."

"Oh, not quite as young as that," returned Arnold. "Let's say a twenty-year old. I've a piece of good news for you."

"Well, thank goodness for that!" she exclaimed. I've just been looking at the morning papers, and what with some people telling us there's nothing to worry about, and others warning us not to be complacent, I really don't know how I'm supposed to be feeling. So I finished up by being depressed."

"Oh, don't say that," said Arnold, removing two dogs from the settee and sitting down beside her. "That Inspector fellow hasn't been worrying you, has he?"

"No," replied Leda. "I'm really beginning to think that he's written the case off just as another of those unsolved mysteries. I've had no questions to answer for weeks, and, so far as I know, Stanton hasn't been arrested yet."

"Good. Well now, Leda, I want to talk to you about this engagement of ours."

Leda slapped him playfully on the shoulder.

"Oh, Mr. Smith, this is so sudden!" she exclaimed. Arnold chuckled.

"I suppose it is," he admitted. "We've taken it for granted for so long now, that we never seem to mention it to each other. I think it's about time that we did. Seriously, Leda, it must have occurred to you that things have changed a lot lately. We arranged the whole thing in the first place to preserve the conventions and spare your sister-in-law's blushes. Although she is no longer staying here, we've just let things drift, but we ought to think about it a bit. You see, we've been living in the same house without a chaperone for several weeks now, and it must look odd to some people. I knew you're very unconventional Leda, but I think far too highly of you to put you in a position which gives anyone the slightest chance of talking scandal about you."

"My dear, I don't care twopence about that," laughed Leda. "Let them talk if they want to!"

"That's all very well," returned Arnold, "but I'm not going to have it, Leda. Oh dear! I'm making an awful hash of this, I'm afraid. Can't you see what I'm trying to say? We can't go on like this, Leda."

Leda turned towards him with an expression on her face which almost transfigured her plain features.

"Oh, Arnold!" she exclaimed. "If you only knew how I've longed for you to say that. I've nearly said it myself dozens of times, but I've always told myself that it wouldn't be fair for me to do so."

Arnold looked even happier than before.

"Do you really mean that?" he asked. "Why on earth didn't you, then? Whatever made you think I should mind? And here I've been feeling quite worried over the possibility that you might take it the wrong way. I really knew you wouldn't, of course: you're so jolly sensible about everything; but I should hate to offend you in any way, and I didn't feel quite sure about it. Well, to think that all these weeks you've been as anxious to get out of our engagement as I have. What a joke! Don't tell me that you're in love with someone else, as I am!"

For the first time since he had embarked so nervously on his suggestion, he turned to look closely at Leda. But she was looking down at the Sealyham which lay on its back on her lap, and was apparently intent on investigating its skin with the same absolute preoccupation which a monkey expends on the same pursuit.

"I do believe that Penny has got fleas," she remarked. Arnold brought his hand down upon his knee with a resounding slap, and rocked with merriment.

"Well, I like that!" he exclaimed. "There you are jilting me, and all you can do is to think about fleas. I know what it is, though. You're trying to get out of answering my last remark. Come on, own up."

He leaned forward, and looked at her face.

"I say, you're not annoyed are you?" he inquired, with some concern.

Leda forced a smile.

"Of course I'm not," she replied, "though I'm annoyed about the fleas. Oh, you can laugh, but it's a serious thing to get fleas in kennels. If the boarding dogs catch them, their owners will never send them to me again, and I make enough money to pay for dog food, out of the boarders."

"That's good," said Arnold heartily. "Not about the fleas, of course. But I must say I'm relieved to know you're not annoyed with me. I was afraid I might be expressing myself awkwardly."

"I think you put it very well," replied Leda. "I can't give you back your ring because you never gave me one, but consider it done. And now, what about the good news? It's Charity Fuller, isn't it?"

Arnold gaped at her in amazement.

"How on earth do you know that?" he asked. "It must be a guess, of course, because she only gave me my answer this afternoon. You don't suppose the whole village knows, do you? We've been very discreet."

Leda shook her head.

"No, I don't think so," she said reassuringly. "We all knew that you found her attractive, on the night that Betty asked her to dine, but I'm sure I was the only one to think it was more than a passing fancy. I suppose it's because I've been in contact with you for so long now that I know all your moods and feelings. Charity is very pretty. I wish you luck."

"Thank you, Leda. I know you mean that. And I daresay I shall need some luck. Charity is so much younger than we are—quite a different generation really—and there will be a few adjustments to be made after we are married, I expect. But as long as we love each other—"

"When are you going to be married?" Leda interrupted. "Or am I going too fast? You're not engaged yet."

"Not officially. I had to talk to you about it first. After all, you might have refused to release me, and as the whole village knows we're engaged I should have to stand by that."

Leda smiled.

I'm not the kind of woman to try and keep a man against his will," she said, "and you know we never pretended to ourselves that it was anything more than a convenience. When do you think of getting engaged to Charity?"

"Just as soon as I can get to a jeweller's to buy the ring," he said.

Leda laughed shortly.

"I said you looked like a schoolboy," she said. "Now you're talking like one. Don't you realise that in the eyes of my relations and friends, to say nothing of everyone in the village, you're engaged to be married to me? What are they going to think if you go about telling them all tomorrow that you're going to marry Charity Fuller? I should be the laughing-stock of the place, and should have to bring an action against you to save my face."

Arnold got up and strode across the room.

"Good Lord!" he exclaimed. "What a fool I am! I never thought of that. Wait a minute though!" He walked back to the settee. You'll have to tell them first that you've jilted me."

"Of course I shall," replied Leda. "Then you can go and get engaged to her in a fit of pique! But you can't do that decently under a week or two. I know you'll hate to have all this delay, but you see, I've lived here nearly all my life, and I should very much dislike to have everyone commiserating with me over a thing like this."

"What am I to do then?"

"Leave it to me, Arnold. I promise you that I'll arrange it all as quickly as I can. You'll have to tell Charity, of course, but keep it to yourselves for a bit."

"Under the circumstances, don't you think it would be better for me to pack up and go to stay at the inn in a few days' time? I can't very well stay here if you're supposed to have quarrelled with me."

"Yes, you'll have to do that soon. I wish we'd never made that stupid arrangement, then you could have gone on staying here and announced your engagement without all this fuss. I shall hate it, Arnold. It's been grand to have you here. We've had such good times together."

He took her hand in his.

"I can't even begin to tell you how marvellous it has been for me," he said. "We're good friends, you and I, Leda. We've always got on so well together. I couldn't think more of you if you were my own sister. You're such a good sort."

"Dear Arnold," was Leda's reply. "I do hope you will be happy, but I can't help wondering whether—" She broke off her words, and placed an impulsive hand on his arm. "Arnold," she said earnestly, "are you quite sure about Charity?"

"Sure about her loving me do you mean? Or about my loving her?"

"Neither. I mean this—now don't be offended will you?—I've always thought it strange that whenever she came to this house, something queer happened. She was here the night before Mother was murdered, and again on the night before Daddy was murdered. When she slept here, there was all that fuss over Frieda. Then when the Inspector did his third-degree on us all, she was the one to break down and confess. I know that he didn't arrest her, but she has an easy influence over men, and perhaps she bewitched him, too. Please don't take this the wrong way, Arnold. I'm only concerned about you. Because, if she did have anything to do with the murders, she'd be quite capable of getting engaged to you, with the intention of doing you some harm. After all, she is a self-confessed murderer, whether she was hysterical at the time or not. Are you sure she's above suspicion?"

"Sure? Of course I am," said Arnold, laughing at her foolishness. "Why, she's no more capable of murder than you are!"

CHAPTER 41

ARNOLD sat at the writing table in the window of his sitting-room at High Bungalow," working on one of the last chapters of his book.

Life had not been easy for him since he had left Leda some three weeks ago, and the one comforting thing, apart from the knowledge that Charity was willing to many him, was that he had suddenly found himself able to write again.

He had taken up his quarters at first at the small village inn, but he had soon discovered that The Fox and Feathers, although outwardly purporting to be one of the old coaching inns, held within its walls none of those comforts which he had anticipated. There were none of the roaring fires, well-cooked meals, good wine, warm beds, excellent service, and goodly welcomes, which the travellers of an earlier century had demanded. He had found it, instead, draughty, damp, and sparsely furnished. The food was badly cooked, and served with none of the refinements of table equipment and napery to which he was accustomed. The water in the bathroom was consistently cold. The landlady, though endeavouring to do her best for him, made no secret of the fact that she had no time to attend to the needs of a permanent guest in addition to her daily work.

Above all, there was no place in which he could write, for his bedroom was unheated, and the room in which he took his meals became a private bar during licensed hours. This was serious, because unless he could earn enough to supplement adequately his present meagre income, he would be unable to support a wife, and at many times during those unhappy weeks, he cursed himself for a fool, and wished he had never fallen captive to Charity's charms.

This, however, was only when he was alone. When he was in her presence, he could not blind himself to the fact that she possessed for him that indefinable and deadly attraction which makes men—and especially men of fifty—do strange and sometimes evil things.

As usual, it was Leda who took matters into her capable hands, and smoothed out his worries for him. Within twelve hours of learning of his difficulties, she had arranged for him to take a bedroom and private sitting-room with a homely widow who lived in a bright, modern bungalow in a quiet corner of Nether Naughton. The rooms were unpretentious but comfortable. The bath water was heated by a gas geyser so that he could have his bath whenever he wanted it, provided that he took it no oftener than once a day, and always remembered to leave the water in the bath as the night's protection against fire-bombs. The food was plain but well cooked and well served; the woman clean and obliging. And if, in her anxiety to ensure that he should be well looked after, Leda had dropped a hint that he was suffering from a broken heart on her account, she could easily be forgiven for so slight a deception.

And now his only trouble was that he was lonely. He dare not be seen about with Charity too often, she rarely visited him at the bungalow, and she only allowed him to call on her occasionally after dark. He missed Leda's loud, cheerful voice shouting to tell him that she was going out or coming in. He even missed the dogs.

But the book featuring Noel Delare which had once seemed doomed to remain as unfinished as Schubert's A Minor Symphony, was now nearly completed.

This evening as he sat at his writing table, he felt suddenly that he was being watched, and, looking up, he saw a face staring at him through the window. Startled, he rose to his feet, and peered back through the dimming light.

Then he smiled in relief, waved a hand, and went to open the front door.

"Come in," he said. "You startled me for a minute. I wondered who it could be. Why didn't you walk in: you know we always leave the front door unlocked."

"I wasn't sure whether you'd be in or not," replied his visitor, "so I thought I'd walk round and peep into your sitting-room."

"Your hands are cold," said Arnold. "Come and warm them by the fire."

She slipped them hastily from his.

"They're all right," she said. "Is Mrs. Bright out?"

"Very much so," replied Arnold. "She's gone off to visit her married daughter at some queer-sounding place, and she won't be home till morning. I wonder you haven't heard all about it: the whole village has been talking about it for at least a week. I believe it's the first time she's plucked up sufficient courage to leave Nether Naughton in ten years, but it appears that her daughter has just made her into a grandmother, so she couldn't resist going."

"Yes, I did hear about that. Aren't country folk simple at heart? Births, marriages, deaths make up their whole interest in life. They assess virtue in a woman according to the number of babies she produces."

"Yes," agreed Arnold, "except that you've got them in the wrong order. It's marriage first in Nether Naughton, if you please! Let me take your coat. I do hope you're going to stay for the evening. No one will know that you're here with me, and I've hardly seen a soul to speak to all day."

"Poor Arnold! Yes I'll stay for a bit, thank you. I should like it. I see you so rarely these days, and I do miss you, you know. It will be all right later on when we can meet openly again, but now it's a rare treat. By the way, how's the book getting on? Is this it?"

She walked across to the table and turned a few pages with the privileged hand of an old friend.

"Oh, it's getting on very well," replied Arnold. "You see I work better when I'm away from your disturbing influence! But I don't know how I'm going to write the last chapter. I can't for the life of me think of a satisfactory ending."

"I should have thought that was the easiest part of the whole book. You've got the reader nicely tied up with clues so that he won't be able to see the wood for trees, while you know exactly who did it."

Arnold shook his head.

"That's the trouble. I don't," he said.

She looked at him to see whether he was joking or not, then began to laugh.

"You don't mean to say that you've got tied up with your own clues! Oh Arnold, I can't believe that!"

"It's true all the same. I've been so careful to invent clues incriminating everyone in the book, that I can't decide which character to choose as the murderer. You see, it's all quite a new technique to me, and there are a dozen and one difficulties that I never anticipated. The trouble is that nobody seems to have any motive."

"But surely you thought all that out to begin with. The motive's such an important thing, isn't it?"

Yes," agreed Arnold, "the most important, I should say, in any crime. But I've written the chapters in such fits and starts that I've never properly visualised the thing as a whole."

She looked down at the manuscript again.

"Well, this seems to be a confession of some kind," she remarked.

Yes, I ve just finished that. It's the murderer's confession but I've worded it so vaguely that it might do for any character. It's all rather worrying. You see, it's awfully important for me to get a good press on this book. It may lay the foundation of a new career for me."

"Yes, I can see that," she replied regarding him curiously. "Well, look here, they say two heads are better than one. Can't we try to work it out together? It won't be the first time I've helped you, will it?"

"Rather not!" exclaimed Arnold. "Why you're part of the book already. If you can suggest the motive, too, it'll be your crime."

She seemed overwhelmed by his tribute.

"I'll do my best anyway," she said. "It would be easy enough to slip another clue in, but the motive's different. It ought to be woven into the plot right at the beginning. It's there when the thought of the crime first enters the murderer's head."

Arnold stared at her.

"Good Lord!" he exclaimed. "You talk as if you know all about it. I think you ought to be writing the book instead of me."

"Not me!" she said, shaking her head. "I never could write. My spelling's atrocious, and my grammar's worse. Well, we'd better make a start. Is that clock right?" Arnold pulled a gold hunter out of his pocket and compared the time it indicated with that of the travelling-clock on the mantelpiece.

"Nearly eight o'clock! Good Lord yes! I thought I was feeling a bit peckish. Have you dined, or can I persuade you to share my sandwiches? Mrs. Bright has left an array of trays on the kitchen table for all my meals. She'll be back at about eleven o'clock to-morrow to get lunch."

"Thanks, I'd like to. I'm all on my own at home, too, as it happens. But I'll go and fetch it for you. I expect there's coffee to be made, isn't there? You do the black-out." Without waiting for his reply, she walked out of the room.

CHAPTER 42

"WE'D better get this story straightened out now," said Leda. "I must get back before half-past ten.'

They had finished their coffee and sandwiches and were seated comfortably in two armchairs drawn close to the gas fire.

"Are you sure you want to bother about my book?" asked Arnold. "You wouldn't rather talk about something else?"

"Of course not. I want to hear how you've worked the plot out," she said. "I know that you killed Mother. Did you murder my father, too?"

Arnold looked startled.

"I—I—" he stammered.

"In the book, I mean, Stupid!" exclaimed Leda. "You needn't look so scared."

"Well—Yes, I did," he admitted. "I described the two murders just as they happened, and I thought I'd make the murderer commit suicide in the end. That's why I wrote that confession."

"Good idea. Have you put the whole family into the book?"

No. Just your father and mother, yourself and me, and a few visitors and villagers to give local colour."

I see. Then it just lies between you and me."

Arnold looked at her in sudden suspicion.

"What are you getting at?" he demanded.

"The motive, I hope,' smiled Leda. "Let's take you first, and see why you became a murderer. You were on the premises, of course. You came here in the first place, knowing that by doing so, you would be living above your income. Therefore you must have had a reason for coming, and I should think you came as an adventurer. Your advertisement was framed to bring replies from people in a good social position. Well, when you arrived, you liked the layout of things, and saw the chance of making yourself comfortable for the rest of your life. You knew that Mother was a rich woman—you knew her fad about taking sleeping-draughts—you knew that the maid had some morphia—"

Arnold gazed at her stupidly.

"I—" he stammered again.

"She told everyone about it," she went on unhurriedly. "You must have known. You slipped into the bedroom, substituted the powders you had prepared for the real ones, and murdered her. You knew she had left her money to her husband and that it meant killing him later, but you were determined to go through with it."

"Leda, what are you saying?" cried Arnold. "How do you know—"

She barely paused in her narrative.

"It was bad luck that the doctor had given her sleeping-powders containing no morphia. You had hoped it would look like suicide. Now they knew it was murder. But you carried on with your plan. You telephoned to Stan, imitating his father's voice, and hoping to get him hanged for the two murders. It all succeeded just as you'd hoped."

"The motive? What motive could I have had?"

Arnold's voice was unnaturally high-pitched.

"Motive? You knew that with the parents out of the way, and the son hanged for their murder, all the money would pass to their daughter, and that she was so fond of you that she wouldn't almost jump at the chance to marry you. There's your motive, Arnold. Money. May I have a cigarette!"

Arnold looked at her in a dazed way as he offered his cigarette case, and she noticed that his hands were trembling so violently that he could not strike a match on the side of the box. She had to take it from him and light it herself.

Then she threw back her head and laughed until tears came into her eyes.

"Good Lord!" Arnold said rather thickly, "Good Lord, Leda, I thought you meant it. I never knew you could act like that. You're as good as Sarah Bernhardt or somebody."

Leda leaned forward in her chair and regarded him searchingly.

"Do you think it's all right?" she asked. "Does it convince you?"

"I think so," said Arnold. "There are one or two details that aren't quite right, but—"

"If you don't think the police would be satisfied, we'd better try the other solution," she said.

Arnold looked at her with a strange expression in his eyes.

"The other?" he asked.

"Yes. In other words, me."

He forced himself to smile.

"You're far too level-headed to commit a murder," he said. "If you wanted money, you'd manage to get it some other way."

"All the more reason why I should be the murderer," replied Leda, "because I'm less likely to be suspected." Arnold shook his head very slowly.

"It doesn't sound right to me," he said. "You're a woman. A woman wouldn't stand behind a defenceless old man and bash his head in."

"Oh, that's what you think!" exclaimed Leda. "The trouble with you is that you don't know the first thing about women. You think we're all like those pale creatures in your old books who fall into a man's arms whenever he chooses to whistle to them, and have no minds of their own. It makes me think of a piece of Shakespeare we learned at school. I know you think me almost illiterate because I don't read many books, but I went to a good school, and I remember this:

"I am a woman. Hath not a woman eyes? Hath not a woman hands, organs, dimensions, senses, affections, passions? Fed with the same food, hurt with the same weapons, subject to the same diseases, healed by the same means, warmed and cooled by the same winter and summer? If you prick us, do we not bleed? If you tickle us, do we not laugh? If you poison us, do we not die? And—"

She paused dramatically and lowered her voice to a whisper—

"if you wrong us, do we not avenge?"

"Jew," murmured Arnold, but she did not perceive his meaning.

"I tell you a woman is just as capable of murder as a man. I am a woman and—"

She broke off abruptly as Arnold lifted his hands and made sweeping tentacle-like movements towards her, uttering queer, deep noises in his throat.

She jumped up from her chair and backed away from him.

"Arnold! What are you doing?"

Her voice rose in shrill, sharp tones.

Arnold opened and closed his mouth like a newly- landed fish, while she gazed at him in morbid fascination.

At length he spoke.

"I—I feel queer," he said in the same thick voice. "I dropped my cigarette. Can't pick it up. My fingers— numb. Feet too. My throat—I—"

His voice trailed into silence.

Leda walked across to his chair, set her foot on his cigarette, and said,

"Come. Try to stand up. I'll help you."

She placed her hands under his arms, and tried to lift him, but he fell back into the chair, where he sprawled uncomfortably.

"No. You can't get up," she said in matter-of-fact tones. "I was wondering how long it would take for the stuff to work. I know the dose for dogs, of course, but they don't give instructions on the label for putting human beings out of their misery."

He stared up at her helplessly, and she laughed at the bewilderment in his eyes.

"Don't you understand?" she asked. "I've drugged you. You ought not to look so surprised. Arnold, you've seen me use the same drug before. I told you then that I usually give it with a good meal. You're one up on the dogs, though. You know how it works."

She lifted his hand up, then released it, and watched it drop back senselessly on to his knee, the fingers twitching.

"You can't get up now. Soon you won't be able to move at all. Then you'll fall asleep. But until then, your brain will be awake. You'll be able to see and hear me, and you'll be able to think. They do say that under such conditions, the brain and hearing are very acute. Well, you'll soon find out whether that's true or not, but you won't be able to impart the knowledge to anyone else because you'll be dead!"

She watched closely the changing expression in his eyes.

"Oh yes, I know that the drug won't kill you," she went on, smiling, "but you're going to die all the same. No, not chloroform. I couldn't risk the smell. Besides it would take too long, and I must get back before the servants return. But there's something just as deadly in this room. That's why I choose these rooms for you to live in. Look!"

She squatted down at the hearth.

"I'm going to turn this fire out." She did so, then looked up at him. "When you're asleep, I shall turn it on again, but I shan't light it—I see by your eyes that you understand."

For a moment she was silent. Then she stood up, and spoke again.

"What a fool you've been, Arnold! You could have had a comfortable, dignified life, with all those little luxuries you like so much, but you threw it all away just like a stupid child. You're not a child, though, my dear, and a man who hasn't learned sense in fifty years doesn't deserve to live any longer."

Arnold lay where he had fallen. His eyes never moved away from the small figure standing in front of the cooling bars of asbestos.

He felt held in one of those nightmares in which one senses danger, but realises with horror that one is powerless to move away from it. But this was no nightmare. It was real.

Here he was, Arnold Smith, held immobile by a drug whose effect he recollected only too well. And there was Leda talking to him quite casually about his approaching death.

Never before, he felt, had he appreciated the nicety of the adjective in that line from Keats:

"So the two brothers and their murder'd man, rode on—"
For, like that man, he too, though still alive, was as good as murdered. Strange that he should think of poetry at such a time. But it was as she had said: his brain was acutely aware of the situation.

Just so, he thought, a man in a condemned cell must feel on the night before his execution.

No, the simile was not a good one, for he had fewer hours than a legally condemned man to live.

But why?

"Why?" asked Leda, repeating the word he could not articulate, so that he would have jumped with surprise, if his limbs had not been paralysed. "I can't think however you came to be a writer at all. You know so little about people.

"Why? I'll tell you. You'll remember asking me whether I had fallen in love, when you broke off our engagement? Well, I promised myself then that one day I would tell you that I had. Shall I tell you the man's name? Do I need to? It was you, Arnold.

"Strange that you should look surprised at that. I suppose you have always looked on me as a woman with no soft feelings. Yet you've seen me often enough with my dogs, and you know I love them. Perhaps you thought I preferred them to men. You are quite wrong. But until you came, I had no chance to become fond of any man. That's why I loved you so much. That's why I became a murderess!

"For of course you know now that I killed my father and mother. You never thought of me as a murderess, did you?

"'Leda is so *sensible*, such a *capable* girl, such a Good Sort.'

"Oh I've heard things like that said about me for years and years. It was true, of course, but why? Because God made me like that so that I could be a comfort to my parents? Such nonsense! It was because I never had a chance to be anything else. What has my life been like in this petty little village, do you suppose, chained down to look after a complaining, snivelling, old woman and an unreliable, bad-tempered, old man?

"Even the war has made no difference. Other districts have their anti-aircraft guns and searchlight batteries, but not Nether Naughton. Oh no!

"Why did you think I replied so quickly to your advertisement? Because we needed the money? Because I wanted to help an evacuee? Not on your life! Because it was the only chance I could see of meeting a man who might marry me, so that I could get out of this rut before I'm an old woman.

"Oh, it was so splendid when you came! We were such good friends, and you really liked me for myself, and didn't pretend to like me because you wanted me to open a bazaar, or get up a dance, or give a donation. It was so many years since anyone had liked me just for myself."

Was she insane? wondered Arnold.

She didn't look it. Her voice was pitched in its usual conversational key. She might have been giving a lecture on rug-making to the Arts and Crafts Association for all the emotion she expressed.

"Yes, we were friends, Arnold," she went on, "but I always knew that it meant more to me than it did to you. I know I'm not attractive like some women. I could only hold your interest by being cheerful and helpful all the time. But if I wanted you to marry me, I knew I must find some better way of attracting you. I knew you found it difficult to pay what I asked for your board here. I saw you economising in the little ways in which most men of property are careless. I knew your future depended on the success of your new book, and I knew that it wouldn't be a success. I don't know much about books, but I know enough of you and of your writing to realise that you could never write that type of thing. You had a flair for one particular kind of book that was fashionable for a short period, and will never be popular again. So I knew you would soon need money, and I knew that if I were rich, you would find me an attractive business proposition."

Arnold was annoyed about her opinion of him as an author, and amazed at her perspicacity. It would all have turned out exactly as she had planned if it had not been for Charity.

Charity!

He had not thought of her once during the evening.

How could he bear never to see her again, never to hold her in his arms? Would she weep for him? He had never felt sure of her love for him, and his mania to possess her was so strong that he had not cared. All that he desired was to make her his wife, since only after marriage, he knew, would she yield herself to him.

Why had Leda chosen to attack him and not Charity? Did she intend to have her arrested for his murder, thus getting rid of them both?

Oh God! To feel such mental torture, and yet be helpless!

"The rest of the story is obvious," Leda went on. "Mother had the money, and she hated me and loved my brother. She never gave me a farthing more than she had to when she was alive. I knew she would never leave me any in her will unless she was forced to do so. So I decided to murder her."

How does the song run? thought Arnold,

"So I *murdered* her one morning—"

It was as casual as that.

"First I made her make that will, not without some persuasion, as you can guess. But I can crack a whip as well as anyone, and she hated the whip.

"No, you didn't see me doing that, Arnold," she said in reply to a flickering question in his eyes. "You surely don't imagine that I should have been careless enough to leave the light on and the curtains drawn back? It was Daddy you saw, and I can only guess that he was using the same persuasion to induce her to write that invitation to Charity. She didn't sign the will until the Friday before she died, and that was what made her write to Stanton, though I don't how she managed to get the letter posted without my seeing it.

"Of course I pre-dated the will after she signed it. It was sheer good luck that made the date coincide with that little scene with the horsewhip that you saw. It was easy to get Frieda's signature as witness. I told her it was a new police form and if she didn't sign, they'd send her back to Germany.

"I got her to leave her money to Daddy so that no one would suspect me. I knew they couldn't prove anything against him, and I knew that he would give me a share in it so that it was as good as mine. Then I discovered that that little gold-digger had got her fingers on him, and that I might not get any of the money after all. I hadn't realised until she dined with us that night how much he doted on her, and I knew then that he must never have another chance to see her again."

"So I *murdered* him one evening—"

The song still rang in Arnold's ears, although this time, it seemed a little more distant.

His mouth suddenly jarred open, and he could not close it again. His lids dropped heavily over his eyes, and all his willpower could not raise them again.

The next moment he found himself staring into Leda's face, which had assumed gigantic proportions, as if she had eaten a piece of the Caterpillar's mushroom.

He realised that she had raised his eyelids with her fingers so that she could look at his eyes.

"So you can still hear and understand," she said. "But I must be quick. Well, there's not much more to tell you.

"I jumped you into making a pretended proposal of marriage, hoping you'd never have the strength of mind to try and get out of it. If that—let's say bitch, though the word doesn't mean much to me in that sense—hadn't started her gold-digging on you, we might have been married by now and you would still have a few more years of life in front of you. I have Betty to thank for it all. It was her idea of fun to ask her to the house that night. She knew that Charity wouldn't be able to resist making eyes at you. She as good as told me that beforehand, and when she suggested that Charity should stay,

I thought it would be a good opportunity to scare the wits out of her. So I put on Daddy's overcoat and hat and went into her bedroom, thinking I could make her believe that his ghost was haunting her, and frighten her away from the district altogether. It would have succeeded, too, if that fool Frieda hadn't gone prying round afterwards. I'd had to leave the clothes in Mother's bedroom in case I saw anyone on my way back to my room, (I locked the communicating door again when I fetched Charity's dressing gown), and she found them there and put them on herself.

"Well, of course, I can't let you get away with your romantic little plan, Arnold. If you won't marry me, I'll take care that you don't marry her. You haven't turned me into a murderess for nothing!"

What will she do next? panicked Arnold's thoughts.

If only someone would come to the bungalow. The door was never locked. Perhaps Cook and Frieda would return unexpectedly and phone to give her an urgent message. They'd be sure to ask if she had come here.

Sure? No, not likely to. She never came to see him. Everyone knew that they had quarrelled. But there must be some way out!

If only Noel Delare had been investigating the murders, he would have ferretted out the murderer by now. But Inspector Driver lacked the imagination to solve such a case as this.

Wait a minute, though; the Inspector had always thought the motive was woven around the greed for money. Wasn't it possible that he was at this moment on his way with a warrant for Leda's arrest? The murders weren't very difficult to solve, once you saw the motive. As soon as Leda had told him that, he had clearly realised the whole sordid thing. And Driver was trained in the strange ways of criminals.

Yes, there was still a chance for him. But Driver must hurry—hurry—

"What a fool you were, Arnold," repeated Leda. "You gave up the gold for dross. Charity will get over your death within a week, and will be off looking for another man. If she'd realised that you had so little money, she would never have wasted her time on you, but she thinks, poor fool, that anyone who has published eight novels or so must be rich! Well, it needn't worry you. It will all be forgotten in a few days' time, and we shall all say it was for the rest.

"For this won't be murder, Arnold, but suicide.

"You're here alone, and you know Mrs. Briggs won't be back till tomorrow morning. This is your opportunity, and you're going to take it. The police will find that no one else has been in the house. I shall take my cup and plate and wash them in the kitchen. But there won't be any finger prints of mine on anything. You see, I've not taken off my gloves since I came in. They're made of flesh-coloured rubber, and you didn't notice them. I didn't overlook any detail in the other murders. I shan't make any mistake in this.

"Yes, Arnold. You're going to commit suicide while of unsound mind owing to grief due to my having jilted you. Plenty of people in the village will be prepared to swear that you were heart-broken: Mrs. Briggs for one. They'll take into account the fact that you confessed to the murders of my father and mother. Oh yes, you were writing the confession when I called this evening. Vague, as you said. It would do for any murder.

"Well, goodbye, Arnold. You'll soon be asleep."

There must be a way out, throbbed Arnold's brain. There must be *some* way out.

He fought to keep away the cloak of sleep which threatened to smother his senses.

You must get out of this. You must get out of it, throbbed his brain.

He snatched himself back from the black abyss which yawned before him.

"Good-bye, Arnold," said Leda again, and this time her words were accompanied by the soft sound of swinging bells.

He heard in the distance the metallic click of the gas tap.

And he realised, as he fell head long into the darkness, that he wasn't going to get out of it!

THE END